Almost Family

D0769644

DISCARDED
From Nashville Public Library

Almost Family

ROY HOFFMAN

35ᴛʜ Anniversary Edition

THE UNIVERSITY OF ALABAMA PRESS
Tuscaloosa

The University of Alabama Press

Tuscaloosa, Alabama 35487-0380

uapress.ua.edu

Copyright © 2018 by Roy Hoffman
All rights reserved.

Inquiries about reproducing material from this work should
be addressed to the University of Alabama Press.

Typeface: Times

Cover images: 123RF.com

Cover design: David Nees

Cataloging-in-Publication data is available from the
Library of Congress.

ISBN: 978-0-8173-5927-0
E-ISBN: 978-0-8173-9219-2

To my mother and father
and all my family

Introduction

In my twenties, when I lived in a studio apartment at 238 West Twentieth Street in Manhattan, I'd sit by my fourth-floor window, a songwriter on the floor above and a dancer below, clacking away on my manual typewriter and glancing out at the street. In the late 1970s and early '80s urban frenzy—I resided next to a police precinct, across from what was called a feminist center, and caddy-corner from an SRO (single resident occupancy), or low-income residential hotel—I felt certain that I would find subject matter more exotic than the leafy block where I'd grown up in Mobile, Alabama.

But as I wrote sketches of stoop sitters and artists, big city dreamers and off-beat strangers, I began to see an image far-away—an old brick house, a blue Formica kitchen booth, a pot of coffee, two women talking. Like many Southern writers who went north to New York, I had traveled 1,200 miles to find myself, in my imagination, right back where I'd started.

For all the afternoons I had sat at that booth and visited with the two women—my mom, Evelyn, and Alberta West, who cooked, cleaned, and helped raise me in the way of the Old South—I had never thought to write a story, much less a novel, inspired by their friendship. It was a complex friendship, of course, employer and employee, white and black, one woman of means and the other having to work. Not family but *almost* family—and in that *almost* existed a great divide.

Indeed, the black maid in the white home had been the subject of scores of literary works by authors black and white—you could fill a bookshelf with the commentaries alone on William Faulkner's Dilsey—and scores [countless] more would follow like Kathryn Stockett's novel *The Help*;

Tony Kushner's musical, *Caroline, or Change*; Susan Tucker's oral history, "Telling Stories Among Southern Women"; and the writings of Jesymn Ward. Within the context of history and politics, the relationship could be interpreted in myriad ways. But I was a son, not a sociologist. My sense of Evelyn and Alberta was bound up in the day-to-day of growing up, the ways each had nurtured and shaped me. Across a range of emotion, in our kitchen and beyond, deep bonds formed. There were tensions, yes, but there were stories and laughter and caring across what could have been a chasm. Not only did they come from two separate communities, white and black, but religions, too. My family is Jewish; Alberta's Primitive Baptist. Each was something of an outsider looking in.

And by the time I, the youngest, was living far away, they went their separate ways. My mom sent me a carbon letter, copied to my three sisters, saying that Alberta had quit, plain and simple, leaving only a penciled note. End of story.

As I sat at my pre-gentrified Chelsea neighborhood window, I began to wonder what the true dynamic of their relationship had been without me and my sisters to fuss over. Had it been impacted all along by the unfolding events of the civil rights movement? Had changing social norms, black and white, in the Deep South and throughout much of the nation, found their ways into the conversations at that blue Formica booth? Or was it simply an expression of the empty nest?

Taking a journalistic approach, on trips home from New York I'd quiz the two women, in their separate homes, about why they had split, but neither divulged an answer. Attempting a magazine story, I talked to Alberta's grown children about what their experience had been, on their side of town, growing up as their mother left them in the mornings to go tend to a white lady's children. For each child the perception was different; for all of them, we were as much in their family as they were in ours. Far-off yet close; neither strangers nor intimates. In the segregated South of our childhood, it was as though we had all come to know each other through the looking glass.

Journalism couldn't take me where I needed to go. Where the door closes, I learned, is where fiction begins. The kitchen booth out my window, and the women sitting at it, were imaginative recreations. I caught the rhythms of their speech— each idiosyncratic in its own way—and heard their voices. If I entered fiction through the kitchen door, it was, in the end, by eavesdropping. Leaning heavily on dialogue, *Almost Family* is as much a novel of the ear as the eye. To free myself up completely, I needed to invent my own landscape; Madoc, Alabama, the geography of my hometown blended with the vicissitudes of other places illusory and real.

But a novel is also a structure, and it was not until I began to alternate points of view, chapter by chapter, one woman then the other, that my fictional characters, Vivian and Nebraska, began to come alive. I chose not to write through their first-person perspectives—nor is there a young man narrating— but to see the world while roosting on their shoulders and ultimately through their eyes. If we are lucky as fledgling writers, we do not choose our first novel so much as it chooses us. Clearly, looking back these thirty-five years, *Almost Family* chose me because there was a story pressing on my central nervous system. I was motivated by a peer group of aspiring authors in New York who met regularly for spirited critique. We dubbed ourselves the Famous Writers Group, inspired by a poetry workshop I'd taken at the Ninety-Second Street YM-YWHA with Muriel Rukeyser, and I was lucky to have my manuscript acquired by Joyce Johnson, an excellent editor at The Dial Press, who'd written her own book that year about her relationship with Jack Kerouac, *Minor Characters: A Beat Memoir.*

No matter how many authors had written about the South, race relations, the civil rights movement, Jewish-Christian relations, family, growing old, coming together and falling apart, I had to do so in my own way. If I was writing about politics, it was politics from the kitchen, the world through the windowpanes. That I was a twenty-something male did not bother me in the least. Had I waited another decade to mature in my craft—or had I simply hesitated, or procrastinated, or talked the story out over too many beers—it might have seeped away. I might have grown apprehensive, too. Why should anyone feel he has the right to appropriate another person's experience, especially a white male the point of view of an African-American woman? It's not only a good question, but also an inhibiting one. That's why we become artists, of course. To throw caution out that fourth-floor window. At age 29, when I published *Almost Family*, I was largely indifferent to what anyone might say in terms of who or what I was entitled to write about. In fact, I encouraged all my writer friends, of whatever background, to write across lines of gender, race, and faith if their stories demanded it, and I still do.

Little did I know that, in Vivian Gold, her husband Edward, and their children, I was creating one of the few Jewish families in the Southern literary canon at the time. In 1973 Eli Evans had published his landmark memoir, *The Provincials: A Personal History of Jews in the South*. The population, in terms of authors with my background, still remained small. As Alfred Uhry inscribed the script of his play, *Driving Miss Daisy*, to me in 1989: "For Roy Hoffman, a fellow Southerner, Jew, and writer."

Nor could I predict that the Nebraskas of the South would seem to vanish, at least to public view. The legions of uniformed black maids, descending from buses, heading to white homes, have gone the way of the buses themselves. Childcare is largely a business; nannies come in all complexions and languages; cooks are for the well-to-do. The Nebraskas of their era often raised, in their own children, the professionals and civic leaders of today. The Vivians, no matter their station in life, wanted to enter the job market. And as the civil rights movement commemorates fiftieth anniversary events—like the 1963 march over Selma's Edmund Pettus Bridge, the 1965 passage of the Voting Rights Act, and the 1968 assassinations of Martin Luther King Jr. and Bobby Kennedy—elders of both races are eager for their grandkids to take measure of what the old folks long ago accomplished, the miles they marched, the fury and violence they stood down, the blood they shed. The triumphs they won.

If the landscape has shifted with time, though, civil rights issues remain with us in new and searing ways. While we have progressed a long way since 1946, when *Almost Family* starts, and 1975, when it concludes, we have miles—some would say light-years—to go. The 2008 election of President Barack Obama—unimaginable to Vivian and Nebraska—ushered in speculation about a post-racial America. That speculation, many would agree on both sides of the political fence, is still a dream. The 2016 election of President Donald Trump was coincident with a newly tumultuous era in our race relations. Selma and Birmingham, symbolic as epicenters of struggle in my generation, have long been displaced by other locales in the South and far beyond—Ferguson, Charlottesville—that are synonymous with confrontation and heartbreak. There seems to be more diversity in politics and popular culture than ever before, yet there are demonstrably more hate groups, too.

Reconciliation? We either become paralyzed by cynicism, or we try. On the novel's centenary, I'm sure we will still be working out the complexity of trying to connect across differences, still reaching out toward becoming what my fellow Mobile, Alabama, author, the esteemed Albert Murray, termed "omni-Americans."

Thirty-five years after its publication, *Almost Family*, I like to think, is not only a time capsule of a time and place but also a living, breathing drama about connection in a quintessential American way. The novel opens with a question posed to Nebraska as she looks out at a Jewish gathering on Mardi Gras Day: "What you think is so different 'bout them?" It's an inquiry that's propelled much of my writing across changing decades and particulars since I first asked it of my characters and now, I realize, also of myself. When our race and ethnicity, our gender and faith, all fall away as we get to know each other, what's left deep inside? What distinctive qualities make us who we are beyond what time and history demand of us?

The answers begin with a kitchen booth and a pot of coffee, voices interweaving, and stories being told.

Roy Hoffman
Fairhope, Alabama

Almost Family

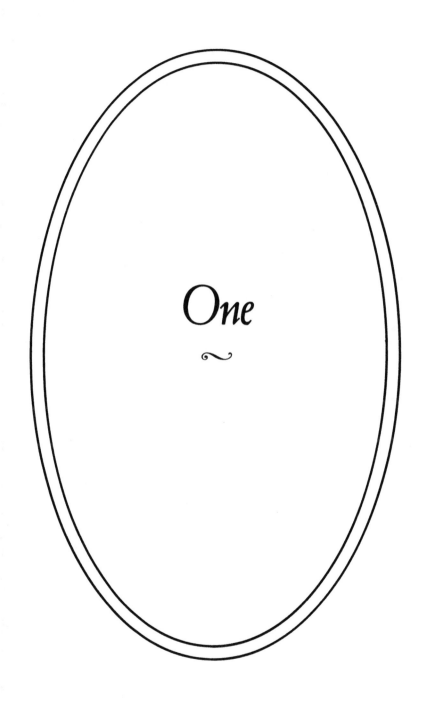

One

1946

"WHAT YOU THINK is so different 'bout them?"

Nebraska Waters shrugged at her friend Mary's question. From the kitchen of the Blooms' house, where she worked as extra help at the Madoc, Alabama, Mardi Gras party, she looked through into the living room and saw the group of revelers clustered. One wore a face like a horned devil. Another, a man, was painted with lipstick and rouge.

Nebraska finished chopping the celery for the potato salad and scraped the pieces into a bowl. "Well, the pastor say they from over in Jerusalem!"

Mary threw back her head and laughed, the muscles in her throat twitching like rope. "Don't you think peoples from over in Jerusalem just like anybody else?"

A small, broad man named Cantor Klein whirled near the kitchen door. Nebraska spotted the black skullcap on his head and wondered if that were part of a costume he had failed to complete. "I guess so," she answered reluctantly. "Course . . . course . . ."

"Course what?" Mary laid out ladyfingers onto a large dish and began to cover them with strawberry preserves. "Ain't no course 'bout it. First of all, Jewrish peoples might *be* from Jerusalem, but they got over here to Madoc now. And second thing, peoples is peoples wherever."

"I guess you right," Nebraska remarked with some reserva-tion. She finished scraping the celery pieces and started chop-ping an egg. Mrs. Bloom appeared at the door. "How're things going, Mary?"

"Fine, fine, Miss Bloom. Nebraska make the sixth day-worker we done hired for the party. It's just the right number."

"Would you have Nebraska catch the front porch with the broom before long, please?"

Nebraska looked up from the egg and smiled. "Yas'm. I'll be there directly."

Mrs. Bloom turned and disappeared into the living room, and Nebraska watched the guests milling and talking, drinking and laughing. More guests arrived, and she could hear Mrs. Bloom greeting them enthusiastically: "Why, Sheryl! Why, Don! How *are* y'all? I was afraid you weren't coming." Edna and David Solomon, Doris and Cantor Klein, Cindy and Daniel Finkle—the family names were pronounced one by one as the guests came up the steps, moved under the streamers hanging from the light fixture, and were introduced to any who did not already know them. The names sounded strange to Nebraska—foreign, and holy.

Nebraska had not known that this was to be a Jewish Mardi Gras party. It was not until she bumped into Mary on the way from her small shack near the Alabama state docks that she found out that the Blooms were Jewish and that most of their guests for the day were to be Jewish as well. Then and there she had confessed to Mary, "You know, I don't think I ever met no Jewish peoples," and Mary had answered, "Just do as I do, say as I say, and everything will be fine. The Blooms is just like anybody else."

And Mary had been right. The Blooms' house, with its high windows and turning fans and Victorian furniture, was just like any other on Governor Street, the main thoroughfare of Madoc and the principal parade route. The party food, too, was pretty much the same—ladyfingers and cold bologna and potato salad and eggnog (though Nebraska did not see the usual party staple of ham). And the people, though they were Jewish, *were* white.

"Miss Mary?" Another day helper stood at the kitchen door. "Miss Bloom want to know if we got enough soft drinks in the garage for later." Mary nodded, and the day helper went back to relay the assurance to Mrs. Bloom. "I swear," Mary said crossly, "if Miss Bloom want me to manage this party, she ought to let *me* manage it and she can go off and worry 'bout somethin' else. I don't like nobody doin' my business for me."

Nebraska cracked another egg, peeled it, and chopped. She hardly heard Mary for watching the guests, especially the one called Vivian Gold.

Vivian Gold was a young woman, about thirty, with finely penciled brows and dark hair swept back in a snood. Nebraska thought of a Hollywood actress as she watched the woman holding a bloody mary not far from the kitchen door. She could overhear part of the conversation.

"It's so good to have you back from Washington." Cantor Klein spoke. "This day is a *simcha*, a joyous time."

The man standing next to Vivian—Nebraska presumed he was her husband—responded warmly. "Yes, Cantor, the war is over. It's a *simcha* for us all."

"We Jews were blessed," Cantor Klein said more somberly. "Only now we are finding out how many"—he paused and looked away at a streamer for a moment, then looked back —"how many Jews were not."

"Let's not be sad today." The cantor's wife took her husband's hand and patted it. "For Mardi Gras we will only celebrate."

Vivian nodded and smiled. Her husband—Nebraska heard someone refer to him as Edward—leaned over and kissed her on the cheek. She waved him away with mock embarrassment. "Honey, are you tipsy!"

"Ain't she a living doll?" Edward asked the cantor, who nodded his agreement. "Ain't she?" The cantor nodded again.

Vivian addressed Doris Klein. "Edward's been a child at a birthday party ever since we got home."

"And you're not?" asked Doris.

"I feel great," Edward said. "Real estate's really gonna take off now, and you know what I'm going to do? I'm going to make my wife a lady of leisure, a princess even!"

"Already she's a princess," the cantor replied, lighting a cigar.

"I've never seen Edward act so silly!" Vivian pouted expressively, broke into a laugh, then reached over and kissed her husband lightly on the ear.

As Nebraska scraped the last chopped egg into the potato salad, added a dollop of mayonnaise, and started to stir the ingredients with a wooden spoon, she continued to watch Vivian Gold, held rapt by the woman's lively manner.

Mary interrupted her eavesdropping. "You workin' anywhere full time now?"

"No." Nebraska saw two large pink splotches on Mary's face, like pale hands reaching over the old woman's neck and temple. For the two years since she and Abraham and their two sons Todd and Junior had lived in Madoc she had not kept a job in any white person's house for more than three months. And, as she had told Abraham, it was not *her* fault. There had been the first woman, the one with the cats crawling over the oven and dining room table and drinking water out of the toilet. When the woman had caught Nebraska grabbing one of the cats by the scruff of the neck and yanking it down from the counter top, the woman had fired her immediately. Then there had been the couple who lived in a house so far from Madoc proper that it took Nebraska nearly an hour to get there every day. And when she did get there she had no place to run and hide when the white man threw his tantrums, shattering glasses and punching doors in jealous attacks on his wife. Then there had been the young couple who lived not far from the Blooms. After three weeks Nebraska and been so entirely humiliated by the young woman's insistence that she ask before eating food from the refrigerator, and that she show the contents of her shopping bag before heading home every evening—since "theft had gotten so bad around town"—that she just went home one night and never returned.

"You never worked a Jewrish house, I take it," Mary said, setting out silverware. "They's the nicest to work for. They understands." Mary glanced up at the clock. "You better stop fussing with that potato salad and go on and sweep the porch."

Broom in hand, Nebraska started out the kitchen and through the living room. Suddenly she heard the word *Randomville* and turned to find herself staring directly into the dark eyes of Vivian Gold. Nebraska asked meekly, "Randomville?"

"Yes, do you know it?" Vivian returned.

"Know it?" Nebraska's bearing came back to her and she knocked the butt of the broom handle against the floor and puffed up her chest. "I was raised up round there. I just moved down to Madoc not two years ago."

"To Madoc all the way from Randomville?"

"Well, my husband Abraham just brung me down with him."

"I've got kinfolk up that way myself," Vivian said.

Nebraska felt Vivian's eyes staring deep into her. "I probably knows them."

Vivian hesitated. "Of course . . . of course they are white."

"I know white, black, red, and yellow in Randomville."

"Does the name Simmons ring a bell?"

"Simmons?" Nebraska put her hand to her lip, figuring. "Oh, yeah. Yeah! Of course I know Simmons, 'cause Lottie used to work for someone lived next door to them. My, my."

"That's my cousin," Vivian explained.

"You know," Nebraska went on excitedly, drawn more deeply into Vivian's gaze, "I even remember the day the Simmons baby was baptized. Lottie worked the big party afterwards. She—"

"I was there," said Vivian. "I probably ate some chicken salad Lottie dished up. Alabama's really not such a big place, is it?"

The whole day began to get tangled up in itself for Nebraska. She envisioned the Randomville baptism and the Blooms' Mardi Gras party fusing into one gigantic gathering. She looked beyond Vivian to the long table of potato salad and bologna and bread and to the white-vested bartender pouring whiskey into tumblers. Someone else put on a mask and whisked through the room looking like a horned devil. Beyond the bartender Nebraska spotted a cook slicing roast beef and looking in her direction with an air of general perplexity.

"I'm confusin' on it," Nebraska said abruptly.

"Pardon?" said Vivian, who had begun to drift into another conversation.

"The pastor told me the people from Jerusalem don't got no baptism."

Vivian looked at her curiously. "What people from Jerusalem?"

"Mary told me . . ." Nebraska tried to resist completing the question, but felt herself hurtling forward. She felt Cantor Klein at her side, staring, she imagined, at her split shoes. "Mary told me this party was a Jewish people's party. I don't remember nothin' 'bout the Simmons or anybody else in Randomville being Jerusalem people!"

Nebraska saw Miss Bloom at her right side laughing uproariously like a mirror image of Cantor Klein, to her left side, laughing so hard he choked on his cigar. In front, Vivian leaned back against Edward and clutched her side, trying to catch her breath in the midst of her own laughing. A dozen more people clustered around, passing along Nebraska's comments, and the horned devil—who Nebraska figured was the real devil dressed up like a play one—lurched toward her as if to drag her off to hell.

As they headed to hell, Nebraska heard the Chickasabogue marching band playing a brassy rendition of "Dixie," with trombones and trumpets rebounding through the room. The high, hard smell of whiskey hit her nostrils. "That 'bout knock me out!" she said over the noise. Someone dressed like a cartoon convict, plastic mask gruesome with a jagged scar running across one cheek, pushed his face up to hers, and someone held her arm fast as the whole group spilled into the front yard.

The Crazy Indian Parade—a satire on a real Mardi Gras parade—rolled down Governor Street. Men and women with red-painted faces and clusters of headfeathers jumped about and threw fake goodies to the crowd. An Indian tossed out a roll of serpentine, which, attached to a rubber band, popped back into his hand as soon as someone in the crowd tried to catch it. One float had an outhouse in the middle with Up North written on the side. An Indian appeared from the outhouse, shaking his flap, and hurled a corncob into the front yard of the Blooms, sending it squarely toward Vivian's face. Nebraska reached up with her broom and swatted it down from the air.

"Sign her up!" the cantor cried. "She could knock crazy a baseball!"

A military school band filed by playing "South Rampart Street Blues." Edna Solomon fired off a spool of serpentine from the porch, and the orange thread, leaping into the air, spiraled down over the table in the front yard.

"How long you been working for the Blooms?" Edward asked Nebraska over the din.

Nebraska called back over the band, " 'Bout a few hours!"

"Cook?"

"Yes, sir, do I. Cook since I was twelve."

"Come work for us."

Vivian, shocked, looked at her husband. "Edward, are you getting carried away? How can we afford help? We've already got expenses as high as the roof of the First National."

Edward sang back over the music, "With real estate booming, we'll be buying up the First National!"

"But . . ."

"But nothing," Edward pronounced. He reached over and shook Nebraska's hand. "What do you say? Give it a try?"

As Nebraska shook back and nodded, a single phrase beat like a litany in her mind: "I gots me a job, I gots me a *good* job!"

To the side of the old brick house stood a Japanese magnolia, and during the first week or two after Mardi Gras every year, little else bloomed save that tree. Its blossoms suffused the rooms with color—a pale red glow seemed to tinge the couch on the porch, the chairs in the dining room, and the dressing table near Edward's closet in the bedroom.

Vivian woke from her afternoon nap, staring straight into the petals that pressed against her window. The backs of the petals were pink, their cores soft white. The creamy texture of the cores reminded her of the creamy, chubby place just behind Rachel's knees. She listened for the chortling of her baby girl from the middle bedroom down the hall.

She'd been dreaming of the train, the brakes of pine sliding by in the Georgia dusk, and Sarah getting motion sick just after passing Macon. She remembered her daughter's slender face pressed against the window in the ladies' room, her dark eyes red and tear-stained. And there was the conductor again with his voice bellowing out the stops like an ornery mule: "Atlaaanta! Biiirmingham! Tuscaloooosa! Maaadoc!"

They had returned to Madoc after two years of Edward's being stationed in Washington. As the train had rumbled south, her hometown had come into view: unfurling first at the edge of the blue-brown water of its bay where the wharves jutted out along the shore, then opening into the downtown with its squat, gray banks and sand-colored courthouse and green-and-brown-fronted stores. The train had chugged to a halt close to the plaque that Vivian had memorized as a child—as had every citizen of Madoc—and that served as the basis for a local belief that Madoc was distinct from, and superior to, all other American towns:

ON THIS SPOT, LOCAL HISTORIANS BELIEVE, THE WELSH-MAN MADOC GWYNEDD, AFTER AN ARDUOUS AND PER-ILOUS JOURNEY ACROSS THE ATLANTIC, THE CARIBBEAN, AND THE GULF OF MEXICO, FIRST PITCHED CAMP IN

THE NEW WORLD—THREE HUNDRED YEARS BEFORE THE BIRTH OF COLUMBUS. THOUGH MADOC THEN TRAVELED SOUTH TO MEXICO IN THE NAME OF HIS KING, A BAND OF HIS FELLOW SAILORS STAYED ON PERMANENTLY AND SPAWNED A RACE OF BLOND, BLUE-EYED INDIANS —THE FIRST TRUE AND NOBLE EUROPEAN BLOODLINE IN AN OTHERWISE SAVAGE LAND.

And they had stepped off the landing board of the sleeper into the heavy smells of the docks—the smells of banana boats, molasses vats, splintered rum kegs, and the iron tracks of the GM&O, where her father used to take her on Sunday afternoons to watch the cars roll in from New Orleans and roll out headed north. The smells that day had reminded her of how hot Madoc was, how damp and steamy come summer nights, and how much she had wrongly recalled it as cool, dry, and sweet when reading the war reports in Washington and dreaming of returning home. The smells had also brought back all that made her uneasy about Madoc: its confinement, its neighbors looking over your shoulder at what you were doing—even, at times, what you were thinking.

Vivian rubbed her eyes, yawned, and got up from the bed. The dream and memory of the trip from Washington whirled away and a more recent memory took its place: a scene from *The Merriest Bachelor*.

Lines she had rehearsed just that morning came back to her:

Why Ronald! You don't . . . don't really think Jennie's going to marry Sebastian, do you? She'll never trap the old coot.

As she recited the lines, she scrutinized herself in the mirror, throwing her arm out in a grand gesture and driving the point home to deluded Ronald:

Besides, if Jennie did snare him one way or the other, imagine what Melissa would do. Shoot herself? Shoot Jennie?

She said the lines again, turning to three-quarter profile in the mirror. Noting her own dark eyes and heart-shaped lips, she thought of another Vivian—Vivien Leigh—and brushed away the thought. An extravagant comparison, she decided.

A large form floated somewhere behind her right ear and vanished into a wall. Vivian stepped to the left to catch sight of it from another angle and saw a dust mop suspended in the air.

"Poor Melissa," came a voice from the dust mop, with Nebraska appearing suddenly behind it. "She's been studyin' on killing Jennie or herself, one, for three days now."

Vivian turned, walked quickly to the bedroom door, and pushed it closed. She calculated that Nebraska had been working in her home not fourteen days, but already she suspected the woman was a touch odd.

The first day in Vivian's house, Nebraska had worn sneakers. After entering and being introduced to Sarah and Rachel, she'd slipped off the sneakers and begun to walk about barefoot. As Vivian showed her where to stack the dishes and where to place the knives and forks, she could not help but watch the large, cracked feet moving over the linoleum floor.

"Nebraska, what on earth happened to your poor feet?"

"Nothin' happened, Miss Gold, just swelled up."

"Honey, feet don't just get 'swolled up' for no reason!"

"My foots been bad since I been fifteen, ma'am."

"Since you've been fifteen! How can you bear it?"

"Sometimes I can't." Nebraska held some drinking glasses up to the light, viewing the mark on their bases and changing the subject. "Did you get these glasses from far away?"

"Those things?" Vivian laughed. "We got those at the filling station. One glass for every ten gallons of gas."

"My, ain't there every kind of 'vantage in driving a car," Nebraska said longingly.

They had not talked about Nebraska's feet anymore that

first day. When Nebraska sat down, however, Vivian slid over some copies of the *Madoc Register* for her to rest her soles on. Sheepishly, she lowered her naked feet on a picture of a girl eating a vanilla ice cream cone.

The second day, Vivian had found tobacco ground into the edge of the living room carpet. Nebraska explained that a bee had stung her left big toe and that she had borrowed two of Mr. Gold's cigarettes for tobacco—which she mixed with spit—to draw out the swelling.

On the third day, Vivian had gone to the store and bought a pair of oversized slippers, medically treated foot pads, and some gauze. After these had been presented to Nebraska, she had wrapped up her feet, donned the slippers, and trudged obediently about the house. When Vivian went into Rachel's room later that evening, though, she had found the slippers hidden under the bed. The next morning Nebraska had explained: "They itched my heels too bad."

As Vivian finished rehearsing her lines for *The Merriest Bachelor* that afternoon and walked back to her bedroom door and opened it, she remembered to make yet another appointment at the podiatrist's for Nebraska (who had failed to show up for the first two). Moving down the hallway, calmly hunting for her daughters, Vivian felt the character of Mona Wright still clinging to her. When Sarah popped out from the hallway bedroom, her ponytail swinging, it was Mona Wright who reached down and lifted the rumpled, dark-haired child. One huge Band-Aid crossed Sarah's elbow and two were stuck on the insides of both calves—marks of her having shinnied easily up a tree, but not so easily down.

"Where's Rachel, honey?"

Sarah pointed to the bedroom. "In there with Nebuba."

Mona Wright gave way to Vivian again. "Dear, the girl's name is *Nebraska*. Can't you say that? *Ne-bra-ska!*"

"Nebuba," replied Sarah. "That's the way Nebuba says it."

"That's not a nice comment. Just because she talks different doesn't mean she talks *wrong!*"

"Yes, ma'am," Sarah said sweetly.

"It sounds like you're making fun of her when you say her name that way."

"But I *like* Nebuba," Sarah protested. "I don't make fun of her. Nebuba! NEBUBA!"

"Hush," Vivian said. "You'll startle Rachel." Coming to the entrance to the room at the end of the hall, Vivian saw Rachel sitting on the floor, haphazardly pushing a wooden block engraved with the letter *I* next to a block engraved with *E*.

"Ice cream," Sarah exclaimed. "She's spelling ice cream!"

"I doubt it," Vivian said. "Besides, half the blocks have been missing since you were that age."

"I didn't throw them into the gulley," Sarah piped. "I didn't, I didn't."

Rachel turned and grinned at them both; saliva drooled down the side of her mouth.

"Don't spit," said Sarah.

"Oh, she's just a little baby," Vivian explained, lifting Rachel up. "She can't help it." She cast a glance at Nebraska, who sat in the couch in the corner with her head tossed back and mouth open. A low sawing came from her throat. Her arms were spread out over the sides of the couch with palms turned upward, as in supplication.

"Mommie, look at Nebuba's feet!"

Nebraska shifted position, settled, and resumed sawing.

"Let her nap," Vivian whispered. She leaned closer and stared at Nebraska's feet, soles the color of clay and crisscrossed with lines and ridges like the Mississippi Delta seen from an airplane. They began to twitch.

"Is she having a nightmare?" Sarah asked.

"Maybe she's just tired," explained Vivian. "Or maybe she's dreaming about running. Maybe she's running from her husband or somebody."

Nebraska stirred again. She started to mumble, the mumble changing into a shout: "Yeow! YEOW!" Her eyes fluttered and opened.

Sarah sprang to her shoulder. "Are you all right, Nebuba?"

Vivian reached out and put the back of her hand to Nebraska's brow. "Do you feel okay? You're not sick, are you?"

"I was having a dream is all," said Nebraska, as in a fog. "A dream 'bout Abraham. He was trying to flick water on my titties."

"What?" Vivian drew her hand away and motioned for Sarah to leave the room. The child resisted and Vivian took her by the shoulder and sent her out.

"I'm sorry to frighten you, Miss Gold. Just saw my Abraham trying to flick water on my naked titties. Wasn't no more than that. He was goin' just like this." She flicked her fingers to demonstrate.

Vivian walked brusquely to the door of the room, then turned back briefly to speak before leaving. "I think you better go start supper, Nebraska. Enough napping for now." After parting she turned back a moment, adding, with an edge in her voice, "Edward likes his lamb chops medium."

❧

The next day Vivian drove the Nash down Governor Street to the small playhouse not far from the Temple. Passing the Temple, she calculated a month to Passover. Azaleas were beginning to push open along its drive.

She passed the parking lot of the playhouse, all the while thinking of Nebraska. She did not yet feel comfortable with the image of a strange woman working in her house—a strange woman who arranged Edward's drawers differently and arranged the dishes in a confused manner and rearranged Vivian's perfume bottles after dusting.

Parking the car along the curb, she got out, seeing Izzy Berman's wife, Margery, peering out through the playhouse door. Margery came out and waved, holding a bottle of nail polish in one hand. "Izzy's sick," she called. "He's got the flu."

Vivian came up to her. "What a shame. Does he have much fever?"

"Not much. He's not big on holding a thermometer under his tongue—or anywhere else for that matter—but it was a hundred one at last tally."

"I'm disappointed too," Vivian said, "but, God, don't tell him that. It's just that finally I got my lines down pat. I bumbled so last rehearsal, it was awfully embarrassing."

"Izzy probably threw you off," Margery contested. "All that boozing during Mardi Gras weakened not only his resistance to the flu, I think it also weakened his brain."

"Izzy's first-rate," Vivian said. She leaned to the side to get a better look through the theater door. "Where are the others?"

"John called off practice altogether. He gave you a ring, but your cook said you had gone out to run some errands."

Vivian sighed. "Will I ever, *ever* become a great actress?"

"Do azaleas bloom in Madoc?" Margery asked, nodding in the direction of a burst of red flowers.

"I have my doubts sometimes." Vivian fell silent a moment then veered toward another question. "How long has Romaine been working for you?"

"Romaine?" Margery figured a moment. "Well, she came to our house when Izzy started working at Lafayette High, and I'd just bought that specially imported lawn furniture. . . . Oh, I'd say three, three and a half years."

"Answer me straight. Doesn't having Romaine around the house make you feel a bit uneasy? Like a lady of leisure or something?"

"Vivian Gold! My self-defeating friend!" Margery put her hands on Vivian's shoulders. "No, it doesn't make me feel uneasy, and yes, it makes me feel like a lady of leisure. I'm always up for a little pampering. Who's not?"

"Well," Vivian began, feeling awkward about disagreeing with her friend. "The truth is, I'm not. At least, I don't think so. I grew up in one of the poorest Jewish families in Madoc—you know that. The thought of having a maid is like the thought of driving a Cadillac. It's just not my style."

"Mona Wright's got a maid in *The Merriest Bachelor,*" said Margery. "When you're Mona Wright you don't seem to have any trouble making it your style."

"Exactly. And Izzy's a playboy with a moustache and a derringer. What does that prove? He still shaves in real life, and I don't think he carries a gun."

Margery dropped her hands from Vivian's shoulders and smoothed down her dress. "Think about it like this, Vivian. Now you've got somebody to help you have more free time. How're you ever gonna be a Rita Hayworth if you don't have time? She's probably got ten maids, one for every room, so she'll have enough time to be a star."

"Margery," Vivian said soberly. "I'm thirty already. The problem is not time. The problem is talent."

"Right. Bull's-eye. Now dig a hole and crawl into it. You got super reviews in the *Madoc Register* for *Play Taps for Suzy.* You want me to pull it out and read it to you right here on the street? I will if you don't quit your moaning."

"That was a one-week run and we had a grand smashing total of one hundred fifty-two adults and forty-eight children," said Vivian.

"So is this Manhattan?" Margery threw up her hands. "Is little ol' rundown, culturally famished Madoc the bright lights of Broadway? I don't see them, but maybe I need glasses." She blinked.

Vivian laughed at her friend's insistence, secretly pleased at the encouragement. "Well, you may have a point."

"So we've decided," Margery began boisterously. "*Your* Romaine gives you time to pursue your theater work, time to become a star. Some colored gal's got a darn good job with a darn good family. And, most important perhaps, Edward is able to give you something special—the luxury of a maid. Don't you think that makes him feel good? Makes him feel like more of a man?"

Vivian's mood turned. "Margery, I think Edward is man enough without having to present me with a Negro cook!"

"Hey, darling, don't get hot under the hem. It's just a figure of speech."

"I'm sorry," said Vivian, walking back toward her car. "Maybe my resistance is down a little bit after Mardi Gras too." She opened the door and climbed in.

"Call me later," Margery called, as Vivian cranked up the Nash and drove off.

A lady of leisure, a lady of leisure. Vivian turned the phrase over in her mind as she pushed the grocery cart by the frozen foods counter and caught an image of herself in the railing of the bin. A thin, dark-haired, convex woman spilled over the silver rail.

Watching her reflection on the rail, she thought of a portrait in the *World of Art* book in the den library. "Madame X" by John Singer Sargent was the painting, and she had paused over it often. In her black gown, Madame X leaned back comfortably against a table, a haughty look on her face. Would not Madame X have maids, attendants, helpers? Certainly a petite French maid in a white lace apron would pour tea—not a cumbersome, sore-footed Nebraska.

Another woman's face moved along the railing of the frozen foods counter. Behind it moved a black face. Vivian looked up to see a middle-aged woman in green slacks and curlers trailed by a gaunt, silver-haired mammy.

Vivian pushed the grocery cart on to the canned goods area. She looked up and down the aisles, noting the different combinations of white women and black women, or black women alone, shopping for white. There were large, handsome, strong-featured black cooks, and there were scrawny, sad, defeated-looking women as well. She tried to imagine Nebraska trailing behind her, turning a can bottom upwards to read the company mark.

No, Vivian decided, the vision didn't click. There was simply no room for a helper, for a shadow, in her life. She would tell Nebraska as sweetly as she could when she got home that their ways must part.

⁓

When Vivian was at least ten houses away in the automobile, she heard the screams. The screams became a wailing, loud and plaintive. She saw the Japanese magnolia dropping blood petals on the lawn as she slowed the car and caught first sight of Nebraska. The woman stood in the middle of the lawn, barefoot, hands clasped, rocking from side to side and moaning.

"What's wrong?" Vivian cried, hurriedly parking the car and rushing across the lawn.

"Sarah!" Nebraska wailed. "Sarah, ma'am!"

"Sarah?" A flush rose through Vivian's body. "What's happened to Sarah, woman? Where is she?"

Nebraska continued rocking from side to side, starting to slap her hands together. "It's little Sarah."

Vivian latched onto Nebraska's shoulders and shook hard. "What have you done with my daughter, dammit?"

"Her foots, ma'am." Nebraska danced as on thorns.

Vivian stepped back in disbelief. "Her *feet?*"

Hearing her child's first screams, Vivian tore into the house, only to find Sarah slung over Dr. Schwartz's large shoulder. Her feet bobbed near his chest, and when her right foot touched his arm, she shrieked. In horror Vivian looked at the foot: its sole, brutally red, erupted with blisters.

"What's going on here, Frederick?"

"Don't have time to talk," he returned, grabbing up his satchel with one hand. "Your cook called and I got here as fast as I could." He lumbered out of the kitchen with Sarah over his shoulder, and as they disappeared into the hallway Sarah's sobs changed to "Mommy!" The bathroom door slammed.

Vivian leaned against the icebox and nearly passed out.

The room turned slightly, then straightened, and all Vivian could see were Nebraska's cracked and swollen feet.

Those feet clung in her mind, and behind them spun shots of dark, unclean places, of Negro tenements, of slum toilets. Over these unclean places the large feet moved, naked and coarse.

The feet moved into her own house and the strange colored woman balanced above them. The feet fell on the carpet of the living room, on the throw rugs of the hallway, on the floorboards of Sarah's bedroom. A sickness crept out of them, an infection that lit up the walls and pillows and beds. The infection leaped to Sarah's feet, igniting the precious white skin.

Vivian hurried to the bathroom and violently pushed open the door. Dr. Schwartz had muffled Sarah's screams in his neck. He kept her pressed close, running water from the tub. "Easy," he said. "Easy . . ." and suddenly shoved the blistering foot under the stream of water and began rubbing it with a rough cloth. Sarah's screams rocketed through the house.

"This damn butter," muttered Dr. Schwartz. "Damn butter!" He clenched his teeth and scrubbed harder.

"What?" Vivian started toward her child, but the doctor motioned her back.

Another scream shot through the house, this one through the bathroom window. Nebraska stood in the backyard, nose pressed to the windowpane. "Oh, Sarah! I rot in hell, Jesus, for little Sarah." Raising her palms in prayer, Nebraska shouted, "Jesus, help Sarah!"

The doctor dropped the brush, pulled Sarah close to his chest, and began to rock her slowly. He stroked her hair and began to croon "The Tennessee Waltz."

"I rot in hell for little Sarah!" Nebraska wailed again.

Dr. Schwartz laughed. "Vivian, go on out and tell your poor cook nobody's gonna rot anywhere this afternoon. Tell her Sarah's the third child this spring who's stepped in a bucket of boiling starch."

"The starch!"

Nebraska's wail rose but subsided quickly this time.

"Yes, yes, the starch. I guess your cook didn't know any better than to slop butter all over Sarah's foot." He shook his head. "Maybe some Edison will invent a decent starch one day you don't have to boil. It'll sure save me a few emergencies every year."

Vivian reached for Sarah, but Dr. Schwartz nodded her back. "Better to let her cry it out for a few minutes, Viv."

Vivian nodded.

The house stilled completely now. Vivian took a deep breath and exhaled. With Sarah weeping behind her, she walked down the hallway, to the kitchen door, and around to the backyard. Through the fronds of a banana plant she saw Nebraska. The woman was slumped in the dirt like a small mountain, sobbing and praying.

Coming up to her, Vivian placed a hand on the woman's shoulder. "It's all right, Nebraska." Vivian jiggled her lightly, but Nebraska continued to sob. After another moment she stopped and looked up, eyes wet and red.

Vivian squatted, searching Nebraska's bloodshot eyes. Had Nebraska possibly detected the fantasy gone through her mind? "Really," Vivian said softly. "It's okay, Nebraska. The doctor says she'll be fine."

"I'm so sorry, ma'am. God forgive me."

"It's all right." Vivian leaned over and picked off a blade of grass from Nebraska's forehead. "Let's go on in."

The small mountain shifted and rose, and Nebraska now stood by her side, leaning on her shoulder a moment before regaining her balance. The two women walked slowly back to the kitchen door.

As they passed the banana plant, the only sound was Nebraska's voice, thick with sadness and relief. "Miss Gold, you got a touch of the angel right round your head, ma'am. I'll stay with you as long as I live."

1948

"Sit up, Abraham. Sit up."

Nebraska grabbed her husband under the arms and tugged him upwards. He blinked, muttered something, and sank back down on the couch.

"Abraham Waters! Don't ever let your chirren see you like this. This ain't no model for young ones to grow up with!"

"Yes, yes," mumbled Abraham, who grabbed the edge of the couch and tried to hoist himself. His hand slipped off and he fell to the cushions. A gentle wheeze of air came from the couch.

"I gots to take care of Todd and Junior, take care of you, and go take care of the Golds' house as well." Nebraska, arms akimbo, shook her head. "How much did you earn last week?"

"Fifteen dollars."

"Fifteen dollars no way in heaven. The union pays twenty for construction. You done drinked up the rest."

"Oh, Gardenia. Gardenia, baby."

"Don't you Gardenia me."

"C'mon, honey." Abraham reached up and fixed his fingers around Nebraska's neck, drawing her to him. When she was in reach of the couch, he sat up and kissed her on the forehead. She nearly tumbled down to him.

A cloud of moonshine—it looked like a white cloud in her mind—surrounded him and now enveloped her. Out of that cloud his face came again, burying into her neck. He moved his hand over her bosom, as though pushing around an object on a shelf.

"Be tender," she said softly.

Abraham unbuttoned her uniform and slid his hand down over her neck, saying, "I didn't drink up five dollars' worth. It didn't cost me but two and a half."

She sat up quickly, fastening her bra. "Is that any way to tell the truth? Coming on to me sweet?" Then she felt herself soften again as he lowered his head, shaking it slowly, saying "I'm sorry" and "You're so pretty this mornin', Gardenia."

"Gardenia" was what did it, made her relax and check the clock only casually to see how long she had before getting dressed again and heading off to the Golds. It was the name she had been given as a young girl in Randomville, given one day when she poured the white woman's toilet water all over herself and her own auntie had said, "My, but don't you smell like a bunch of gardenias?" From then on, Gardenia had been the nickname by which she was known—a nickname such as every child of the country had, a free pass to being someone slightly different, slightly more glamorous.

The toilet water she now used—she bought it for thirty-five cents at the five-and-ten—was barely noticeable in the heavy cloud of Abraham's liquor that lifted them both away, their arms entwining, mouths crossing, knees sliding over one another. Stroking her husband's back, Nebraska felt the knife scar from four years ago like a soft ridge under her fingers. She had needed a year to feel comfortable touching that scar. Now it was a secret place that was hers alone, like a sign of trust.

After twenty minutes she laid her head back against the arm of the couch and saw the clock spinning upside down, looking like three o'clock from her position. She calculated backwards and the time became nine thirty. She pushed Abraham gently off her chest, fished up her uniform from the floor, and slipped it over her legs. She stood, buttoning the front, and went to wash the smell of whiskey from her neck and face.

The water gurgled over the shiny tin sink by the window. She pushed open the window farther with her elbow and looked at the warehouses of the state docks behind the line of trees. The day was muggy, and already hot. The faint haze settled to the base of the trees. Every week she seemed to see a new warehouse being built. There was talk that one day Madoc would be as big as New Orleans.

After waving her hands dry, she walked back to the couch, picked up a blanket, and laid it over her husband. Kneeling down, she kissed him on the throat, drew the blanket off his chest so he would not be too hot, and doubled it over his hips.

༄

While the bus rambled through downtown Madoc, Nebraska reflected on the last two years. The Blooms' house slid by the soiled bus window and she could almost envision the Mardi Gras party out front. Miss Bloom had died from a stroke the summer before while swimming at Madoc Bay. Nebraska's friend Mary had taken a job with a cousin of Miss Bloom's. She said a prayer for the white woman who'd been so kind and allowed Mary to hire her that day to cook and clean.

That whole celebration came back to her, and again Mary explained to her about Jewish people. "I ought to go visit Mary this evenin'," Nebraska said to herself.

"Hey, Nebraska."

It was not Mary who called her name now, but a younger woman, who pushed through the crowd of white-uniformed maids and cooks heading uptown this morning. Immediately, Nebraska recognized the bony face and sallow eyes. She scrunched down in her seat.

"You goin' to Miss Gold's?" the woman asked.

Nebraska replied tartly. "Where'd you think I was going?"

Without noting Nebraska's response, the woman asked if she could have a seat. "Seat's free, Romaine," Nebraska said.

"How is Miss Vivian?"

"Fine, thank you. And Miss Margery Berman?"

"Fine, fine."

Nebraska tucked her dress under her thighs and inched closer to the window, hoping to avoid further conversation.

"Young Howie is having his *Bar Mitzva* on Friday and Miss Margery's all in a tizzy." Romaine's voice crackled in the air.

"Is that so?" Nebraska turned around to look at Romaine but the woman had struck up a conversation with another cook, who had just pushed her way to the back of the bus. The voice crackled: "Lu Ann? Why, she looked like somethin' the dog drugged in."

Nebraska twisted toward the window again, watching the street pass by. A minute later she heard Romaine. "Nebraska, did you just ax me somethin'?"

The bus chugged to a halt and two women clambered off. Romaine said good-bye to one woman making her way to the door for the next stop and at the same time struck up a conversation with two more women just entering.

As the bus turned down Iberville Street, a street parallel to Governor, Nebraska watched the nose of the vehicle move beneath a magnolia limb and start down the wide, newly paved road. *Ching ching.* A hand reached up from a seat and yanked the halt cord. *Ching ching.* Nebraska wrinkled up her nose from the smell of busted foam cushions under sweaty legs. She glimpsed Romaine opening her purse and taking out a compact. The smell of cheap perfume mingled with the foam rubber, seeming like a soured version of the toilet water she had doused herself with that morning.

Holding the mirror in front of her nose, Romaine flared back her lips and picked a sliver of food from between her teeth with the nail of her little finger. She moved the mirror up to her left eye. "Ooh, I do look bloodshot!"

Watching Romaine, Nebraska was reminded of Margery Berman.

"Such a shame," Romaine started. "Miss Gold looked so poorly when she was over visitin' Miss Berman last."

"What do you mean?" Nebraska questioned.

"Oh, kind of runned down. Kind of sad. Kind of like she was blue or whatchumcallit."

Nebraska reached into her purse and took out a mint. The bus shifted gears and lumbered by the palatial Duchamp house. A black man was pushing a hand mower alongside the walk of the house and a cloud of grass blades spun about his legs. Nebraska sat up straighter in her seat and spoke. "I haven't seen Miss Gold look poorly or whatchumcallit in the two years I've known her. She's always the pitcher postcard of health!"

"Nebraska, it ain't no embarrassin' thing for a woman to miscarriage a child."

"What?"

"That's what Miss Berman told me was wrong with Miss Gold. And she should know! They is near best friends."

"Don't talk 'bout Miss Gold like that."

Romaine turned away to wave at a friend.

"And listen to me when I talk to you," Nebraska went on.

"Lord, Nebraska, I *am* listenin'. But you ain't listenin' to *me*. It ain't no shame for a woman to miscarriage. Just a little blood passin' on away is all."

"I know what it is," Nebraska returned sharply.

"Miss Margery done lost one once. And I lost one not a year ago." She lifted her long arm and latched her spindly fingers on the halt cord. *Ching ching.* "Course," said Romaine coolly, "I figured you knew. Miss Margery tells me everything, so I figure Miss Gold would trust you the same."

"Hush, you," Nebraska hissed. Romaine stood and made her way to the door. When Romaine was just out of earshot, she added, "You're as bad as that white nothin' you work for."

❧

Five hundred times—that's how much Nebraska figured she'd passed the mailbox on the corner of Iberville Street, turned under the canopy of the magnolia tree at the entrance to Magnolia Court, and headed down the quiet, water-oak–lined street leading to the house of the Golds. Every time she passed the large olive-colored mailbox, she wondered how many letters had been dropped there, how many bills, how many checks, how many postcards and letters to children who had left Madoc and moved north to Atlanta, or even New York, for good.

Maybe she had walked down the street more than five hundred times, she speculated as the Golds' house came into view (she took Thursdays and Sundays off and received two weeks vacation a year). She caught an image of Vivian in the kitchen window, the woman's dark hair mixed, as in a painting, with a reflection of cane bushes on the pane. Vivian was a princess in her small castle, the prince gone off to sell real estate for the kingdom. Was she not a picture postcard of health?

Nebraska paused to drag in the garbage cans from the curb. She stopped near the window and thumped it. Vivian looked up, startled. "Hello, Nebraska" seemed to move silently from her lips.

"Hello, Miss Gold," Nebraska answered, imagining that she spoke silently as well.

"I heated up some coffee for you," Vivian said, turning the pages of the *Madoc Register* as Nebraska entered. She stopped turning at an advertisement for shoes, bent over the page, and scrutinized the boxy black shapes. "Aren't these pumps the ugliest! I wouldn't be caught out of a closet in them."

"You look real good this morning, Miss Gold," Nebraska said brightly, pretending to look at the pumps but really scanning Vivian's face for signs of depression.

Vivian reached over and opened the curtain an inch more to allow light to stream in. Facing Nebraska, she said, "Take a look at my rouge. Do you think it's on too heavy?"

"No, no. It looks good! You always got good natural color anyway, but it don't hurt none to high it up a bit."

Vivian looked back down and started turning the newspaper. "Well, Edward says, 'Vivian, I don't like you to paint yourself up, 'cause you look like somebody out of the circus.'

Then, if I don't use makeup, he asks me why not. Men are hard to please. Maybe I will join the circus."

"Abraham's the same," Nebraska commiserated. "First he says, 'Nebraska, you's too fat,' then he goes once around the house, comes back, and says, 'Nebraska, you's too little!' I know I ain't too little, but I also know I ain't too fat." She hesitated. "Is I?" She turned once around as she had seen a fashion model do in a newsreel.

Vivian, watching Nebraska's turn, answered slowly, "You're fine, honey. You have a build that's . . ." She paused, choosing her words carefully. "That's right for you." She nodded. "Don't let a man's complaining get under your skin. Once you do, there'll be no room left there for yourself. Men don't want to be married to a real woman, they want a dream woman."

"Yas'm," Nebraska said indignantly, "they want movie stars."

Vivian nodded wisely.

"Of course," Nebraska continued, "Mr. Gold's already got him a movie star."

"Don't be ridiculous," said Vivian.

After reaching for her purse and drawing out a neatly folded, yellowed newspaper clipping, Nebraska read, "Vivian Gold's performance in *The Merriest Bachelor* was stunned."

"The word is *stunning*," Vivian corrected, "but *stunned* says it better." She shook her head. "I can't believe you carry that old review around. It must be a fossil by now."

"I likes to show it to my friends when they ask me about you." Nebraska folded the paper away. "I even showed it to our choir leader last month."

"Nebraska, have you been out sipping sherry with Margery?"

"You know I don't drink, Miss Gold."

"Well, when y'all start in on my acting, you both start sounding, as my mother would say, *shikker*. I'm *not* an actress. I'll *never* be an actress."

"Hm, mm," said Nebraska, impressed. "You sound just like that Scarlett woman in *Gone With the Wind* right now."

Abruptly Vivian stood, walked over to the stove, and lit a flame. "God, woman, you can be so exasperating sometimes." She poured some already brewed coffee into a pan.

"And Mr. Gold could have played Clark Gable if he'd growed a moustache!"

"Nebraska! Would you please stop that right now. Besides, I hated that movie. It made all of us down here look like a bunch of hillbillies neck-high in magnolias."

"My granddaddy was in the Civil War, I hear tell," Nebraska said proudly as she took off her street shoes and hunted for her work shoes in the closet. "Went to fight in place of a white Georgia farmer." After finding the shoes and slipping them on, she headed back and took a seat opposite to where Vivian had been sitting. "He busted his ankle, though, and ended up brushing down horses."

Vivian resumed her place at the table. "Well," she said, "my grandfather surely wasn't in the Civil War. All I know about him is that he was in Russia, trailing from village to village, when the cossacks came and wrecked his home. Poor old soul."

"Don't we got common upbringings in different ways!" Nebraska remarked, trying to sound cheery but immediately realizing she sounded grim. Vivian, rustling the newspaper, did not seem to pay the comment any attention.

"Doesn't Trish Green look dreadful in this Junior League photograph?"

"You in there?"

Vivian peered closely at the photograph on the society page, then closed the paper quickly. She turned on the radio at the kitchen table, but as soon as the sound came out, turned it off. She looked out the window. "I hate these curtains. Ugly blue. Blue's so in these days it makes me nauseous." She opened the paper again and stared blankly at the daily horoscope. "Do you want to know what your horoscope says, Nebraska? I wouldn't even dare to read mine."

"No'm."

Vivian began to turn the pages slowly again.

"You know, Miss Gold," Nebraska said gently, "I feels very comf'able talking to you."

"That's nice," Vivian answered without looking up.

"I hopes you feel comf'able talking with me."

Vivian pushed the paper away and looked up. "No, I'm not in the Junior League photograph. They don't allow . . . don't allow Jews."

In her mind's eye Nebraska saw Vivian curled up on the bed, clutching her stomach with one hand, her other hand pressed to her mouth. The broken child streamed out of her.

"Oh, not being in that club don't upset you, Miss Gold."

"No." Vivian looked at her hard. "It doesn't upset me. It galls me."

"Well, I can't belong to it, and I sure don't feel none the sorrier."

"It seems," Vivian said, "that if I were a Negro, I wouldn't even want to be part of the Junior League. I might even have my own Junior League."

"Is it like the choir?"

"Yes, I guess you could say that, but a choir selects you on how well you sing, and the Junior League selects you on how good your last name sounds."

"I likes the name Gold. I likes it very much." Nebraska wondered exactly when Vivian had lost the child, and where she had been at the time. Had it been on Wednesday night, when she was at a foot-washing, or Thursday afternoon, when she lay with Abraham, listening to the radio?

"Nebraska, you know that you sound like my mother sometimes!"

"And you know," Nebraska pressed, "the Gold family is one of the nicest, and *cleanest*, families in all Madoc. I talk to a lot of cooks and maids and you find out some terrible, I mean *terrible*, things about white folks' houses."

"Really?" Vivian, suddenly attentive, bent over closer to Nebraska. "Like what?" she asked in a voice close to a whisper.

"Oh," Nebraska said, instantly feeling a touch coy, "just things."

"Just things? What things?"

"Oh, well," said Nebraska, taking her time, "like how a certain dentist and his wife don't have their sheets changed but once a month, or how a certain judge and his wife don't even . . ."

"Yes, go on."

"Don't even flush the toilet!"

"I'll be," Vivian declared, screwing up her face with disgust. "What some people!"

"Yas'm. Or how Mr. I-can-not-tell-who slips out on his wife evenings and the poor cook's gotta make up excuses for him or she'll get fired."

"Who is it?"

"I-can-not-tell-who."

"You can tell *me*."

Emphatically, Nebraska shook her head.

"Nebraska, you can tell me anything, everything. Really. I can keep a secret better than anybody in this town."

Holding steadfast, Nebraska eased toward her question. "Miss Gold? Do you feel you can tell *me* anything?"

Vivian put her coffee to her lips, looking down into the edge of the cup.

"Do you?" Nebraska persisted.

"Yes, of course," Vivian said quickly, then added, "Well, you've only been here a couple of years, dear. It . . . It wouldn't be natural if I felt I could tell you everything. It takes time for people to . . . to really get to know each other."

"Could you tell me if somebody in your house was sick?"

Vivian nodded.

"Or had some kind of woman problem?"

Vivian's eyes misted over. Faltering, she asked, "Honey, are you sick?"

"Me? No, ma'am! I was just wonderin' if anybody here was having a problem. If they was, I'd sure want to help out."

After a few seconds of silence, Vivian asked in a voice quiet yet direct, "You found the towels?"

Bluffing, Nebraska answered, "Yas'm, I did."

"I thought the blood would rinse out in cold water. I guess I didn't do it soon enough."

"Blood!" said Nebraska, shocked upon hearing the actual word. Trying to cover that shock, she went on, "Oh, yas'm, you gots to wash out blood right away."

"I hadn't meant to get pregnant. But I knew it the second I was. I also had this feeling it wasn't going to work out. Strange. It's just this *feeling*, like a chill. You know?"

"Yas'm," said Nebraska, and feeling guilty that she had drawn out Vivian's confession—and now her sadness—felt she owed her the name of the mysterious adulterer. She also wanted to reach out and hold her hand comfortingly, though felt she could not after tricking her into telling. "It was Jimmy McGee, the car dealer, who was slippin' out on his wife. But seein' as how they moved from Madoc to Lafayette, Louisiana, this past summer, I don't guess it really makes no difference to nobody noways."

But Vivian didn't seem to be listening.

❧

That afternoon Nebraska changed the sheets in Edward and Vivian's bedroom. As she lifted the top sheet and popped it with her wrists, the white fabric billowed and turned. She popped it again.

This time the sheet seemed to hang suspended in the air, as if caught by a draft of wind, or by souls lifting it upward, blowing it back, lifting it once more, then dancing over the drifting, changing contours.

She started to pop the sheet a third time, but before it could flutter all the way back to the mattress it took on a life of its own, soaring and dipping, a cloud in seesaw.

Above that cloud, which now changed to a white wing rising toward the ceiling, the face of the lost child appeared in front, then behind, then beneath, as though the child were an angel playing hide-and-seek.

Alongside that child two others arose—the child Nebraska had lost in a miscarriage two years before starting to work at the Golds, and then the child she had given up at the age of sixteen when the yellow-faced woman with the rag around her head had jabbed the knitting needles high up into her belly. She had been made to walk back and forth in the woman's shack with the knitting needles still inside, until she collapsed; then she was taken to pass the child's life into a stream.

They came and turned, and as the sheet stilled and their faces turned yet again, then vanished, Nebraska said a prayer for her own, then a prayer for Miss Gold's, remembering the Hebrew she heard them read on Friday nights when lighting Sabbath candles, remembering *Boruch Atto Adonai,* and saying it so softly that only the unborn children could hear.

1951

AUGUST WAS SO HOT and damp that all Vivian could do was lounge on the inner tube attached to the pier by a long string. Madoc Bay was quiet, and the only movement of the inner tube was created by the flux of the tides, a slow current that spiraled in toward Point Hope or spiraled out toward the dim, small skyline of downtown Madoc on the opposite shore. The inner tube turned this way and that, revolving, bobbing, growing hot or cool as the sun flickered across it. And Vivian was plunked down in the middle of it, the bottom of her flowered bathing suit tracing the water, her feet dangling and casting shadows on the sandy bottom, her hands from time to time disappearing like half-sunk toy boats.

While she floated, her gaze passed along the open waters of Madoc Bay. Around one side of the bay, on a small peninsula, was the Old Dixie Country Club, the waterfront establishment with its sweeping grounds and green bungalows and gleaming clubhouse, where, it was said, every Alabama judge and congressman had special guest privileges. Vivian had visited the Old Dixie only twice, each time wishing she and Edward could be one of the few Jewish families allowed to join. The Old Dixie was renowned for its social gatherings, its bridge parties of slender, high-cheekboned ladies nodding and cooing as red-vested black boys scampered about with pretzels and frozen daiquiris.

At the Old Dixie the Confederate flag flew just beneath the United States flag, and golf carts roamed the impeccable Augustine grass with round, red attorneys inside. On Saturday night at the club a dance band set up show at the outdoor bandshell at Bourbon Point, and the high-cheekboned bridge players and round red attorneys danced peppy fox-trots to "Tallahassee Lassie."

Vivian drew her hands through the water toward the inner tube, and the float spun her about so that she directly faced the pier she was tethered to and the crab lines hung from its sides. When those crab lines were drawn taut, Sarah, lanky and sloe-eyed, and plump, curlyheaded Rachel, came out with long nets and bent over the lines, dragging them up slowly, watching for the whiskers and eyes, then quickly scooping.

Edward had picked up the mortgage to the small house the summer before. It was low, green-shaded, and unassuming; its back windows overlooked a wooded yard where the cedar trees formed a boundary with the house next door. In one of the rooms of the house, Vivian's mother, gray and watchful, stayed from time to time, and in another, Edward's parents—his short, bullish, Romanian father and his milky-complexioned, tranquil Romanian mother—stayed as well. When the sun dropped in the late afternoon, they all came down to the end of the pier and slipped off their overgarments and walked down the steps into the water. With Vivian amidst them, floating and turning, they'd paddle about, gossiping in Yiddish, exclaiming in German, questioning in Romanian, while Vivian answered back in the only language she knew or ever cared to know: the languid English of Alabama's Gulf Coast.

Her father, Moishe, had died the year before—a poor yet elegant Russian Jew who had stumbled from job to job as a young immigrant, finally ending up in Alabama, where his older brother, Benjamin, had landed a job with a traveling medicine show. Moishe was the pragmatist, Benjamin the romantic. When Benjamin saw a vision of Jesus Christ on a country road one afternoon and converted to Christianity, folks came from miles around to see the Jew changed to a Baptist. Moishe had refused to go to the baptism. He had stayed in Madoc, tending his store, talking incessantly of the sorrows of the Old World and the frustrated expectations of the New.

And oh, Vivian thought, how her father had loved to float! He had once lain in this same bay, smoking a pipe, his large, hairy feet sticking out of the water like fins and his smooth belly surfacing periodically. While he had lain there, inhaling, exhaling, tamping the end of the pipe against the butt of his hand, he confessed that his religion meant almost nothing to him, nothing but the burden of being different. "Maybe Benjamin had the right idea. Maybe. Maybe. Maybe." His *maybes* had been as constant and rhythmic as the ripples the breeze set up on the bay.

Maybe it was Edward's refusal to embrace *maybes* that bound Vivian so closely to him. "I know who I am. I know what I do. I know what my beliefs are. I know my hopes for the future." Edward had once spoken in such a way as he swam about with Vivian clutching onto his back. Later, when he had rolled over, skeeting water high into the air, he remarked that he was only joking in his self-assurance, but Vivian knew that he wasn't, that Edward was a man who felt comfortable with the world about him, whereas she, like her father, was the child of *maybes*.

Her father's touch had been tentative those Sunday mornings when they had gone to the GM&O station and watched the trains chug in and out. Edward's touch was very sure. His fingers were not the long, tobacco-stained ones of a father, bending and hesitantly brushing his child's hair, but the broad, certain fingers of a husband, moving up through the water, coming over her shoulders, rubbing and embracing her. They were the fingers of a man who cared for her more consistently than she felt she could ever care for him, or for anyone else for that matter. There was no *maybe* in his touch. There was—only love?

Vivian lay back on the inner tube and felt the sun on her thighs. She recalled Edward, on a purple July evening, diving into the water from the pier's end and, on surfacing, holding his bathing suit up to the sky. He spun the suit about like a lariat and flung it back onto the pier, then swam out on his belly and made a surface dive, the white curve of his buttocks appearing and disappearing, the bubbles of his breath heralding his coming to the surface again.

Edward had made another surface dive, and Vivian had felt his body pass close beneath hers on the inner tube. His hand brushed over her leg to her ankle, then ripped her off the float. She screamed, her scream cut short by the water as Edward dragged her under. His face loomed close to hers through the murkiness and changed to another face—a face she had never seen, the face of the man who lived in the lake of her childhood summers and met girls under water when they were alone and gobbled them whole!

The man's face pressed against her, his lips crossing her neck. He lifted her out of the water, and as Edward's face returned, the strangeness of his touch had lingered, as though he were still the creature beneath the lake. When he reached behind her and unclipped her bathing suit, she had finally relaxed, and her husband's strangeness was gone. He peeled the suit down over her shoulders and full white breasts. He held her closer and moved his hand down her back, his palm sliding smoothly over her in the water.

Then Vivian had seen his eyes, always brown, but suddenly gold-flecked in the fading dusk. He came into her and the gold-flecks were in her own eyes. They became the same body, same hands, same mouth.

Looking up from the inner tube now at the pier, and feeling the sun warm on her belly, she longed for Edward to appear right now by surprise, to dive in and startle her, to snatch her thrillingly off the float.

✧

Though Vivian usually hated to get her hair wet, she had done so on purpose this August afternoon. Now, stepping out of the shower at the back of the house, she brushed it out and, wrapped in a kimono Edward had brought her from New Orleans, walked to the room at the end of the hallway. Behind the door a radio played. "THIS HALF IS BROUGHT TO YOU BY NEW RINSO, WHICH CONTAINS SOLIUM, THE AMAZING SCIENTIFIC SUNLIGHT INGREDIENT."

Vivian knocked and heard a radio voice say "GREETIN'S AND SALUTATIONS, ANDY, BROTHER MYSTIC KNIGHT OF THE SEA!" Vivian knocked again and a voice—it sounded like Nebraska's —asked gruffly, "Who's there?"

"It's me," Vivian said, then loudly repeated "me" over the noise of the radio. After being invited to enter, she pushed the door open and peered in. Nebraska sat in a rocker, flowered shift coming to just above her knees. Rachel and Sarah, shirtless in shorts, lay on the bed, eyes wide as they listened to the broadcast. Vivian's mother, Sosha Brooks, sat on a rocker near the window and inched her chair closer to the radio.

"What did Andy just say?" Sosha asked. "Something about a commotion?"

Nebraska translated: "Andy said Sapphire's done seen Kingfish with another woman and she's gonna give him a concuction on the head when he gets home!"

Rachel rolled over on her stomach and faced Sosha. "Grandma, can't you hear?"

Sarah wagged her finger and imitated Andy. "Sapphire's gonna give you a *concuction!*"

"What was that he just said?" Sosha asked, leaning over.

"Holy mackerel," Nebraska said. "Kingfish says he's afraid Sapphire's gonna sue him for separate maintenance."

Rachel glared at Sosha. "Grandma, can't you hear?"

"I can hear fine," Sosha retorted. "I just can't understand pickaninny talk."

Vivian stepped into the room. "Mother, that's an awful thing to say. Apologize to Nebraska."

Nebraska waved her hand in the air and scooted her chair

closer to the radio. Andy's voice roared out: "WHY, KINGFISH, SAPPHIRE AIN'T SAID NOTHIN' 'BOUT NO SEPARATE MAYONNAISE!"

"I understood that," Sosha said, her mouth crinkling with laughter.

"Mother," Vivian persisted, "please apologize."

"Miss Gold," Nebraska said, "your momma ain't said nothin' wrong. That's just the way colored talk up yonder in New York."

"Mother, I've never heard you use that word before."

"What word? *Pickaninny?*" Sosha began to rock steadily. "It's only another way of saying *shvartzeh.*"

Nebraska spoke with irritation. "I can't hear if everybody's gonna talk. I invited y'all into my room to listen, and now y'all want to chew fat."

Vivian, exasperated, rubbed her hair with a towel, then shook her head to dislodge a drop of water from her ear.

"My teacher said you should use a Q-tip to get water out of your ear," Sarah said.

Nebraska turned up the radio and the *Amos 'n' Andy* show blasted forth. "Miss Sosha," she called over the dialogue, "did you know the people on *Amos 'n' Andy* ain't even really *shwatsas*? In real life they're white folks."

"I *knew* they sounded peculiar," Sosha returned. "I bet they're from Texas."

"You should be extremely careful with a Q-tip," Vivian instructed. "The general rule is never put anything in your ear smaller than your elbow." She bent her head to the side and began to slap her temple in order to loose the drop.

"Miss Gold," Nebraska blurted out, "you look like a crazy woman."

Sarah bounded up from where she lay and stood on the bed, surveying her mother's efforts, then catching sight of herself in the mirror, asked, "When am I going to get breasts?"

"In good time," said Vivian, still swatting her head.

Static cut across the radio dialogue and Nebraska fiddled

with the receiver. "You know, chirren is growing up too fast these days. We might have done everything when we was little, but we didn't want to *know* everything."

"Your mother developed when she was thirteen years, maybe fourteen," Sosha said. "I don't think you need ask more about it."

"Thirteen?" Sarah started to bounce on the bed, keeping an eye on her chest. "I'm already twelve! I'll never catch up!"

"You're not twelve," Rachel remarked. "You're only eleven."

"What do you know?" Sarah came back. "You're just a baby."

"I'm not a baby. You're a baby."

"You're both babies." Vivian's tone was stern. "Here y'all are carrying on, bickering, turning Nebraska's bed into a trampoline. You won't even let Kingfish get a word in edgewise."

Sarah squeezed her nipples, drawing them out like elastic. "I want to be big," she said, throwing her head back and speaking to the heavens. "Like Nebraska!"

Sosha rocked forward on her chair and, almost tipping over, slapped at Sarah's hand, just nicking her little finger. "Don't pull on yourself," she said fiercely. "You'll go lopsided."

"Sarah," Nebraska said, "Granna's right. It ain't good to pull on yourself."

"But what if I don't get breasts?" Sarah's voice became frantic. "All the women in the bathing suit ads have breasts!"

"Confucius say," Vivian advised, "One must be most patient."

"But what if I don't?"

"Well," answered Vivian, growing amused, "maybe, when you do a swan dive . . ." She began to sing: "You will fly through the air with the greatest of ease . . ."

"Mother!" Sarah kicked in frustration at the foot of the bed and caught her foot under the railing. She fell down over Rachel, who pushed her off and stood up, kicking back. Like a tragic heroine, Sarah turned and tossed, flailing arms at her little sister.

"Vivian," Sosha said icily, "this is the price you pay for letting them go about with half their clothes off." She muttered something in German.

Holding her hairbrush in the left hand, with her right hand Vivian reached for Sarah's foot. "Settle down, you two. This isn't a zoo."

Sarah kicked out blindly and knocked Vivian back a step. Vivian took a swipe with the back of her brush, missing Sarah and hitting Rachel, who began yelling. Nebraska rushed up from the chair, picked up Sarah, and carried her bodily to the corner. "You kick at your momma like that?" she asked at fever pitch, setting the child down. "You know you wasn't raised like that!"

A knock sounded sharply at the door. Everybody fell silent. "Who is it?" Vivian asked, going to the radio and turning it off, knowing full well who it was.

The door opened and Edward stood there, briefcase in hand, straw hat pushed back on his head. "Is the Battle of Madoc Bay getting revived in here?" he asked hesitantly, as though he was afraid the answer was yes. "Can I get somebody ammunition? Torpedoes? Peashooters?"

Vivian leaned over and kissed him pertly on the lips. "Oh, honey, we were just listening to Nebraska's radio program is all. And talking."

Nebraska wiped her forehead and sat back down on the rocker. "Yes, sir," she said, nodding. "That's all we was doin'."

That night Vivian could not sleep. The rocking of the inner tube stayed with her and made the whole room rock. When she did doze off briefly, she dreamed she was still in the water, and saw blue crabs and flounder swirling beneath her. The swirling made her dizzy.

Finally she rose, took a motion sickness pill, and walked out onto the porch. The night was luminous, the sky patched with cirrus clouds. The pier, eerily, looked like the long back of a prehistoric creature.

After unlatching the screen she walked barefoot down to the pier. She stepped on a cockleburr, extracted it, and continued on to the pier, her feet drumming quietly on the wooden crossboards.

She began to hum "Stars Fell on Alabama," then changed to "Mobile," then stopped a moment as a star, firing brightly, streaked toward shore and disappeared. She made a wish: that everyone she loved should be healthy, and happy. As though in response, heat lightning lit up the sky.

She remembered a night when she was a teen-ager and had crawled out a window onto the rooftop of her parents' house. For hours she had sat there, watching the velvety sky flash with heat lightning, recalling what her uncle Benjamin had said about stars, clouds, and people's eyes being glimpses of God. Then she had asked herself incessantly, until the question became a drone in her head, "What's life all about?"

Looking up, Vivian saw the bay house and had, after all these years, what seemed to be an answer to her question. The house, and all the people in the house, were what life was all about. The answer, though, was not the one she wanted. It was blunt, and unexciting.

She began to feel as though she had borne that house and all the people inside, who now were multiplying endlessly, as in mirrors. There was no room for an actress there, no room for a different Vivian. The only Vivian there was room for was the Vivian who gave birth and fussed about the kitchen and humored her daughters when they fretted.

Shouldn't the presence of Nebraska in that house enable the two Vivians—actress and mother—to thrive equally? Why did Nebraska add to the concerns of family, as if she were one more child who needed attention, one more life reflected in endless mirrors?

She coiled up her hair with her right hand, eased the screen door open, and walked into the house. Rachel, sleeping on a couch in the corner, turned and muttered. A bat clung to the screen. Crickets pulsed. She moved down the hall toward her room.

Before going in to where Edward slept, though, she noticed a crack of light coming from the end of the hallway. Tiptoeing there, she put her eye up to the keyhole of a door. Nebraska sat alone, motionless, reading.

"Are you okay?" Vivian whispered through the keyhole.

Nebraska, looking up startled, put her hand to her ear.

"Are you okay?" Vivian whispered a little louder.

Nebraska nodded. She closed the book, stood with a short groan, and came to the door and opened it.

"What are you reading?"

"Book of Timothy," Nebraska answered softly.

"Is it good?"

"It's the Good Book."

"Do . . . do you feel okay? You look a little sad."

"Well, yes, I guess I am sad. A little."

"Tell me. What's the problem?"

"No problem." Nebraska looked away.

"Is it the heat?"

Nebraska shook her head.

"Well?" Vivian leaned over in order to catch Nebraska's diverted gaze.

Nebraska closed her book, looking back at Vivian now. "I guess it's just this ol' bay. It makes me blue."

"Aw, honey, it makes me blue, too, sometimes."

Nebraska thumped her chest. "It makes me blue right here."

Vivian nodded. "Yes, I understand."

"And I guess what's more is . . ."

"Go on."

"Guess what's more is, my family they so far away over in Madoc."

"Your family?" Vivian took a small step back. "Well . . . well, you do see them on weekends."

"Yas'm." Nebraska hesitated. "But it ain't enough. My chirren need me more."

"But . . ." Vivian began, nonplussed. "But, Nebraska, Edward and I thought, well, thought this was kind of like a vacation for you too." She raised her hands, gesturing to the house. "Isn't this place kind of special for you? We know a lot of folks who'd give anything to spend a month on the water."

Looking down at the floor, Nebraska nodded and started to back into her room.

"We're only out here a couple more weeks," Vivian went on. "Won't the time fly?"

Nebraska said nothing.

"Look," Vivian said cheerily, "I've got a solution. Have your family come out here and spend a night. Yes, that's the *perfect* solution."

"Out here?"

"Yes, that's what I said. Out *here*! Hazel, who works for Molly Granger, had her family out one night. They stayed in the old slave quarters out back of the Grangers' house. Of course, I would never have y'all stay in any ol' slave quarters, even if we did have them."

"Some slave quarters is fixed up nice," remarked Nebraska, but Vivian reached over and put her hand on Nebraska's forearm before she could finish her comment.

"You mean too much to me and Edward for us to make you blue. Have your family out, please, Nebraska."

❧

"I didn't expect seven of them!"

Under her breath Vivian spoke on the telephone to Doris Klein. "Really, Doris, don't you think that's a bit of an abuse of my generosity? Don't you?"

Doris's voice buzzed back.

While Vivian responded, saying, "It's a good thing Nebraska and I prepared a lot of chicken and potato salad," she craned her neck out from the kitchen where the phone was, and watched the Waters brood sitting solemnly in deck chairs near the beginning of the pier. Todd, with oxlike build, looked about with a deadpan expression. Abraham, wearing a straw fishing hat and holding a cane pole, stood motionless as a statue, looking like a model for the Gold's Western Wear calendar. The caption read SLEEPY TIME DOWN SOUTH.

"I wish," Vivian continued, "that Rachel and Sarah had not disappeared. You know, I think Nebraska's family appears to be uncomfortable, out of place. Her oldest boy even looks terrified."

Doris's voice rose a pitch.

"I'm not sure who all the others are. They're four girls. Nebraska introduced one as her cousin's daughter, two as friends, and the fourth she just called Wanda or Wenda or some name like that."

Doris's tone became indignant.

"Well," Vivian replied, "I appreciate your concern. Maybe it won't be so bad. I better go on out, though. They look *so* uneasy! Okay. Bye-bye."

After hanging up, Vivian wiped her hands on a dish towel, mustered her confidence, and leaned out the window again. "Anybody like some iced tea?"

Nebraska scurried into the house. "Miss Gold, you ain't gonna wait on *us*. That's right nice, but I'll do it."

"No," Vivian returned, "I'll do it."

"We'll both do it."

Vivian carried the oatmeal cookies and napkins, and Nebraska the tea and tray of glasses. They set down the items on a french-grille table, and Vivian sat down pertly on the edge of an empty chaise longue.

"My, Nebraska," she said, "Todd and Junior are getting so big and fine-looking."

"Thank you," said Nebraska, clearing her throat. She awkwardly held an oatmeal cookie.

"And Abraham," Vivian went on, "you're looking so good yourself these days."

"Thank you, Miss Gold."

"Well!" Vivian slapped the arms of the chaise longue and raised her enthusiasm a level. "Another oatmeal cookie? Anybody?"

Todd put up his hand sheepishly.

"Well, go ahead and have one then."

The boy reached out, his hand seeming large and blunt to Vivian as it fumbled for a cookie. A cookie toppled onto the ground and he bent to pick it up. Vivian bent down also, and Todd's hand brushed right in front of her. She drew back, startled by the heavy musk odor of his body.

Working to conceal her embarrassment, Vivian latched onto a new topic: "Why don't we have a fishing contest?"

Nobody responded.

"We have a few more poles in the house. Maybe y'all will catch some trout."

"Can you catch croakers out here?" Abraham asked.

"Croakers? Certainly. But you can't eat croakers."

"We eats 'em."

"Oh, you do?" Vivian smiled weakly. "Of course, I forgot what good fish they are."

"Oh, yas'm. We always catch croakers off the bridge goin' to Lafayette Island. Nebraska fry 'em up quick with onion and a little garlic and they real good."

"That . . . that's interesting." In her mind Vivian retraced the road to Lafayette Island. Frequently, as Edward's Nash had rolled across the bridge, she had remarked at the large number of colored folks standing along the pedestrian walk, their fishing poles held patiently over the water. She had once told Edward that they looked like beings come from another planet.

"Miss Gold," said Abraham, "you ever drove over to Lafayette Island?"

"No, I don't think so."

Todd, standing, stretched and became taller than Nebraska. He could not be much older than Sarah, figured Vivian, even though his stature was nearly that of a grown man.

The girl named Wenda pulled out a pack of cigarettes and motioned to Todd. He tugged out some matches from his pocket, struck one, and, cupping the match in his hands, lit her cigarette. She nodded and puffed vigorously.

Vivian slyly noted Wenda's face. She resembled Nebraska around the eyes, but her nose was slenderer and her lips more delicate. Her complexion was light brown.

Todd spoke. "If you tell me where the other poles is, I'll go get 'em."

"I'll show you," Vivian said, glad to have the opportunity to break from the gathering.

Once in the shed behind the house rooting about for the poles, Vivian asked Todd, "Shall we get a pole for Wenda?"

"For Wenda June? No'm. My sister don't like to fish."

"Your sister!"

"She don't like to fool with the bait."

"Yes, of course. I wasn't thinking."

"You think we might catch a ground mullet?"

"Todd, how old is your sister?"

"Ground mullets is better than croaker," Todd said, then answered: "I guess Wenda's 'bout nineteen, twenty. I forget."

"Nineteen or twenty?" Vivian calculated fearfully, thinking, "Nebraska would have borne her when she was only fifteen!"

Before she could chance another question, they were within earshot of the pier. They passed out the poles and some dead shrimp Edward kept in the icebox for bait, and the group filed respectfully out to the end of the pier.

Nebraska leaned back under the awning of the gazebo at the end of the pier and began to fan herself with a Kleenex tissue. The three girls took off their shoes, rolled back their skirts, and dangled their feet in the water. Wenda June walked to one corner and lit another cigarette from the butt of the first. Todd, Junior, and Abraham fished. Vivian sat and watched their lines floating out and corks suspended. She envisioned Nebraska at age fifteen, suckling an infant at her adolescent breasts.

Junior's cork disappeared. "Miss Gold, Miss Gold, I got somethin'!" He pulled on the line and the cane pole doubled over like a twig.

"Yank it up," Nebraska yelled. "Yank it, boy!"

Junior yanked. A flat, hat-shaped creature rose into the air and came hurtling toward the pier. With a smack the thing landed, its body shuddering, its nostrils flaring and beadlike eyes revolving.

"You done pulled up a devilfish!" Abraham said excitedly.

"I know what it is," Todd announced proudly. "I know 'cause I seen one in science class. It's a stingaree."

"Get y'all's foots out of that water," Nebraska said briskly to the two girls. "Get them out! It's dangerous!"

Todd reached down and dragged a jackknife blade along the tail of the stingray. He cut out the barb and held its serrated edge up to the sky. "There's poison in this stinger," he said boastfully. "Watch yourself."

Vivian put her face close to the barb and noted the saw-teeth. "Ugh." When she turned back, she saw the Waters clan convened under the gazebo.

Abraham acted as spokesman. "Miss Gold, thank you for having us out. The last Greyhound back is in half an hour and we think we can make it if we start now."

"But you just got here."

"Yeah," chimed Todd, "we just got here." His grown man's face, pouting, became a little boy's.

"Todd," Nebraska said sternly. The boy walked reluctantly to his mother. While bending close and whispering to him, Nebraska pinched his arm.

Vivian moved toward them. "At least let me give you a ride to the train station."

"They'll be all right," Nebraska insisted. "It ain't too far to walk."

"No . . . no, you go on with them." Vivian halted, looking at the brightening face of Nebraska. "I can manage things here by myself for a few days."

Nebraska walked over and pecked Vivian on the cheek.

When the brood had trailed back down the pier, Vivian stood alone, arms enfolded.

"It's too confusing, all too confusing," she said out loud, then addressed the expiring stingray. "You try to be a mother, it's hard. You try to be an employer, it's hard. You try to be a friend, it's hard. You try to be all three and it's impossible!"

Feeling quite burdened with these considerations, Vivian peeled down to her bathing suit, stepped down the ladder into the bay water, and dog-paddled to the inner tube. She crawled belly-down onto the inflated circle and flipped over on her back. With the sun beating down on her chest and thighs, she waved her hands in the water, spinning toward the skyline of Madoc on the opposite shore.

1952

Nebraska felt life take root inside of her in the fall. It was a vague, discomforting feeling, as if an internal compass were veered off course. She felt bloated, and her breasts became sore. For three weeks, on and off, she felt as if she had the flu, vomiting up her breakfast.

Of course, she knew it was not the flu, as the sensation was a familiar one (five times familiar, counting her one miscarriage and one abortion), but this time, perhaps because of her age, she felt the compass swing the most sharply. "Get me off this ship!" she said anxiously to her daughter, Wenda June. "Get me off this tossing ship!"

That ship stayed under her as she left the apartment in the federal housing project and boarded the bus and fussed and cleaned about the house at Magnolia Court. It was as if the carpets and floor tilings were swaying beneath her, like the carnival ride at the Greater Gulf State Fair in which the floor of a room swung one way and then the other while all the people inside screamed delightedly, trying to hang on to the walls that were revolving in the opposite direction.

She called in sick four times in those three weeks, and during the fourth week said to Wenda, "Take this note to Miss Gold and tell her you gonna work for her until I feels better."

"I don't want to work," said Wenda. "Not for any white woman at least."

"Wenda June," Nebraska said angrily, glaring up at her from the couch, "if you can't make it up in Detroit and want to come back here to Madoc, what more kind of work you gonna do?"

Wenda shrugged. "I hate the South."

"This is your home," said Nebraska, with the weight of having been through the conversation many times before. "And if you want to stay in your home, I can't keep making it for you. You gots to get out and work yourself."

"I can go to the state docks. They got work there."

"So go there! Like you said you was gonna do before. But for right now you go on and work for your momma at Miss Gold's."

"Why can't Daddy go there and work? He ain't doing nothin'."

"A man don't work cleanin' and cookin'. Besides, Abraham's waiting for another construction job, Wenda. You know that. The union say there's nothin' right now."

"He can't hold on to a job when he does get it."

"Wenda! Don't carry on like that, child. I'm sick and tired of you wantin' to drag us through the dirt. If you don't like it here, then leave."

"Well," Wenda answered indignantly, "I'll take the note to Miss Gold, but I ain't gonna work there." She grabbed up the paper and stomped out the door.

Nebraska laid her head on the pillows of the couch—a new one, still covered in plastic—and looked up at the light fixture. "The gov'ment likes things to be regular," Romaine had told her. "They gonna make sure each housing unit is 'zactly the same."

" 'Zactly the same" meant: a porch, a living room, a kitchen, a downstairs bedroom and two upstairs bedrooms, and a bathroom with a small window overlooking the backyard. The backyard, already a garden at Nebraska's, was surrounded by a chain link fence that led to the next backyard, and so on down the line. Nebraska's apartment was the fourth from the street, in a line that stretched for twenty-five apartments. The whole apartment house looked like a long barracks, except that the brick was new and shiny and there was a neat walk between one apartment house and another, with patches of dirt planted with clumps of Augustine grass. The area where the old Waters shanty had stood was now bulldozed away, and a street was paved there to give easy access to the docks. From the top step leading to the backyard, Nebraska could just make out where her old house had stood. Beyond it she could see the riggings of steamships, the eerie latticework of cranes and hoists, and a building boldly painted with MADOC LUMBER COMPANY.

" 'Zactly the same" also meant hot and cold running water, steam heat, and drapes. And it meant, as Nebraska lay there thinking, "No more wind comin' through the chinks during winter."

She had invited Vivian and Edward out to the apartment three times, but they had postponed accepting the invitations. Nebraska began to suspect they simply did not care to come. "That's funny," she had said to Abraham, while lying in the bed, " 'cause it was Mr. Gold who made sure I got a good place here. He fixed up all the papers and everything and told me 'Now, Nebraska, private housing'll eat you up alive the way things are going. I know 'cause that's my business. One bad landlord will make your life miserable. So you're better off taking advantage of what the government has to offer.' "

Abraham had shaken his head when Nebraska told him that, saying he didn't quite understand what Mr. Gold had meant, but also saying that Mr. Gold was smarter than him and his hounds put together, so it must be true.

"You every bit as smart as Mr. Gold," Nebraska had returned. "Just 'cause you can't read or write good don't mean a thing. I sometimes think Mr. Gold, for all his education, would forget to put his pants on in the morning if Miss Gold didn't dress him."

At that comment Abraham had howled, saying, "I guess there is every kind a way o' bein' smart."

Nebraska had nodded, rubbing some cold cream that Vivian had given her on her face.

"But it's so new and *so* beautiful!" Nebraska exclaimed quietly to herself now, as she lay, one month with child, studying the room. The light fixture was round and frosted, just like the one in the back hallway of the Golds' house. "Maybe one day I'll have a whole house just like theirs," she said brightly, patting her hands together like a child." "How'd you like that?"

"Who is you talkin' to, woman?" came a low voice from upstairs.

"Ain't talkin' to nobody but me and my baby," Nebraska called. She had been unaware that Abraham was awake.

"Why aren't you at work?"

" 'Cause I'm sick."

"With what?"

"With my baby, fool. You know that."

"I think that baby's affectin' your mind, Gardenia."

"I think whiskey's done affected your mind already, Abraham."

"I ha'n't been caught talkin' to myself."

"Ain't talking to myself! I'm talking to my baby. To my . . ."

"To what?"

"To my baby. I haven't thought up names yet."

"Why don't you call it after me?"

"It's not a boy."

"How we gonna afford another baby, boy or girl? Miss Gold gonna keep you on if you carryin' around a little baby?"

"Abraham, if you want to talk to me, you come down the stairs where I can see you. I'm pregnant and sick and you making me shout." Nebraska drew her hand up to her forehead to gauge her fever. She felt she had none. She reached down and felt her pulse, trying to ignore Abraham's comment.

Abraham appeared, his pants, though baggy, neatly pressed, and a light cotton shirt on unbuttoned. "This shirt of Mr. Gold's is a little full on me. It's a nice-lookin' one, though."

"Hm, mm," Nebraska agreed. "Do you really think it'd make any difference to the Golds if I had a baby?"

"How you gonna stoop and mop and all if you got to watch an infant?" Abraham came down the steps and went to the front door. He opened it and inhaled. "That damn paper mill's stinkin' to Jesus."

"Don't curse on the Lord, Abraham. Jesus, forgive him."

"I think you'd better study on how you might lose your job, Gardenia."

There was a knock at the door. Nebraska turned to see Wenda June followed by Vivian. Her heart raced as she sat up quickly, pressing one hand to her hair to straighten it and fluffing a pillow with her other. "We was just talking about what a beautiful shirt Mr. Gold gave Abraham." She stood weakly, smoothing down her nightgown. "Come for a housewarming, I see."

Vivian entered hesitantly and glanced up at Abraham, who nodded hello. "I'm sorry you're sick, Nebraska. I went on and called your friend Mary to come in until you feel better." She stopped and looked around. "My, my, it is a lovely new place."

"You're not mad with me?" Nebraska blurted out.

"Mad?" Vivian looked at her inquisitively. "Why should I be mad?"

" 'Cause I'm sick."

"Because you're sick? Why in God's name would that make me mad?"

" 'Cause . . . 'cause . . ."

When Vivian's face broke into a smile it reminded Nebraska of the first moment she had seen her at the Mardi Gras party, of the way her eyes had flashed and her expression had changed and flickered. "I couldn't be mad with anybody right now, honey. As a matter of fact, I think I'm probably the happiest woman in all of Madoc."

Nebraska stared at her, waiting for the explanation. "Did you win a sweepstakes?"

"A sweepstakes? Yes," said Vivian. "Of a sort."

"What sort?" Abraham asked.

"Abraham," Nebraska said gruffly. "Could you go on back upstairs and let us talk private a moment."

As Abraham walked back upstairs reluctantly, Vivian came and sat on the edge of the couch. She picked up Nebraska's hand and placed it on her belt buckle. Quietly and with great self-assurance she said, "Nebraska, dear, we're going to have another baby!"

᧞

As fall turned to winter, then winter to spring, Nebraska felt the bond thicken between herself and the fetus, and, in a different way, between herself and Vivian Gold. Time and again she replayed in her mind Vivian's response when she had announced her own pregnancy: "Nebraska, Nebraska, that's so wonderful, so fine." After placing Nebraska's hand on her belt buckle, Vivian had done the same in return, placing her small, light-brown hand with its smooth red nails against Nebraska's belly. For that moment as each touched the other, felt for the life beginning to flower in the other, Nebraska imagined their children would be cousins.

This feeling of kinship grew in her even more when the two women walked the streets of downtown Madoc side by side, nodding and waving at the white women Vivian knew and at the black women Nebraska knew. Together, Nebraska and Vivian took up most of the walk. Nebraska, already well over two hundred pounds, put on little weight with the pregnancy. Vivian, weighing only a hundred and ten or so to begin with, ballooned with the child.

"Now I know what it's like to be fat," Vivian said as they strolled through the downtown to meet Edward one day.

"Other children hadn't made you so big?"

"No, no. Maybe I'm going to have a boy this go-round."

"That would be nice," Nebraska said, thinking, in fact, how good a boy would be for Vivian and Edward. Certainly, they loved their girls, gave them everything children could want, but it seemed only right for Edward to have a son. "You know," she went on, "Abraham loves his boys. He loves his girl, too, but the boys is special."

"Hm, mm," said Vivian, stopping a moment to push her dress a little to the side as it had moved off-center on her stomach. "I don't think we'll go over the bay this summer, not with my baby and all."

"Having a boy would give Mr. Gold somebody he could take to play baseball. And take fishing."

"I'd love a boy, Nebraska. You know that. Of course, I'd love to have a baby girl too."

"One thing for sure. Boys ain't as much to worry about when they get to be teen-agers. They might act wild, but you don't have to watch out they go and get themselves . . ."

"Get themselves in trouble," Vivian completed.

"Yas'm. In trouble."

"Well, my girls don't have that problem yet, thank God. Besides, I think they can follow a good example."

"Do you think the good example's what's needed?" Nebraska asked as they turned a corner and came to the edge of Dauphine Square.

"If you don't practice what you preach, Nebraska, what good is it?"

The water oaks of the square cast a shade in front of them as they strolled along. A squirrel leaped in front of them, stood on its hind legs, wriggled its nose, then leaped away. The morning's heat rose from the walk.

Nebraska felt the confession coming. "Miss Gold, I had my first pregnancy and was confusin' on why!"

Halting in her steps, Vivian turned to her. "What do you mean?"

Nebraska shook her head, running her hands across her dress. "Did not know why, ma'am. Had trouble puttin' two and two together. Nobody ever told me nothin' 'bout God's ways."

"You mean you didn't know for certain that . . ." Vivian meted out the words slowly. "Didn't know for certain that one thing begot another?"

As Nebraska shook her head and softly said no, she became fourteen years old again. Standing in the middle of the country grove where the white plantation boss had taken her, she lay down, overcome with the heat of the Indian summer. When the man lay down next to her and his coarse red hands touched her shoulders, she was puzzled; she was startled and confused when his hands jumped to her chest. He began to push and grab at her skin and she shouted, "Let me up!" He laughed and forced his mouth down onto her throat. As she fought to stand he pressed down on her with his whole body, half naked now, heavy as a workhorse, raw and foul-smelling as the underside of a workhorse. Then she was drowning, sucking for breath, gulping at the butt of his elbow that jammed against her mouth. He tore into her; she screamed. He clamped a hand over her mouth and she screamed again, the scream splitting in two and skipping like fire through her split body. Suddenly she could breathe again, and she lifted her head up and watched him walk away, heading for trees, clutching his trousers to his ghostly white backside. Then she cried. She cried every day that week and vomited every day the next week, then stopped crying and stopped vomiting and told no one. After five months, with her body swelled, she visited the yellow-faced woman with the rag around her head, who mourned: "You done got a little baby in you from sittin' in the outhouse, and there ain't nothin' I can do about it after all this time." In June, in a bed prepared for her by Wenda, the pastor's wife, she gave birth to a girl, and she held her baby close, knowing in her bones the yellow-faced woman had lied about how she'd gotten it.

The recollection broke around her as Vivian turned to go through Dauphine Square. "Miss Gold," Nebraska said sadly, "up in the country, we didn't know nothin'. We used to believe every kind of devil's talk and hoodoo about babies. I thought babies was somethin' that came out of . . ." She hesitated, embarrassed. "Well, I'll just put it this way: I used to think babies came out of nowhere."

"The lack of education is an awful thing," Vivian lamented. "You know, my own mother didn't even tell me about the woman's cycle. Can you believe it? Of course, I'd have never had happen what you did, because she did warn me, over and *over*, about men. But when I got the visitor my first time I thought I was, plain and simply, going to die."

Nebraska stamped her foot to shoo away a squirrel. "Well, I know more now than anybody could ever want to know."

"Me too," Vivian said, laughing.

"And you watch. Now that you know everything to tell, you gonna have a boy. That's just the way the world is. Yas'm, it is."

❧

Edward Gold's office was a large, tidy room lined with filing cabinets and maps of Madoc. There were aerial maps, surveyors' maps, topographical maps. There was a calendar from Gold's Western Wear—his parents' store—turned to the month of May. A painting of a man holding a fishing pole was on the calendar with the caption SLEEPY TIME DOWN SOUTH. A pitcher of ice water stood on Edward's desk and a fan turned its slow *clackity-clack* overhead.

To Nebraska, Edward Gold's office seemed the axis around which Madoc turned. As he'd point to those maps, showing what parts of the city were being sold, which were being developed, and which were becoming mobile home parks or shopping areas or church sites, he seemed to be a young prince divvying up his kingdom.

Vivian's cousin Barbara—everybody called her Babs, even little children—sat at the front desk, answered the phone, and typed Edward's correspondence. Babs was once described by Edward as *zaftig*, which Vivian explained to Nebraska meant plump, but Romaine explained—as she heard it from Margery Berman—meant not only plump but *sexy*. Nebraska was partial to Vivian's explanation of the word, but sometimes feared Mr. Gold was partial to Romaine's.

Babs was short and buxom. Her face was round and pale as meringue. She seemed inclined, Nebraska decided, to wear dresses tight enough and loud enough to catch men's eyes as far away as Fort Deposit. In a scarlet dress today—the top button was popped off—she greeted Nebraska and Vivian as they took chairs by the window overlooking Dauphine Square and waited for Edward.

"Wh-why how y'all?" Babs asked, and giggled nervously. "Hot, hot, ain't it?"

"We're fine, fine," Vivian answered.

"Two pregnant women is quite a sight," Babs said.

Nebraska nodded. "We'd frighten away anything."

"Babs," Vivian asked, smiling sweetly, "when do you expect Edward back?"

Babs twirled a card file and glanced around. "Maybe he stepped out the back door to get a newspaper. That man follows Dow Jones like some men follow horses."

"You don't have to tell me," Vivian remarked. She admired a vase of flowers on Babs's desk. "Pretty mums. From a client?"

"A client?" Babs giggled. "Vivian, you make me sound like a lady of the night, and I haven't even been taken to the picture show in two years." She blew off a fly that alighted on the lilies. "Edward gave me these. Just to brighten up the place."

Babs's hands moved anxiously over the telephone, the paper clips, the typewriter. First she dusted, then she neatened. *Clackity-clack,* sounded the fan.

"Those flowers done brightened up Miss Babs too," thought Nebraska to herself, leaning back in the chair and feeling the kicking of the child in her belly. She said a prayer of thanks for having her Abraham.

Restlessly, Babs began to jiggle a drop chain around her

neck. "Did you see this crescent moon Edward gave me for my birthday? It was from Vivian, too, of course."

"It looks pretty with what you're wearing," Vivian offered, straining to be diplomatic.

"My," Nebraska added. "It looks right nice next to your Star of David."

Babs grinned. "Aunt Sosha gave me the Star."

There was a sudden commotion in the back room. "Babs, hon'! You got to get this hell hole straightened up back here." Newspaper under arm, Edward stomped in. When he saw his wife and Nebraska he blushed the color of a Rome delicious, regained himself, then spoke tenderly. "Ah, the two mothers!" He blushed the apple color again and, still blushing, walked over to Vivian and kissed her on the lips.

Babs turned away.

"Ooh, it's kicking!" Vivian said.

Nebraska joined in. "Mine's kickin' too!"

Babs screwed up her face. "I'd hate to have something inside of me kicking."

"Me too," Edward seconded. He placed his hand on Vivian's stomach and looked to the side like a doctor listening through a stethoscope. "He's a real tiger!"

In what seemed a spontaneous gesture, Edward reached to Nebraska and placed his hand over her navel. Just as quickly he seemed to want to draw it away. His hand, large and ruddy, hair crisp along the knuckles, looked lost against her uniform. Nebraska realized it was the first time in six years Edward had ever touched her body.

"Another tiger!" Edward said, less boisterously, removing his hand, swallowing uneasily.

"How's business, hon'?" Vivian asked.

"Great. Handled two plots for Jake Silverstein out by Rabbit Bayou, and just got a call from Shel Friedlander, said he might have some clients for me, some rich Yankees wanting to invest south."

"I hate those cigars Mr. Silverstein smokes." Babs patted

her foot. "Why don't you outlaw cigars in the office?" She giggled.

"Don't do that," Nebraska said, looking about at all the impressive paper on the desks and the maps on the wall. "I'd be out of a job, too, if that happened."

"You wouldn't work for free?" Vivian asked.

"You pulling my leg, Miss Gold?"

"Aw, Nebraska," answered Vivian coyly, "I've got my feelings bruised."

"Some of us have to work for a living," Babs started. "If we don't get paid, *we* don't eat."

"Oh!" exclaimed Vivian, and continued pointedly. "I never realized that!"

"And slavery's over," Babs added.

"Where'd you read that?" Vivian asked. "I haven't seen today's *Register* yet. Is it in there?"

"Vivian, Vivian, don't fight with your cousin in here," Edward said.

"Tell that to Babs," Vivian said.

Edward bent over and kissed his wife. "This is a business office, sweetheart. Let's keep family feuds for someplace else."

"Yes," sniffed Babs. "This is a place of business. A *serious* place."

"Babs!" Edward cautioned.

"I was just agreein', Edward!"

"Change of topic." Edward took a deep breath. "I've got a question. Have you thought anymore about names for him, or her?"

"It's going to be a boy, Nebraska says." Vivian smiled. "And if it is, I want to name him after you."

"Vivian, you know that's not possible."

"Why ain't it possible?" asked Nebraska, puzzled.

"Because," Edward explained, "the Jewish tradition is to name the child after someone deceased. It's a way of keeping not only a name alive, but also the memory of the deceased relative."

Nebraska nodded, thinking how wise Edward seemed when he talked about religion. She loved the rich, slow tones of his voice. "I see," she said, but suddenly grew fretful.

"Fiddlesticks," Vivian said. "You're so big on tradition. I want to make my own tradition."

"Well, my children might be Reform Jews, but my parents were staunch Orthodox, and I'd just as soon cling to something of what they gave us. I didn't wrap *tefillin* every morning just to throw away history."

"Maybe I'll name him after my uncle Benjamin," Vivian conceded. "Even if he wasn't Jewish."

"Why not name him after your father?" Edward asked.

"Name a child Moishe in twentieth-century Madoc, Alabama? You want him to get beaten up every day at school?"

"I likes Ben," said Nebraska.

Edward faced Nebraska. "Well, what about you? Have you a tradition in your family of deciding names?"

Nebraska laughed. "My momma named me after a train side."

"Wh-what?" Babs said with amazement.

"Yas'm, it was the first thing she saw after I was born, and a white man at the plantation told her *Nebraska* was written on the side of the boxcar. She couldn't read herself, they tell me."

"Are you gonna name your baby after a train?" Babs asked.

"This is modern times, Miss Babs," Nebraska answered. "If I've got a boy," she went on with great assurance, "I'm gonna name him Abraham, after my Abraham and your people's Abraham."

"That settles that," Babs giggled. "All these babies make my head swim. Glad I don't have one to name. I'd just let it run around without a name, I'd have such a hard time deciding what to do!"

"And if it's a girl?" Edward asked.

Nebraska grew worried again. "Mr. Gold, can I ask you a question? Can somebody who's not Jewish name her child after somebody who is Jewish even if that somebody who's Jewish is still alive?"

"Well," Edward said, "I don't see why not."

"It ain't bad luck?" Nebraska asked.

Edward shook his head.

"Well, in that case, if it's a girl," Nebraska said, folding her hands together and smiling slyly, "I gots the best name of all."

"Wh-what's that?" Babs asked, cupping a hand behind her ear.

Nebraska took a deep breath and pronounced in rich, slow tones: "Vivian!"

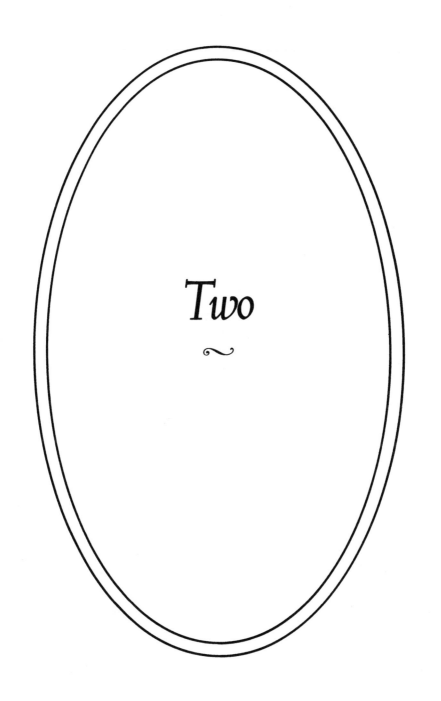

Two

1953

THE *bris* was meant to be a family celebration, but enough close friends came to make it seem like a party. There was Sarah, of course, perched in the corner, wide-eyed at the infant balling its hands in the crib. There was Rachel jumping about, first holding on to Nebraska's print dress and then scurrying over to Vivian and pulling at her wrist. "Please, honey," Vivian said, "go visit with Nebraska, but don't upset her in the chair." When Rachel went to Nebraska and looked at the baby over her shoulder, its dark face puckered and its bright pink tongue poking from its mouth, Nebraska said, "Go hold on to your mother." Rachel settled for the hand of Edna Solomon, the designated godmother, a tall, brisk woman in a smart summer suit. Babs had invited her friend Mimi from across the street, a frail, highstrung young creature. In one corner Doris Klein sat with her husband, Cantor Klein, who started to smoke a cigar but tamped it out for hygienic purposes when the *mohel* frowned at the smoke drifting about the room.

"Rivka, how are you?" Vivian asked Edward's mother. Rivka, bending over the baby's crib, looked up and nodded, smiling broadly. She turned back to the crib.

"And you, Poppa?" Vivian asked Saul, Edward's father, who was sneezing into a handkerchief.

"I am *kvell*ing," said Saul, wiping his mouth. "*Kvell*ing!"

Edward, his coat off and suspenders drawing his pants up

to his midriff, strode across the room. "I sure hope y'all are *kvel*ling. It's not every day you've got a new grandchild, a grand-*son* no less!"

"My *tateleh*," Rivka said, bending farther into the crib, "my precious *tateleh!*"

"Did I have a *bris?*" Rachel asked.

Vivian turned and saw Edna Solomon with Rachel on her lap. Edna looked up and silently mouthed a question: "Can I explain?"

"Oh, don't be silly, Edna. She knows she didn't have a *bris*. You don't have to explain anything to my daughters."

Vivian glanced from Edna to Nebraska, whose baby girl, Vivian's namesake, was vomiting a small, white stream of milk. Nebraska reached up with the towel that lay over her shoulder and wiped the infant's mouth. "All this commotion's got Viv going round," Nebraska huffed. "I'm sorry, sweet pea." She stroked the child, whose eyes closed once, opened quickly, then dropped shut.

"Vivian sure does sleep a lot," Sarah said, coming over and stooping down to peer into the baby's face. "You'd think she was a little kitten."

"Infants sleep a lot," said Rivka, who smiled warmly at Sarah. "You slept that way too. I remember."

"Don't stand so close to her," Nebraska warned. "You got germs."

"I don't have germs."

"All peoples got germs, sugar. Ask any doctor."

Vivian spoke: "Sarah! Leave Nebraska be."

"Oh, I feels like I got a crick in my back." Nebraska sat forward. The abrupt motion caused her infant to loll its head and curl fingers around the edge of the towel.

"Help her," said Edna.

"I'll do it," Vivian offered. Slowly, she walked to Nebraska, the stitches where she had given birth to Benjamin— seven pounds, eleven ounces—irritating her mildly. "Here, let me, Nebraska." She took little Vivian and raised her up, motioning to Sarah to move the towel onto her shoulder. The infant, after wriggling a moment, settled back into sleep. Vivian could smell the cornstarch and talcum on the tiny body, could look from the corner of her eye and see the black face pushed up against her neck. The lips were perfect as petals. The ears were small, delicate shells.

While watching the *mohel* converse with the rabbi and the cantor near the bowling trophies that had been her father's, Vivian turned back and forth, soothing the sleeping baby. Benjamin slept, too, his body pink as jam in the crib. She walked over to him and bent to the crib. "My sweetheart," she whispered. Benjamin opened his eyes, round and damp, making liquid sounds with his tongue, the bubbles frothing over his lips. Vivian reached down with her free hand and touched his tiny chest. It was no larger than her palm and felt frail as porcelain. Then she felt his diaper. It was dry.

Hadn't Nebraska said she would have a boy? The prediction crossed her mind as Benjamin kicked the end of the crib and, at the same moment, Viv turned her head and yawned. This time, though, as Vivian glanced down at the baby on her shoulder, the face did not look as flawlessly formed. The talcum and cornstarch smell cloyed. Briefly, she imagined having given birth to this child with the flat, wide nostrils and coffee bean eyes. Glancing over at Nebraska, who was being fanned by Rachel, she thought of this baby girl as being large and round and sore-footed one day. Might she even work as a housekeeper for her son?

Edna Solomon was suddenly close upon her. "Not just one baby but two!" She went on under her breath, "You're not thinking about switching them, are you?"

Vivian took up the joke. "They're both so beautiful. Which should I keep?"

"Keep the boy," Rivka said, who had overheard. "He's white, first, a Gold, second, and third already the *mohel* has come."

Vivian reached down and unhooked Benjamin's diapers.

His tiny penis stood straight as a matchstick. The foreskin was a tiny, wrinkled hat. It had occurred to Vivian the day before that she had seen the genitals of only two other men in her life—her husband and father. During the Jewish community dances more than one young man from the Temple had brushed against her leg ever so lightly as they danced, and more than once she had pulled away, imagining what those faint imprints looked like in the light of day. They all became her father, who, until she was nine or ten, sometimes turned in such a way when taking off his shorts that she caught full view of his body. The dark place below his abdomen was the place that she had re-created secretly on those boys at the Temple dances. Only her marriage to Edward had made her see man's sex as natural, healthy.

Then there had been her son next to her that morning eight days ago. His penis was not the dark place of the boys she had grown up with, but was bright and God-formed as the eye or hand. She was astonished by the thought that her female organs had created male organs, had retained a power for years that now was crystallized in her son.

A tiny scrabbling came at her breast. She turned abruptly from looking at Benjamin to Viv, who was hunting for a nipple. Standing straight with a jolt, she lurched the infant from her shoulder. Viv's mouth stretched wide and she began to yell. "Hush," Vivian said.

The child began to scream. Nebraska, holding her back with one hand, bounded from the chair and reached for the child.

"She's all right," Vivian said, rocking her. "She just got startled and took fright."

"She pulled on you, didn't she?" Nebraska asked with great concern.

"Naw! She's been perfect."

"She did, Miss Gold. I'm sorry. A baby won't take milk from nobody but its momma, but they'll pull on just about anybody."

"Nebraska, you don't have to tell me that. I did breast-feed Sarah."

Rivka cut in: "No milk is better than a mother's milk. A bottle is for nothing."

"Rivka, we are of the old school," Doris Klein said. "This modern way, though, it is not bad. With a bottle the baby is as happy. And"—she lowered her voice—"the poor mother does not end with breasts that drag to her *pupik*."

"We should start soon," the rabbi said. A lean, olive-complexioned man with a vandyke beard, the rabbi repeated his request and his voice, slow and drawling, sounded like a gunslinger's.

Benjamin started to cry and Vivian reached down and lifted him. "He's afraid, Rabbi."

"A son of Edward Gold afraid?" the rabbi said. "Down around the Rio Grande there's an expression for a brave man: 'He'll do to ride the river.' I bet little Benjamin will do to ride the river."

"I'll make preparations," the *mohel* said. "Edward, come with me." He looked around. "The godmother?"

Edna raised her hand. "But I've got an upset stomach," she warned.

The *mohel* shrugged. "We will tell you when to bring in the boy."

With Edward at his side, the *mohel* shuffled off to the back of the house, where a bedroom had been prepared for the ceremony.

Sarah appeared with a warm bottle. "Nebraska told me to get this for Benjamin."

"Thank you, dear," said Vivian, slipping the bottle into Benjamin's mouth. The baby's cheeks drew in and the milk oozed through the nipple. "I think a *bris* is pagan," Vivian exploded suddenly. "Why can't the circumcision be done in the hospital like civilized people do it?"

Saul Gold spun about like a man slapped across the face. "My own grandson not have a *bris*?"

"It's crude!"

"For the son of a *shiksa*, is crude," Saul said.

"Don't call me that!" Vivian said. "I know you've always called me that behind my back. But don't say it to my face. My son is the child of a Jew—a Reform Jew. *We* believe in hospitals, and doctors."

With a cold look Saul silenced her, then turned dramatically and stomped off to the back of the house.

"Miss Gold, Miss Gold," said Nebraska, rising from her chair and coming over. "You's exhausted from all this to-do. It's got you out o' sorts."

"You've offended my husband," Rivka said sternly. "You've offended us all."

"My Vivian can say as she'd like," Sosha countered. "She's my daughter."

"*Goyim.* The Reform Jews in Madoc are *goyim,*" Rivka said.

"And the Orthodox Jews are descended from peasants," Sosha came back.

"Quiet! Everyone!" Doris Klein shouted. "This is a *holy* day."

Nebraska whispered to Vivian, "You gone and got all the old folks upset. Let me take Benjie and you go on back and discuss this thing out."

"You're right, Nebraska. I'm just plumb tired. Maybe that's all there is to it." She gave Benjamin to Nebraska's keeping. "Peace, everyone. It's my fault." She left the group and searched the back of the house for Edward's father, but found him outside. He was standing under a pecan tree, looking up at the the billowy clouds. He held a lit cigar; smoke curled up toward the green sheaths of the pecans.

"Poppa . . ." she started.

Keeping his back to her, Saul turned and went into the house.

As Vivian trailed in, she felt her body wanting to sag beneath her. Fighting back tears, she came to the room where the men were congregated. Sosha and Rivka sat against one wall, not speaking to each other. Doris folded a clean cloth for the *mohel*, who sat in the middle, an empty chair—Elijah's chair—next to him. Near the *mohel* sat Nebraska with Benjamin on her lap, the bottle in his mouth, and little Viv pressed up to one half-exposed breast. The men, looking everywhere but at Nebraska, chatted uneasily.

Vivian leaned against the doorway, thinking what a bizarre group portrait they made: a Negro madonna and her *minyan* of Jewish disciples. She could not help but giggle.

With laughter starting to run through her body, she watched the *mohel* reach over—eyes still averted—and take Benjamin from Nebraska, then place him on the chair of Elijah.

Nebraska, wide-eyed with nervousness, still clutching Viv to her breast, tiptoed toward the door of the room. She crossed the threshold to Vivian, whispering, "Miss Solomon got a sour stomach and *made* me bring him in," and closed the door respectfully behind her.

After the circumcision the men broke up their gathering and then tension in the house seemed to break up as well. Saul Gold hugged Vivian, then hugged Vivian's mother. "We should make a toast to Moishe," he said, "a toast that he should have been here for his own grandson's *bris*."

"Babs!" Sosha called out again. "Babs! Go get the wine."

Babs and her friend Mimi had been sitting on the porch since the guests first arrived—talking and giggling, pinching off clusters of wisteria that brocaded the gutter along the edge of the roof. "I don't know why there's all this fuss over a little baby," Babs called back, pulling off some petals, crushing them between her thumb and forefinger and flicking them over the steps, which began to look covered by a lavender carpet. "I would *never* have a baby. And if I did, nobody would make a fuss, I bet."

Inside the house the upbeat tempo of the Glen Miller band

filled the room and Edward started to dance with his mother. Nebraska tapped her foot, and Rabbi Solomon asked Doris Klein to be his partner.

"For this I am too old," Saul said.

"I know one thing," Nebraska remarked, turning her head with disapproval, "you'd never see a Baptist preacher dance!"

"I've seen some Baptist preachers shake," came Rabbi Solomon, at the same time twirling Doris Klein so fast that her heavy rouge seemed to fly off her cheeks.

"Oh, yes," Nebraska went on, smiling. "Shake when they got the spirit." Holding Viv tightly with one hand, she raised up the other and trembled it. "The spirit of Jesus Christ, amen!"

"The spirit of Jesus Christ, good *yontif*," the rabbi cracked.

"Babs!" Sosha shouted again.

Babs leaped up from her chair on the porch, opened the screen abruptly, and passed through the room, making a beeline for Edward in her bright orange dress. She brushed against him, and when he stepped back from her, he bumped the rabbi. The rabbi laughed, pulled Doris close, pushed her away, pulled her close, then spun her out like a top.

In a few minutes Babs reappeared from the kitchen, holding a silver tray with a bottle of Mogen David and a cluster of glasses.

Looking up, Vivian saw another image of herself in the mirror above her mother's couch. She saw a Vivian who had dreamed of being a starlet, and was now surrounded by parents, children, friends. They moved about her, danced about her. There was no path through them all to the door, out the door, to the glamorous world beyond.

Sosha took a sip of the wine and handed a glass to Vivian, who touched it to the lips of the other Vivian she continued to watch in the mirror. The wine, perfumy and sweet, ran over her tongue as the woman in the mirror tipped the glass and swallowed.

A cry unheard by anyone else—by the dancing rabbi, or the frowning Babs, or the reclining Edna—was heard by Vivian.

She walked quickly through the room and toward the sound of that crying. "Benjamin . . ." She repeated his name more loudly.

In the bedroom the *mohel* sat with Benjamin on his lap. The baby's penis was bandaged; cotton swabs, dotted with blood, were nearby. While Benjamin wailed again, the *mohel* stroked the child's brow.

"With me he fusses," the *mohel* said quietly. "With me he is mad."

Vivian peered at her son's lips. They were wet and purple. "What's wrong with my son!"

"Wrong?" the *mohel* said. "Today he has known pain. May he not also know pleasure? The two drops of wine I touched on his lips you see." He nodded to a chalice. "Drink." Vivian lifted the chalice and sipped the wine. "Now take your son."

The *mohel* began to pack his bag. "I must go back home to New Orleans today. I came four hours at dawn on the train this morning because your father Moishe was a friend of mine." He looked at Vivian sternly. "A good Jew Moishe was not." He shrugged, then smiled. "But a *mensh* he was!"

He finished packing his bag, nodded, and left the room.

After Vivian calmed Benjamin, she carried him back through the house. At the entrance to the living room she paused and watched the men standing about the *mohel*, shaking his hand; saw Nebraska holding and patting Viv; saw Saul, noticeably fatigued, sitting on the couch holding his dimmed cigar.

With delicious energy humming through her limbs, she felt her body beginning to glow. She turned back and forth with Benjamin in a small, snug world all their own.

❧

For the two months that Nebraska took a leave of absence, Mary took her place. Whereas it had once been awkward for Vivian to have Nebraska going over the objects of her house, balling up the socks, cleaning the glasses, it now was so familiar that it felt even more awkward to have another woman going through the identical motions.

Mary was so old as to be called ancient. Regardless of her years, she could talk up a storm: "Miss Gold," she said during her last week at Magnolia Court, chewing on gum or false teeth (which, Vivian could never be quite sure), "is it true that Jewrish peoples make love through a hole in the sheet?"

"Where on earth did you hear such a thing as that?"

"Little Ronald Bloom once read it to me out of a book. Say the peoples don't think it's clean to touch. They cut a hole betwixt the bedsheets to make babies from."

"Have you seen a hole in our bedsheet?" Vivian waited for an answer. "If you have, I suspect it was scratched by squirrels or something."

"Now, Miss Gold, don' get riled with me, ma'am. I's just axin'. How'm I gonna know what is truth and what ain't?"

"Ax away," Vivian said sarcastically.

"Ronald say the Orthodock or somebody do that. Old-timey Jewrish peoples."

"The word is *Jewish*."

"Say they eat meat off one dish, milk off one dish, and cut up the sheets. Baptists wash feets, but we don't do nothin' like that."

"Some Jews," Vivian explained, "do keep separate dishes for meat and milk. Edward's parents, for instance. That's because they're Orthodox." Vivian looked out the window to see if her ride was coming down the street.

"Whenever I works at a Jewish home," said Mary, chewing, her old jaws moving up and down and the white-mottled face bunching rhythmically, "I washes the sheets real good. Yas'm, washes them right, so you don't worry if what Ronald Bloom done told me ain't no lie."

"You are the most obstinate cuss I have ever known, Mary!"

"When you get to be as old as I am, you gonna cuss too." Mary cackled so loudly that Vivian was certain it was not a real laugh.

"You ought to go into the movies, Mary."

"I could play an old blackface, yeah?" Mary threw back

her head and laughed so loudly that Vivian wanted to put her hands over her ears.

"They haven't even had blackface for twenty years."

"I could play it anyways!"

Though Vivian could not have imagined a shriller laugh than before, she heard it now. It was a laugh that shot up the sides of the walls, then came down slowly, like rain from the windowsills.

"Sometimes," Vivian said crisply, "I think you insist on playing it now."

"Miss Gold," Mary said on a change of note. "Do you hate niggers?"

"What—what do you mean?"

"Niggers, black folks, coons. We all knows white peoples thinks Negroes is stupid."

A tightness gripped Vivian's throat. "That's—that's absurd!"

"Nebraska says you one o' the nicest white ladies I gonna ever work for. I told Nebraska all the Jewish peoples is nice. Yas'm, I reckon. I told Nebraska all 'bout that before she worked that Mardi Gras party how many years ago."

Vivian struggled to order her words and speak clearly. "People are people, Mary. I try to judge people on their individual merits."

"But you *do* think niggers is a li'l stupid, don't you?"

"Of course not!"

"But Nebraska say you do."

"Nebraska! Why—why, I don't believe it. I've never treated her with anything but the highest respect." She saw the automobile coming in rescue down the block. The floor moved an inch beneath her. Heat washed her forehead.

"But she say—"

"I don't care what Nebraska Waters says," Vivian snapped. The heat washed from her forehead to her neck. "I'll have you know that I treat Nebraska better than just about any white woman treats her help I know of!" The words gushed out. They came in a torrent that tasted bitter upon leaving her mouth.

"Yas'm, yas'm," Mary repeated quickly, her face working with chewing. "You's one o' the best, but I was just speaking the simple truth."

Vivian cut in. "Do we have the same meaning of truth, Mary?"

"Yas'm. The truth is that all white folks thinks niggers is stupid."

"I won't even allow that awful word to be used in my presence!"

A tapping came at the window and Margery Berman pressed her face to the pane. Her features were spread out across the glass. She looked trapped in an invisible cage.

"I've got to go," Vivian said sharply.

"How're you?" Margery pushed open the back door and addressed both the women.

"I's fine, fine," said Mary. "I think I got Miss Gold a little upset with all my talkin', though."

Old Mary minced and grinned as she spoke, and Vivian thought silently, You two-faced old bitch!

"Oh," Margery explained, "don't let Mary get you upset. She's as bad as my Romaine. Those two could talk until the cows come home—with bulls behind them, no less."

"It'll be a cold day in Hades or Madoc, Alabama, one, before some bull follows this ol' cow." Mary howled.

"Mary, Margery and I are going to drive you home. I think it's time to call it a day."

As Mary gathered her belongings, Vivian said to Margery, "I'm absolutely humiliated by what that old crone told me," but before she could finish, Mary reappeared, shopping bag in hand and round, flowered hat set neatly over her silver hair.

"When's Nebraska coming back?" Margery asked as they drove first to Sosha Brooks's house to pick up Benjamin and Rachel, then headed through the downtown to the housing project near the docks.

Rachel, in the car beside Mary in the back seat, asked, "Is Nebuba gonna come back soon?"

"It's Nebraska," Vivian said. "First I had to break Sarah of it, now you. For the hundred thousandth time, it's Nebraska!"

"Is Nebuba gonna, huh?"

Benjamin woke from a nap. Vivian stroked his cheek with the back of her hand and lifted him to her shoulder. The car moved smoothly past the appliance shops and bank buildings of downtown and turned by Dauphine Square.

"Nebraska'll be back on Monday, sugar," answered Mary, moving her hat back and forth into proper position.

"Are we going to visit Nebuba?"

"No!" Vivian noted the buildings passing by and dropping away, then changing to the buildings at the outskirts of the black section of town. "No," she said again. "Absolutely not."

Large houses in a state of disrepair stood along Dexter Avenue. In one, the windows were knocked out and the ample white porch peeled badly. Someone had scrawled DEATH TO THE KU KLUX KLAN on its side wall with blood-colored paint. Vivian clasped Benjamin tightly, and when Rachel asked what the words meant, said only "Hush, dear, you ask too many questions."

Toward the far end of Dexter Avenue marquees hung over the entrances to large movie theaters, some abandoned. Church steeples rose above the building tops.

"Is that Madoc?" Rachel asked.

"Yes, yes, that's Madoc," Mary said. "Colored Madoc."

"Lock your door, sweetheart." Margery reached back and locked Rachel's door for her.

They passed the last of the wooden houses, the shanties that moved off toward the river, and came to the outskirts of the federal project. WELCOME TO GOLDEN CASTLES, read a sign, but two letters were painted over and the sign became WELCOME TO GOLD CASTLES.

"How golden is it?" Margery asked wryly.

"To some of us, it's the Promised Land," quipped Mary.

Could Nebraska really have said what she did? In Vivian's mind Nebraska sat, again occupying the chair in her mother's house. The *bris* returned clearly, and Viv, her namesake, her godchild, lolled her head and looked back at her as if she knew Vivian felt nothing but love for Nebraska. Or did she?

A thought seized hold that would not let loose: What if Nebraska decided not to return?

The chain link fences in the backyards of the projects slipped by the car. Old women sat on rockers, their feet in house slippers, their hands hung into big shiny buckets as they shelled peas. "What if she doesn't?" Vivian whispered to Benjamin, who was cradled peacefully in her arms.

"There's Abraham," Mary said excitedly, and leaned over from the back seat and tooted Margery's horn. Next to Abraham on the porch of the Waters's apartment was Wenda June, still and sullen.

"Keep going," Vivian insisted. "We don't have time to say hello."

The car rode along, slowing once for a group of children to clear the street. The kids, engaged in a game of stickball, stood to the sides of the car and stared through the windows as Vivian and the group passed. Vivian turned on the radio. The news came on. She turned the radio off. A small child sat in the middle of the street, naked. Margery honked. A reed-thin woman raced out and grabbed him up, grinning back at the car.

"I'll tell you, the way some parents allow their children to . . ." Margery began, but fell silent.

"Here 'tis," Mary said. "Thank you all for escorting me home. See you all tomorrow." She pulled her belongings to her hip and dragged them from the seat as she got out, pushed the door closed with her foot, and started off toward her apartment.

Margery drove to the end of the block and started to circle it in order to head back to the downtown. Where she drove there were still red-brick buildings under construction, and buildings with MADOC LUMBER COMPANY written on the side could be seen over a clearing. Cranes, like bizarre river creatures, bent over the treetops.

A softball bounced in front of the car and Margery eased on the brakes. A child bounded across their view. Before she could gather momentum again, a man came wobbling down the middle of the street. She slowed.

"That fool. Why doesn't he get out of the way?" Margery honked the horn. The man turned and faced them with a wild, popeyed expression. Margery stopped the car, threw it into neutral, and gunned the motor. The man advanced.

"That black idiot," said Margery fiercely. She slapped her hand down on the horn and gunned the motor until it roared like a storm beneath them.

Vivian clutched Benjamin and held Rachel's hand. "Margery," she said evenly, "be patient, he'll move." A moving truck rolled up behind them and began to honk. Vivian glanced in the rearview mirror and saw two shirtless black men high in the cabin of the truck. One had his face hidden behind a whiskey bottle.

Margery started to back up, but the truck continued to block her way. "Take a nap," Vivian said to Rachel, and pushed her daughter down into her lap.

"I wanna look out the window!" Rachel wailed.

"Shush! Put your head down!" Vivian pressed her daughter's face against her leg and rubbed her neck. The black man seemed to stare straight at her. As he came closer she made out a deep scar along the right side of his face. She held Benjamin more tightly and he began to fidget and whine.

When the man moved closer still, Margery put the car into neutral again and gunned the motor so hard Vivian feared the car would explode. "Margery, stop it! I've got my children in here!"

"That black bastard," Margery shouted. "You stupid nigger! Get out of the way or I'll run you down!"

Near the brink of the hood the man struggled to tear off his shirt, his eyes popping out farther when the cloth would not give.

Margery started to throw the car into forward.

"No!" Vivian screamed.

Before she could engage the gears, the man spun around and, as though the air were being sucked out of him, crumpled to the ground. Blood seeped like mud through his dark green shirt and over his waist. As he writhed on the concrete, a knife handle flopped under his arm.

As the car shot into forward, Margery turned the wheel hard. They lurched around his body, bounded up on the curb and skidded over the sidewalk. She brought the car back to the street and the buildings of the project whirled by them, children leaping from the path of the automobile. In the rearview mirror, Vivian watched the men clamber down from the truck and bend over the man on the street.

Sobbing uncontrollably now, she kept Rachel's head pressed tightly against her leg so that she could not see, and muffled Benjamin's crying against her neck.

"These damn niggers! These animals!" Margery's hands on the steering wheel turned hard and white.

Vivian could say nothing. Before her the man's face clung to the windshield, eyes jiggling wildly. She held Benjamin so tightly he squirmed, and thanked God her son did not yet have the faculties to see and understand.

1954

Wenda June walked to the wall and bent over to peer at the calendar from Gold's Western Wear. Above MAY was a picture of a camellia girl: a rosy-cheeked blonde in a dress as pink and large as a giant camellia. Behind the camellia girl a line of boys from Madoc Military Academy stood at parade rest. The caption read MADOC, ALABAMA. HOME OF BEAUTY AND PRIDE.

"Beauty and pride, shit," Wenda June said.

From the newly upholstered couch Nebraska watched her daughter and winced when she spoke. She did not reprimand her, though. It was enough to see her healthy again after the collapse.

That awful night was still stark in her memory. Only two months after Viv had been born, Nebraska came in from the pen where Abraham had been delousing his hound dogs, and neither Viv nor Wenda June were in the living room. "Wenda June?" she had called. Only Todd, studying his geography lesson on the porch, had answered back. "I heard Wenda go upstairs like she was in the middle of a hurricane, Momma. I figure she was mad about something."

When Nebraska had trudged up the stairs, she saw Viv lying flat on her back in front of the bathroom door. "What have you done with my baby?" she asked angrily. It was then that she heard the noise: a clattering of objects against the wall. When she broke the lock on the door with her body's force, she saw Wenda standing in front of the toilet tossing her head back and forth, gasping, dragging down every brush and talcum container she could find and throwing them into the bowl. Wenda yanked at the handle on the toilet to make the things go down, but the commode heaved back, already flushed dry and jammed up. In another moment Nebraska had latched her arms around her daughter. Within the hour, Todd had borrowed a car and gone screeching to the colored hospital with Wenda.

The colored hospital (even the doctors called it that) had once been a general hospital that admitted black patients in one half and white patients in the other half, but the new white hospital built and subsidized by the Protestant Church Society had siphoned off its white clientele until it was left almost entirely to colored. In the black section of town, just beyond Dexter Avenue, the hospital was an enormous hulk with Corinthian columns. Every time Nebraska went there to visit Wenda she felt as if she were walking into a picture postcard.

The picture postcard was destroyed once she entered, turned to the left, and climbed the three flights of stairs that went to the mental ward. Gnarled and jittery old men sat in chairs whittling imaginary ships or shouting "I'm gonna fly outen that window there," all the while pointing to a water faucet or radio. Youngsters were in the ward too—fine, strapping lads who walked about with sad, fixed expressions and girls who mumbled incessantly about babies and corn bread and death.

The first visit to the mental ward had caused Nebraska to take her cross from her pocketbook and squeeze it tightly. During the second visit, when Wenda June was sitting up in a chair resting, she took out the Holy Bible and thumbed through it to the Book of Revelations, then read quietly of the time when the world would be plagued with wars and sickness and wondered if the mental ward of this colored hospital was not some part of the Lord's promise already come true.

The third visit she held Wenda's hand and walked her to the window and looked out across the city. Beyond the buildings of the downtown she could make out the trees of the white neighborhoods, the neatly culled gardens and trimmed lawns, and the spotless playgrounds. Did people have collapses there, she asked herself? Did mothers come in from the backyards and find their children beating their heads against a light fixture, or trying to flush a house out of existence by throwing it piece by piece into the commode?

On the fourth visit she had walked to that same window and, looking out, realized that she had spent most of her waking hours for almost the last decade at a house in that white section. The white neighborhoods seemed wrapped in auras, as if mental anguish beat about the families there like a moth beats about a windowpane. The mental anguish threatened but never reached beyond the pane, never pierced through the comfort, the wealth.

On that fourth visit the young doctor in charge of the ward, an impeccably groomed man, a graduate of Tuskegee and Howard, told Nebraska that Wenda June could go. "Your daughter's not mentally ill, Mrs. Waters. She's just suffering from the strain of—"

"Strain of what?" Nebraska interrupted defensively. "I do everything for her I can."

"Mrs. Waters, I'm sure you do. But you must realize that sometimes Negroes . . . sometimes Negroes can't bear the frustrations of their world. Your daughter is also mulatto. That adds a factor. She hates Alabama and talks incessantly of returning to Detroit. You see, Mrs. Waters, all colored people in the United States are victims in some way. Wenda June has seized on that truth and distorted it to the point of emotional turmoil."

"Alabama's the most beautiful state in the union." Nebraska drew herself to full height. "Wenda June's just spoiled. It's plain as can be."

"Take care of her, ma'am. Try to find something to occupy her mind, something really constructive." The doctor led Wenda out from a back room and asked Nebraska to sign three papers, on which she placed an X instead of signing her name so that no one would have a record of her being in the hospital.

That doctor's words came back to her as Nebraska lay on the couch and continued to study Wenda June, who in turn studied the calendar. The doctor's words had confused her: "seized on that truth and distorted it." What did he mean exactly? One by one, like detonating capsules, the words became clear to her and Wenda June seemed to walk through them like a penitent through fire.

"Wenda June?" She clapped to get her daughter's attention. "How'd you like to get a job?"

"I'm not well, Momma. Didn't the doctor tell you that?"

"Don't get smart with me, Wen. You know I know you been sick. But the doctor also said it was good for you to get something to help you relax, maybe some kind of work."

"Work for white folks?" Wenda screwed up her face. "Maybe I can work for this pretty camellia girl in the calendar. You think she needs somebody to straighten up after her after all them military boys in the picture get finished taking her to bed?"

"Hush up," said Todd, who sat in the corner bouncing Viv on his knee, sticking out his tongue and clenching his teeth until Viv squealed delightedly. "Hush up talking like that or Daddy'll whup you good. And if he don't, I will."

"If he *doesn't*," Wenda corrected icily, "not *don't*. You're such a dumb southern nigger you can't even talk right."

"And who are you? Lena Horne?"

Wenda turned back to the calendar, smoldering. "You should have stayed in the crib. That's where you still belong. You might have even died there if we were lucky."

"Wenda June!" Nebraska swung her body around to the edge of the couch and shook her head sadly. "Take that back!"

"Yas'm. I take it back." She spoke sullenly.

"Todd, apologize yourself."

"I'm sorry," he muttered.

"Wenda," began Nebraska, rising, "Miss Gold tells me her mother, Sosha Brooks, is needing someone to help her two or three days a week. She's such a nice Jewish lady from over in Germany. We used to sit together and listen to Kingfish by the hour over at Madoc Bay."

"Kingfish don't come on but for a half hour," said Todd, then added, "I mean Kingfish *doesn't*."

Wenda pursed her lips and made a motion like spitting. "Do I have to clean toilets?"

"You don't have to clean nothin', sugar. Just fetch tea and crackers. She ha'n't been feeling good lately. Needs somebody to wait on her a little is all."

"What about that little thing who lives with her? Why can't she do it?"

"Babs?" Nebraska shook her head. "Babs works. And she ain't no little thing. She's a growed woman." She detected her daughter's resistance softening.

"How much she pay?"

"A lot. Two dollars a day, meals, and bus money."

The young woman looked up at the ceiling and drew imaginary numbers with her finger. "I could get enough money to make it back to Detroit."

"Of course," Nebraska said quickly. She went to the telephone, determined to make the call before Wenda changed her mind. She called Sosha Brooks and made the appointment for Wenda June to start the following Wednesday.

"I might go, but I ain't gonna like it," Wenda said.

"Oh, you can't help but like it. She's nice people."

Wenda walked briskly to the front door and left the apartment, slamming the door behind her.

"Listen to me, Todd." Nebraska spoke hotly. "If there's one thing you promise me in this life it's got to be never to get fustrated or worked up over who you are. No, sir. If you do, you'll be having a distortion like the doctor says Wenda's got. And I tell you, sweetheart, I couldn't stand another one in the house. No, sir, I couldn't."

The sheet of paper came that next week, slipped under the door as a ghost might sneak through a vent or imperfectly closed window. On it in big block letters was printed: BROWN VS. BOARD OF EDUCATION. A VICTORY FOR NEGROES. COME TO THE TALK GIVEN BY PASTOR ALFONSE RAY NEXT MONDAY AT HOLY MOUNT BAPTIST CHURCH.

When the paper came Nebraska was at home on the couch, peeling her stockings down over her feet after a long day at the Golds'. She spotted PASTOR ALFONSE RAY before anything else and got up to see what the pastor had his name on.

"What that paper say?" Abraham asked from the kitchen, where he sat at the table, hunting for the baseball game on the radio. "It sellin' or preachin'?" He turned his attention back to the dial. "This damn baseball. Where are you, Madoc Warriors?"

Nebraska picked up the paper and held it aloft for Abraham, who called back, "I can't see that far, Gardenia, and even if I could, what make you think I'd be able to read it when I ha'n't been able to read nothin' till now?"

"No difference," Nebraska said. "I can read good enough but I can't tell you what this means." She proceeded to read the notice aloud.

"Oh, I heard somethin' on the radio 'bout that, Gardenia. Up in Montgomery they talked to some big state man who called it 'Black Monday.'"

"Black Monday! What went on? People start fallin' down dead in the streets?"

Abraham laughed. "No, no. You can read but you talk foolish sometime. Black *peoples'* Monday. Somethin' to do with mixin' up colored with white in the schools. Say that's gonna happen now."

"In Montgomery? Montgomery, Alabama?"

Nebraska's question was answered by the sudden screech of a radio announcer: *"Steeerike two!"*

A single picture of Montgomery rose to her. It was a white-hot day in July and she was twelve years old. She had gone with her auntie from the plantation to get an official birth certificate. In sight of the capitol building itself, just as her auntie pointed with her long arm and said, "Nebraska, that's where this whole state is runned from, just like the main house on a plantation," a stately white man in a seersucker suit and panama hat approached them. "That's a judge or congressman, one," said her auntie. As the man glided past them her auntie said cheerily, "Mornin', Congressman." The man turned, looked at them coldly, and snapped, "I am not a congressman, nigger. I am a senator!" Ever since that day, Nebraska had figured there was no place where people were meaner than in Montgomery. Shoot, she thought to herself, they ain't even got Mardi Gras.

Junior appeared at the back door carrying Viv on his shoulders. He ducked low to make sure the baby's head would not bump against the door frame. Nebraska looked at his massive hands holding the child as she took her from him. "Look at this, Viv," Nebraska said sweetly, fanning the piece of paper in the air. "Maybe you and Benjie gonna go to school together. Miss Gold and I can come strollin' in, arm and arm, to pick up our chirren."

"Viv might go, but I ain't," Junior said instantly.

"Gonna be a lot of Negroes, honey, not just you."

"No mind. There'll be nothin' but fightin'."

"Junior!" Abraham spoke from the kitchen, the clamor of the Madoc Warriors game behind him. "Don't get all agitated." He turned down the radio. "This Brown-Education stuff got somethin' to do with Kansas, or someplace way away like that."

"Kansas?" Nebraska turned and glared at her husband. "You just told me it happened in Montgomery!"

"Gardenia, Gardenia, you listen more foolish than you talk. They was just *pronouncin'* over it in Montgomery." He turned up the radio again. "I got enough politickin' for now."

Nebraska folded up the piece of paper and put it in her pocket. "Viv, me and you's gonna move to Kansas. We gonna move to Kansas where the world is natural, like it s'posed to be."

"Not me," Junior warned. "On white people I feel just the same as Wenda June."

～

"My two darlings," Nebraska said. She, Viv, and Benjamin climbed onto the downtown Madoc bus.

"Them two is yours?" The bus driver raised his eyebrows.

"Yessir. My white one and my colored one." She grinned and led them down the aisle, past the few white men on the very front of the bus, and settled down in the area at the front of the black section. She dragged a small carriage along and set it just along the side of the seats.

Another woman with a black and a white child got on the bus. The woman, older than Nebraska and lanky as a bean pole, had the children trailing behind her. She paused in the front of the bus and the white child climbed onto a seat while she continued to the back with her own. In another moment the white child, a boy of five or so, leaped up and came to the back. "Nelda!" he implored. "I want to ride with you."

"Billy Smith," the woman answered sternly, "go ride up front like your mother said."

The boy whined. "Nelda! Come ride up front with me!"

My, my, Nebraska thought as she watched the scene, what all this racial business do to the children. Got 'em going every which away.

Nelda took the boy's hand and slapped his wrist. "Go back on up front now." The child went reluctantly to the seat just behind the bus driver.

A fat woman in a hat covered with plastic oranges and pineapples was sitting next to Nebraska. She reached up and tugged on the cord and stood to get off. When she passed out of the seats and into the aisle, Nebraska took a blanket from her bag, doubled it over and set it down on the seat, then placed Viv and Benjamin next to each other and steadied them with her hand. Viv looked out the window, blinking in the sunshine. Benjamin sat straight, as if transfixed by the ashtray attached to the seat in front of him.

"Oh, them's pretty babies," came a crackly voice.

"Hey, Romaine," said Nebraska, feeling herself growing smaller in the seat. "What brings you out into the downtown this hot afternoon?"

After settling into the seat opposite Nebraska, Romaine looked at her with one yellowish eye—she had lost the other eye a year earlier when she had climbed on Margery Berman's roof to clean out a drainpipe and slipped and skidded face first into the branch of a crape myrtle tree—and said, "I wisht Miss Margery would have some more little ones. They is precious as lambs."

Nebraska half turned away. Romaine's one-eyed stare looked like a whammy.

"I's out to hunt down some special silver polish for Miss Margery," Romaine continued, turning back and forth, as she always did, seeing who else was on the bus. "Hmm. I'd give anything to sit next to them two lamb dolls."

In order to avoid any more fuss on the matter, Nebraska offered the seat to Romaine and took hers in exchange. Romaine bent over Viv and Benjamin and began to make faces that, thought Nebraska, could frighten the devil into taking up religion. The children seemed both rapt and puzzled.

The bus stopped again and enough people climbed aboard to fill all the seats. One middle-aged white man walked with a smart mahogany cane down the aisle, made his way to the end of the white section of the bus and scanned about for an extra seat. He looked at Nebraska. She looked over at Romaine, now dandling the babies, then looked down at the tips of her shoes. Her feet began to pulse. Her whole body began to pulse.

The man, hovering over her, latched onto a strap to keep himself up as the bus started. The bus stopped. The driver leaned around the metal railing behind his seat and said above the passengers' chatter, "Can't find a seat, mister? Maybe somebody oughta let you rest your legs, don't you think?" Nebraska felt the needle scrutiny of the driver, and continued to feel the growing pulse in her body. The pulse became an angry one.

She was seized by the desire to keep her seat, to shout back "I ain't gonna budge!" and to fold her hands in her lap as neatly as if she were sitting in a church pew during one of Pastor Ray's sermons. Had a black woman ever done such a thing before? She glanced over to Viv and Benjamin, who seemed to stare at her in such a way as to suggest they *knew*. "I can't let them see me give up my seat for anybody," she said to herself. "I will not move."

Before she could form the real words in her mouth, however, her body moved in a pattern directly opposite to her conviction. Almost automatically her hand clasped the top of the seat in front of her and she stood, feeling the angry pulse fall down about her feet much as a gown might fall to the floor after the straps slip from the shoulders.

She reached up and pulled the cord. "You can have this seat if you want," she said with mock sweetness to the white man, who said "much obliged," and sat down brusquely. She went on. "You can have this seat because me and my babies was gonna get off here anyways."

Nebraska grabbed up Viv and Benjamin, nodded "good day" to Romaine, who looked about with her one eye to see what the rush was all about, then walked quickly from the bus, the carriage clattering down the steps behind her. Finding herself by the five-and-ten-cent store, she parked the carriage by the bicycle rack and entered. Carrying both children in one arm, she wiped the perspiration from her brow. She put the children on the ground, and immediately they scrambled in opposite directions.

She caught Viv near the chocolate counter, lifted her, and raced to the lingerie counter, where an elderly woman bent over Benjamin, saying, "Peep eye, I see you," and wagging her finger.

"He don't need no pee pie, lady," Nebraska said roughly, and gathered up the boy.

With the children in both arms she walked in a daze through the sports section and the underwear section. Baseball bats and footballs became sheer stockings and frilly petticoats. Bras clung to pink-tinted mannequins. One mannequin's arm was twisted backwards and a sale pocketbook hung over the wrist.

The white man with the mahogany cane turned the corner and approached her. She came to the corner of the household appliance section and the man disappeared. "Am I losing my mind?" she asked out loud. "I should have kept my seat! I'll be actin' like Wenda June before long." The man reappeared behind the aquariums in the pet department, then vanished. "Is this what the doctor calls the 'distortion'?"

She turned the corner of the pet department and passed by the long counters where colored customers sat. Beyond them, closer to the window, white people sat sipping on cups of coffee and looking over newspapers.

Benjamin began to squirm. Viv began to move about restlessly. "What y'all want, sugars? Y'all want to know where Nebraska's goin'? Even I don't know that. Just know I should have done otherwise than I did."

Benjamin wriggled harder.

"You must be thirsty, honey. Where's the water fountains in this place?"

She found the fountains against a back wall of the store. One was marked "colored," the other "white." The man with the cane appeared, vanished. "I'll show you," she said violently.

She pressed her foot against the fountain marked "colored" and took a sip, then, looking about to make sure no one was watching, pressed her foot against the fountain marked "white." She held Benjamin up to take a drink, then leaned over herself for a swallow. As if there were a protective shell over that fountain, though, she turned away, unable to cross the barrier. Instead, she held Vivian up to the clear "white" stream and pushed her little face to the arc.

⁓

"It's good, but it's not good. It's good but it's not good." Edward Gold paced back and forth in his office and spoke to Nebraska.

As Edward paced, Nebraska smoothed out the piece of paper she'd kept crumpled in her purse for over six months: BROWN VS. BOARD OF EDUCATION. The rest of the letters moved into a sea of brown creases where a Coca-Cola had spilled three weeks earlier.

"You see," Edward continued, "I'm afraid all these bigots down here, all these self-righteous, so-called God-fearing folks, are never gonna see a mix of kids in the schools. Is the Supreme Court going to come down here in person and take the children by the hands to the classrooms? Of course, suppose that integration *does* succeed. Well, in that case . . ." His expression became long and sad. "In that case, Nebraska Waters, all hell's gonna break loose in Madoc and everywhere else between here and the Mason-Dixon Line."

Nebraska nodded. Behind Edward she saw the maps of the city with their arrows and numbers. The maps looked like ragged clouds from which faces, as long and sad as Edward's, emerged.

"Take a look here." Edward pointed to the mouth of one face that emerged from a map. "I've got some property here. And I've got a lot of clients who've got property over here." He pointed to the eyes of the face. "Those two areas are important school districts—white school districts."

She nodded again, watching the faces recede, listening to the tension build in Edward's voice: "You know what's to happen if Negro children from here start going to a white school over there? Do you?"

"Yes, sir," Nebraska answered. "I guess they'll have white and colored jumbled together."

Edward gave an uneasy laugh, then continued. "Certainly,

all jumbled together. You're absolutely right. But what about around the schools, the neighborhoods around the school? The neighborhoods where we've got a little money tied up?"

"What the neighborhoods got to do with the schools?"

Edward brought his hands together and twisted them. "The answer to your question, Nebraska, is simple. The bottom's going to drop out of the real estate market. It's going to drop out of the housing market. Nothing will be worth anything."

"How come?"

"Because . . ." He hesitated. "Because the cold facts are that as soon as colored children start going to school in a white neighborhood the whites are going to start getting the hell out. And who's going to buy the property? Colored people?"

"Maybe they can put up another housing project."

"Lord help us. Uncle Sam will pay us a hundredth of what the property's worth."

"I got a friend named Aljean who works out at Woodmill. It takes her near 'bout three quarters of an hour to get all the way there on the Madoc bus. She say there ain't no Negroes within fifteen miles of Woodmill. How they gonna get chirren from over where I live all the way out there?"

"Beats me, Nebraska. Maybe they'll take them out in U.S. Army tanks. And you know what?" He walked closer, putting his hands on the edge of Babs's desk and looking Nebraska straight in the eye and lowering his voice. "Between you and me those s.o.b.'s deserve whatever's coming to them in a place like Woodmill. Their neighborhood is already restricted. In my book that means one thing in particular: no Jews."

"So there you are," said Babs, entering the back door of the office with several packages bundled up against her mint-green dress top. "I been looking all over for you, Nebraska." She moved to Edward's desk and plunked down the packages, then started to remove them one by one to her own desk. "Figured you'd be sitting and enjoying the nice cool air in Dauphine Square, relaxin' on your day off, feedin' pigeons."

"I won't relax till after Judgment Day, Miss Babs," Nebraska said, motioning subtly with her head for Babs to fix her dress, which was askew on her shoulders.

"I'll probably be fetchin' something for Edward even then," remarked Babs, and turned and grinned at her boss.

"You got the pitchers?" Nebraska asked, reminded of the purpose of her visit to Gold's Real Estate.

"Yes, yes," Babs answered. "Just hold your horses. I went and got some extra copies made just for you."

After situating all her packages, Babs slipped a brown envelope out of her purse and took out the photographs. She fanned them out on her desk top and bent over them with a longing look. As she straightened her dress top with one hand, with the other she isolated some snaps of Edward standing at the beach in a bathing suit. "These are for me." She giggled. "So I'll remember him like he was before starting to put on weight."

"Me put on weight?" Edward chuckled, patting his stomach.

"Nebraska, you're feedin' him too good," Babs said.

Nebraska scanned, with delight, the photographs meant for her. In one, Vivian Gold and Rachel sat in a swing, a jungle gym and willow tree behind them. In another, Sarah and Rachel stuck out their tongues at the camera. In a third, Benjamin toddled across a seemingly infinite lawn with a cocker spaniel in a suspended leap at his side.

"My, these are good pitchers, Miss Babs. Sarah looks so growed up in this one."

"She'll be getting her learner's permit for driving a car pretty soon," Edward remarked proudly. "Anyway, Nebraska, do you understand the implications of that sheet of paper now?"

Nebraska shrugged. "Understand it as good as I can."

"Wh-what are y'all doin' all this understandin' about?" Babs huffed. "Some secret?" As though she were suddenly not interested in the answer, she started busily fussing about her desk and taking some new curtains from one of the packages.

"Don't worry," Edward said. "It's nothing personal. We're only talking about mixing races in the schools."

"*That'll* be the day!" Babs straightened her dress again. "Nothin' changes around Madoc. I'll be sitting in this office chair this time come nineteen hundred and ninety-nine, if I live that long, and everything will be exactly the same as it is today. Nothin' but nothin' changes in Madoc. Nothin' but everybody having more babies."

Nebraska picked up the copies of the photographs made for her and said quickly, "Thank you. See you tomorrow, Mr. Gold, and see you real soon, Miss Babs," and left the office. The fall day was crisp, and she walked across Dauphine Square, stopping to look at the goldfish swimming sluggishly about in the fountain. She continued on in the direction of Dexter Avenue.

When home, she climbed the steps with a flush of energy, exhilarated by the cool air, and entered the front room of the apartment. Abraham's gift to her, the photograph album, lay black and glossy on the coffee table.

Before taking off her sweater or kicking off her shoes, she began to flip through the pages of the album she had started to fill with photographs out of boxes that morning. There was the picture postcard of the bank at Randomville, Alabama; the card of the Mississippi Bridge in New Orleans that the Golds had mailed to her on their last trip there; and another postcard of a cartoon Mexican in a sombrero, sent to Vivian and Edward by an old army friend and salvaged from the Golds' garbage by Nebraska.

Next came the photographs of her family: of Abraham, taken at a country fair; of Wenda June and a girlfriend snapped in front of a columned building in Detroit; of Todd holding Junior on his shoulders on a church outing at the beach; and of Viv cradled in Nebraska's arms the fourth week after her birth.

"My, time flies, flies, flies," Nebraska said under her breath, and shut her eyes tightly for a moment, repeating the phrase. Dots drifted across her retinas, and she imagined them as all the children in the world not yet born. She opened her eyes, and the picture of Viv goo-gooed back at her.

Sliding the photographs of the Gold family out of the envelope, she placed adhesive corners on them, licked the corners, and stuck the pictures onto the page opposite the shots of her family. She stood back a moment to survey the mix—Waters to the left, Golds to the right—then changed her mind.

Unsticking the Gold photographs, she put them in the back of the album, on the last page, in order to have unbounded room left for her own family. Running shy on adhesive corners, she trudged upstairs to hunt for some more.

Not finding any in the bureau in her and Abraham's bedroom, she went into Wenda June's room and opened the top drawer where paper, pencils, and assorted odds and ends were kept. Before her, gleaming, was an exquisite silver butter knife.

Astonished, she lifted the knife up and held it to the light. A capital *B* was engraved delicately on the handle. After scrabbling about in the papers, she uncovered another *B*-engraved piece of silver, this one a serving spoon. A realization struck her that made her legs want to give way.

She walked to the edge of the bed, sat down, and put her head in her hands. "Oh, Lord," she said quietly. "Oh, Lord, forgive my baby Wenda June 'cause she know not what she do. She done gone and stole from Miss Brooks. Oh, Lord, forgive my poor sick child."

1958

Vivian looked over the clubs in her golf bag and speculated on which wood to use for the tee shot of the first hole. "What about the two-wood, ma'am?" asked the caddy, a balding black man in cleats, baggy brown trousers, and a T-shirt that read OLD DIXIE COUNTRY CLUB.

"Yes," Vivian said, "the two-wood will be fine."

Since 1956 the Golds had been members of the Old Dixie —part of its discreet, yet clear, Jewish quota. The two oldest and most powerful Jewish families in Madoc, the Altmans and the Finks—both with money in oil and paper mills—had been members of the club since its inception in 1910. The Golds, like several newer and less illustrious arrivals to south Alabama, had won their invitations only after decades of proving themselves promising, upwardly mobile members of the Madoc business community. When Edward had received his invitation through a friend in the chamber of commerce, he said to Vivian somewhat sheepishly, "The Old Dixie would never even have acknowledged the presence of my parents or yours, but—but it would be a tremendous advantage to our future in Madoc." At first Vivian had protested, but then had been quietly thrilled that her family would be able to walk, unrestricted, under all those moss-laden trees. And when Margery Berman had said, "I wouldn't join the Old Dixie, even play golf there, if they paid me all the money in the world," Vivian had answered with measured patience, "Just because you and Izzy applied and were rejected, please don't say it was anti-Semitic."

The caddy slid the two-wood from the golf bag and mopped off the head with a towel he kept tied to his belt. "Here go, Miss Gold," he said in a low, scratchy voice.

"Thank you." Self-consciously Vivian repeated, "Thank you, Rochester."

If the caddy did not look and sound so much like Jack Benny's Rochester she had seen for the last year on the television set Edward had bought her, she would not have felt so awkward calling him by his name. Now that the shambling, grinning, "Yassuh, boss!" valet came into her living room once a week, she could not help but suspect the caddy of acting a part himself, as if he were secretly preparing for a venture to the bright lights of New York or Hollywood to nail down a Stepin Fetchit role.

Maxine Grenoble went up to the tee first. As she took her practice swing, a list of stereotypes rolled across Vivian's thoughts: Aunt Jemima, Uncle Tom, Sambo . . . blackbird, spade, coon, ape. The list degenerated into epithets of horror. Alongside that list another arose: Rich Jew, tight Jew, kike . . . She remembered a high school assignment to read *Oliver Twist* at Lafayette High and how, when she came to the character called "the Jew," she cringed and put the book down. And when the Madoc Players had decided to stage *The Merchant of Venice,* in the late 1940s, she'd convinced them to stage *As You Like It* instead, arguing that *The Merchant of Venice* was too somber and academic. It had really been her unwillingness to see Shakespeare's Shylock standing on the stage, shouting "A pound of flesh!" that had fueled her repugnance for the play.

Maxine lined up her shot, drew the club back and up in a slow arc, then smashed the ball down the center of the fairway. "Good 'un," said Rochester.

"Yes," added Cissy Vance, the third member of the threesome. "You powdered the *h-e-* double *l* out of it."

Did Maxine Grenoble ever feel she was the victim of a stereotype? Vivian watched the high-cheekboned, lightly freckled blue-eyed woman whose husband was heir to the Madoc Lumber fortune. Scotch-Irish on one side, French on the other, Maxine's third claim of lineage was what she referred to as her "beloved Confederacy": a grandfather with enough land in Tennessee to build another Madoc on and a great-uncle who had served as a cavalry officer to Robert E. Lee. Vivian had described Maxine to Nebraska as being "old Madoc," or "Madoc blue blood," to which Nebraska had obstinately replied that "blue blood" sounded like a sickness she wouldn't even wish on one of Abraham's dogs.

Cissy Vance—whom Vivian had described to Nebraska as "not old Madoc by a long shot, but would love to be"—teed up next and hit a sharp slice out of bounds. "Sorry, Miss Cissy," said her caddy. Cissy turned and glared at him.

Vivian, up next, cracked a shot that followed the exact arc of Maxine's ball. As she made her way along the fairway with Cissy and Maxine, there was satisfaction in having hit the ball so. After all, Maxine was one of those strong, lean women who had played golf since the age of ten, received instruction since the age of twelve, and been presented with monogrammed clubs on her sixteenth birthday. Walking alongside her five foot, nine inch frame, Vivian—five foot three—felt her own stature increase.

A minute later, as Maxine began to work her way toward the one topic of the day Vivian dreaded, she felt her body shrink again.

"Well, Vivian, what do you think about the news?"

"News?"

"Little Rock," Maxine said.

"Oh, you mean that little article in the *Register* this morning?" Vivian saw the front page headline again: GOV. FAUBUS CLOSES LITTLE ROCK SCHOOLS. Under the headline were two photos, one from the previous fall of a black girl being escorted to class by a National Guardsman, another from just yesterday of a city official placing a padlock on a schoolroom door.

"That *little* article?" Maxine took some ointment from her pocket, squeezed some on her palm, and began to rub it on her forehead. "I didn't want to say anything about it in earshot of the caddies, but I tell you, it makes you wonder about the world's sanity, still trying to mix colored and white. They put a dozen students in the Little Rock schools last year, and what happened? The whole city's shot to hell."

Vivian stared at the distant golf balls: tiny white flecks on a bright green sea.

Maxine went on. "Do you realize how lucky we are in Alabama to have politicians who can tell Uncle Sam to get his grubby paws off our backs? And he gets them off too! We don't need some bighearted"—Maxine lowered her voice—"fat-assed Washington screwball giving us directions on how to live our lives. We do just fine, thank you."

"Well . . ." Vivian's throat became dry. She coughed, then forced herself to protest, though meekly. "I . . . I don't know about that."

"Don't know about what?" Maxine came sharply. "How would you like to walk into your house one day and catch your daughter necking with a blackbird? Would you?"

Vivian watched the golf balls float seemingly farther into the distance.

"Of course you wouldn't," Maxine answered haughtily. "I don't know you well, but I know you better than that."

"But, Maxine"—Vivian caught a sidelong glare from her partner—"Maxine, just because they go to school together doesn't mean they're going to be marching down the aisle together."

"Ever been to Paris, Vivian?"

Mutely, Vivian shook her head.

"Well, you see enough chocolate and vanilla combos there to make you sick for a year. Of course, it's always chocolate men and vanilla women! Didn't Edward ever tell you that joke?" She looked around to make sure the caddies were out of earshot. "You see, there's this colored fella who walks into a white bar, pounds his chest, and shouts, 'Ah sleeps wi' white women!' He goes into another white bar, this time kinda drunk, pounds his chest and shouts even louder, 'Ah sleeps wi' white women!' So then he goes into a third bar, drunker than a coot, pounds his chest like a damn drum, and shouts at the top of his voice, 'Ah sleeps wi' white women. AH SLEEPS WI' WHITE WOMEN!' Finally this little white guy at the bar turns around and says real cool, 'I don't blame ya', buddy, I wouldn't sleep with a nigger either.' "

When Maxine had finished laughing to herself, Vivian replied icily, "No, Edward's never told me that joke. He's got a better sense of humor than that."

"Okay, okay, some jokes are funnier. There aren't any *truer* jokes, though."

Remembering all the stories she'd heard of white men abusing black women, and then fixing on an image of Wenda June Waters's slender Caucasian features, Vivian shook her head. "I think you're taking this whole thing around the world and back when it needn't be taken any farther than the corner. Little Rock needs time. Alabama needs time."

"No, ma'am," Maxine answered. "I'm taking it as far as it should be taken. Desegregating the races is unethical. It's immoral. And it's un-Christian."

Like a shotgun blast "un-Christian" exploded near Vivian's face. She tried to disregard its sting the way Edward would, taking the term as an inappropriate choice of words, nothing more.

They arrived at the golf balls. Maxine hooked her shot to the left of the sand trap. Readying to swing, Vivian thought to push her shot to the opposite side of the green in order to avoid further talk with her partner. Her shot bore right as planned; then, as if an avenging spirit had entered the ball, it curved left and rolled alongside Maxine's.

"Miss Gold, Miss Gold," Rochester said. "You's gettin' good. Yas'm. You be beatin' Miss Noble 'fore long."

Vivian nodded, working to conceal her chagrin.

The two women took out short irons for the approach shots and quickly walked ahead of the caddies. Cissy had sliced her ball a second time and was two fairways in the distance.

"What does your girl say about all this?" Maxine asked, flicking off a speck of turf from the head of her iron.

"Rachel?" Vivian asked, baffled. "Or Sarah?"

"Not your daughter, honey. Your cook! Montana, Africa, whatever her name is. She told it to me on the phone, but I have an awful memory for names of colored."

"Nebraska Waters is her name," Vivian said. "I guess Nebraska's for integration. Why shouldn't she be? She's got a precious little girl who's quick as a fox. She wants the best education possible for her, just like any parent."

"The last girl who worked for me said she'd never have a child of hers go to school with whitey. That's what she called us, 'Whitey'! She told me that the same day I saw her spit in my food!"

"Well, Nebraska's never spit in my food," Vivian said as she watched the sand trap loom larger, like a welcome beach beyond the bright green sea.

"How do you know?"

"That's ridiculous, Maxine. I know because I know. I know because Nebraska is a fine, upstanding woman, Negro or white."

"You don't think she ever would?" Maxine raised her eyebrows as she finished the question.

"Heck, no, I don't," Vivian said forcefully. "You know, Maxine, colored people are different from each other like white people are different from each other. For example, take this colored woman named Mary who worked for us when Nebraska was out having a baby. Mary told me the most awful things about how colored feel about white. When I told Nebraska about what she'd said, Nebraska explained, 'Miss Gold, Mary done had a father lynched from a tree and set out on an open casket in the middle of town. Folks came from all over to take his picture, and some white man even made a postcard that said *One Less Nigger*.' How can I blame Mary for telling me the things she did?"

"What's your point, Vivian? What's your damn point?" snapped Maxine. "I'm not saying we should string up every Uncle Remus from a tree. What I'm saying is what your Mary is saying and what Nebraska would say if she wasn't scared you'd kick her out the door: We don't want them, and they don't want us!"

The words were burning on Vivian's tongue. "The schools, Maxine, are for the public, the *whole* public."

Though they were still several yards from the golf balls, Maxine stopped and turned to her. "Honey," she began, "you sound just like a liberal Je—" Maxine's mouth tightened and the half-uttered word blew away in the breeze. She finished sourly: "Where's that damn Cissy? She's going to slice herself right into the Gulf of Mexico."

By the time the golf game was over, the conversation had wound from a further discussion of Cissy's slice, to a detailed account of everyone's children, to a speculation on who would be the new golf pro at the Old Dixie; it stayed far clear of anything resembling racial topics. The women then parted ways into the locker rooms, later meeting on the veranda for drinks. From the table where they sat, Vivian could see the Golds' bay house in the distance: Nebraska would be sitting in the back room, reading the Book of Timothy as the sun went down.

"What time are the boys expected?" Cissy asked.

Maxine answered. "Brad said they'd get here right about six. Isn't Edward driving them out?"

Vivian nodded and turned to see the men at that very moment stepping between two bungalows, laughing, faces red as the late afternoon sun.

"Who are the others?" asked Cissy.

Behind the three husbands strode four other men, three of

them tall and brawny and one wiry and small. When the small man spoke, the others fell silent; then the whole group burst into feverish laughter.

Maxine spoke through a yawn. "Did they bring along a stand-up comic?"

"Oh what fun!" Cissy said, voice full of a good time.

By the color of Edward's face, Vivian knew that he and probably the others had a sizable amount of whiskey hammering through their blood.

Brad Grenoble whistled through his teeth and shouted lustily, "Look at those sexy golfers," before stumbling into his wife's lap.

Maxine shoved him off. "Brad, don't you come falling all over me when you can't even see straight."

Edward, his head bowed like a humble knight, came forward, took Vivian's hand, and gave it a slobbery kiss. "Mrs. Gold, the fairest of the fair."

Vivian drew her hand away and wiped it on her shorts. "What unfortunate gland causes the male to become totally obnoxious when drunk?"

"The only gland they've got that we don't," Cissy said, grinning and waving to her husband, who stood sheepishly beside the others.

"Shut up," Maxine said under her breath. "It's not a gland anyway."

Cissy, blushing, shut up.

"Such a fuss!" Brad exclaimed. "Such a fuss, and we've come with a dignitary in our midst."

"A dignitary!" Cissy said, springing back to life.

"Yes, a dignitary," Brad said, puffing out his chest. He turned to a man behind him—a hunkering giant in a green-and-yellow-checked coat with an unlit stogie in his mouth. The man stepped forward majestically, nodded, and introduced himself as the bodyguard of the next governor of Alabama.

"Who's the next governor?" Cissy asked, craning her neck

as though the next governor were to be found hiding behind a bungalow.

It suddenly dawned on Vivian who the small man with the shiny pompadour was. She recognized his face from the billboards and bumper stickers and the *Madoc Register*. He was the politician recently defeated in the 1958 Democratic primary.

"May I introduce," the bodyguard said, making a sweeping gesture with his arm, "Judge George Corley Wallace."

"I thought his name was *John*," Vivian whispered to Maxine, who glanced back with "You little fool" written in her expression.

With great aplomb, Maxine stood and shook the politician's hand, saying, "Why, this is the best surprise I've had all year, Judge Wallace." She winked at him. "So pleased to make your acquaintance, *Governor*."

Cissy followed suit, her intonation identical to Maxine's.

Maxine, beaming now, asked, "What on earth was so funny?"

"Oh," Wallace said, hiking up his pants, "nothin' I can repeat in front of you ladies. Just a few ol' nigguh jokes is all."

Again the men burst into laughter. Vivian watched Edward closely. He laughed loudly with the others. At the same time he did so, however, he looked back at her, blushing deeply behind the red whiskey glow of his face.

"You know," Wallace went on, rocking slowly on his feet like an orator, "the only reason I lost out this go-round to Johnny Patterson was he had more nigguh jokes than me. But believe me, ladies, I will not be out-nigguhed again!"

Everyone except Vivian laughed heartily. She felt the green sea of the golf course rise up around the veranda. Alone she sat, marooned on an island in that sea. Sharks plied the water around her, and Edward became one of those sharks.

Quickly she rose. "Mr. Wallace, nice to make your acquaintance," she said drily. Startled, Wallace held out his hand to shake, but she turned away from the small, plump fingers and walked quickly to the parking lot.

Edward caught up with her by the portico shade next to the Old Dixie front office. He latched onto her shoulder and his whiskey breath lashed against her. "What do you mean, tearing off like that? Don't you know who the hell that man is?"

"I know who he is," Vivian answered hotly. "He's a little racist."

"Listen, Viv." Edward stood directly over her and spoke an inch from her face. "Don't believe any of that nigger joke crap. He doesn't take it any more seriously than I do. How can he win in Alabama if he *doesn't* play the racist. He's a capable man. It's just politics."

"Does that mean you have to play the racist too?"

"Aren't I in politics as well? Isn't everybody? Do you think I can swim upstream in the middle of this thing and come out ahead?"

"And Benjamin?"

"What do you mean, *Benjamin?*"

"Benjamin." Vivian stood firmly as she talked. "What will Benjamin think of you?"

"Benjamin's five years old, Vivian. Are you crazy? Don't drag the children into this."

"The children are already dragged into it." She surprised herself by speaking with such fierceness to her husband. The words bolted out of her as Edward stood suddenly quite still, pursing his lips like a little boy about to cry "I wanna be part of the gang." She went on: "It's the children who are being used as everybody's excuse for hating people who just happen to have a different color of skin."

"It's more than skin."

"You're drunk, Edward." Vivian turned to go. "And you're God damned unbearable right now."

As she backed away, Edward lunged forward to stop her. He tripped over a potted plant and went sprawling on the neatly clipped grass in front of the office. "Don't go, don't go." He looked up at her with cow eyes and beckoned with outstretched arms. "I'm sorry, baby. You've never seen me like this before."

"You're absolutely right. I've never seen you like this before." She jangled the car keys. "I'm going home. Stay and whoop it up with the menfolk. Y'all just have a grand ol' time."

ᕲᕗ

When Vivian arrived home it was evening; at last, blue-gray light clung to the magnolias and dogwoods. The Japanese magnolia, long bare of its petals, pushed its dark green profusion of leaves against the windows of the playroom (the porch had been walled up to make an area for Ping-Pong table, bridge table, and bar).

Though Vivian had been tense all the way home, she relaxed upon seeing the house. It was her asylum from the outside world—the world where grown men, like silly children, sorted and arranged according to a person's complexion, religion, and last name. "Colored and white," she said to herself wearily, "colored and white. Why is the whole world becoming a question of colored and white?"

She parked in the garage and walked to the kitchen door. The kitchen light was on and she saw shadows of heads nodding and bending over the driveway. She crept up quietly to surprise the children and Nebraska, who was staying with them. The first person she caught a good glimpse of was Viv, her hair in cornrows, tied up with twists of newspaper, her eyes large and staring at some object on the table. Next she saw Benjamin standing on the bench of the breakfast nook, his elbows on the table, leaning forward. His foot wiggled with excitement as he also watched. Even Rachel, dressed in her pedal pushers, hair in pigtails, leaned against the icebox, staring at something. It was unusual to see her thirteen-year-old spending free time with the younger children, as she was just at the age when she'd rather pass the time alone in her room, with radio, record player, or telephone.

As the evening was warm and the window was open a

crack, she could hear Nebraska speaking in low, mysterious tones. She eased up farther and saw the black woman sitting against the bench opposite Benjamin. A glass of water was in front of her. Nebraska's expression was serious, rapt, as if she were in a state of hypnosis.

Nebraska spoke slowly. "Hoodoo is what you call the ways of spirits mixin' with men. Hoodoo is somethin' powerful and somethin' mean if you don't know how to use it. Used to be a woman up in the country, round Randomville, said she knew a hoodoo that could call down hants from the cemetery."

"What's a hant?" Rachel asked, stepping forward a bit.

"A hant is a hant," Nebraska answered. "A spirit, a ghost. 'Ceptin' hants comes from the hoodoo."

Benjamin wriggled his foot fiercely and reached to the center of the table. His small hands, grubby from picking at some cake or batch of brownies, suddenly spread wide. Nebraska reached over and popped him gently on the wrist and he jerked away. "Leave the horsehair alone, Benjie. Gonna mess up the hoodoo. Just hold still while I conjure." She paused. "Where was I? Oh, yes."

Nebraska droned softly and Vivian imagined Edward driving home with the husbands of Maxine and Cissy and with George Wallace and his bodyguards in the back seat. "Sit here, Mr. George Wallace," Nebraska would say. "Stay right still and let me tell you 'bout hoodoo and hants." Mr. Wallace, hair combed back like a wave at Madoc Bay and small eyes flashing, would sit as bug-eyed as the children as he watched and listened. Would the politician tell nigger jokes then? And if he did, would Nebraska call down some spell to flare his nose and blacken his skin, then ask him what he thought was so funny?

Nebraska's voice rose a pitch. "Once I knew a man who almost died. Had the colic. The hoodoo woman said to my sister Maryland, 'Go and fetch some weeds, some red clay, and some cow tee-tee.'" Benjamin giggled. "Shush, boy. Listen. So my sister did what she was told and come back to the hoodoo woman who mixed them all up and gave it to the man to drink.

Called it Minnie's weed tea. Not six days later the man was up and hoein' in the field!"

"Put in the horsehair," Rachel said excitedly, pointing to the center of the table.

Nebraska held out her hand as in a trance and fingered up what Vivian presumed to be a hair. Ducking down so as not to be spotted, she thought to herself, So *this* is what goes on when I'm not around! She rose again carefully and peered at the ritual.

Nebraska brought her hand down slowly over the glass of water, then opened her fingers. Benjamin pushed his face so close to the glass that Vivian could see his left eye as if it were in a fish tank, ballooned through water.

"Where's the worm?" Benjamin asked.

"Quiet," Rachel breathed. "If you keep talking, the hair might not change into a worm. You might frighten it."

"Can't nothin' frighten a worm, sugar, when it takes a mind to change outa the horsehair." Nebraska kept her sight trained on the glass. "Nothin' but bad hoodoo. Course, this is good hoodoo."

"A fish scares a worm," Viv remarked.

"Viv's so smart," Rachel said. "Isn't it true she's got a very high IQ? That's what mother told us."

"Hush," said Nebraska, still watching the glass, then added, "That's what they tell me at the play school. She takes after your momma."

"Where's the worm?" Benjamin asked impatiently.

Nebraska jiggled the top of the glass with her hand and the water sloshed about.

Benjamin squealed. "It's comin' alive! Nebuba, it's a worm comin' alive!"

"Look," Rachel shouted. "LOOK!"

"Hoodoo is workin'," Nebraska shouted. "It's turnin' and shakin'!"

Heart aflutter, Vivian stood to try to catch a glimpse of the conjured worm. Immediately Benjamin spotted her through the window and pointed to her. "Mommy, Mommy, it's Mommy!"

Nebraska looked up, face stricken, and quickly pushed her hand across the table, knocking the glass to the floor. "What a terrible accident," she cried. "Look what I've gone and done."

When Vivian opened the back door and entered, Benjamin leaped to her, throwing his arms around her neck, giving her an allover kiss. Beyond his kissing and slurping she saw Nebraska hurriedly sweeping up the broken glass and dumping the pieces into a brown bag. She folded the bag into another bag, saying, "Well, I think I'll just go on outside and juke this mess in the garbage can instead of leaving it here in the wastebasket." She moved for the door.

"So," Vivian inquired, training her sight on the bag, "how have y'all been passing the time?" While she waited for the confession, Benjamin jumped down and scampered back toward Viv.

"Oh," Nebraska passed off, "same as always on Saturday evening, just watchin' TV and eatin' waffles."

"Nothing else?"

With sealed lips, Nebraska shook her head and disappeared out the door. Vivian turned to Rachel, who shrugged and wandered off to her room.

"So what's been going on here?" Vivian asked Benjamin and Viv, who stood near the icebox. They began to giggle, then scampered out the back door after Nebraska, slamming the screen behind them.

༄

On Sunday morning a week later Vivian lay awake in the bed, watching the light fill the room and move up the dressing table, over the perfume bottles, across the chest of drawers, where Nebraska had, as always, neatly balled up and stored Edward's socks. Was there ever a time when it did not feel natural to have some other woman's hands fixing those socks? She tried to remember, but could not.

She envisioned Margery and Izzy Berman and Romaine.

She envisioned Edna and David Solomon and Sunny. She saw Maxine and Brad Grenoble and Hattie. It was as if there were three-way marriages, double vows. The white woman existed for her husband and family. The white man existed for his wife and family. The black woman existed for the white woman, the white man, the white family, and her own husband and family.

She drew two huge family trees on the ceiling with an imaginary pencil. Her own family stretched back to Russia and Germany, the branches moving over the wallpaper to the beginnings of life in the Middle East. Nebraska's family stretched back to Africa, its branches ending beyond the mirror in a dark forest of earth's creation. Were not Isaac and Ishmael brothers, as the rabbi had said in a recent sermon? (Edward had said the rabbi should discuss Torah and not politics, but she felt differently.) Was there some point in antiquity where her fathers had been Nebraska's fathers?

Edward rolled over and opened his eyes. "Awake already?" he asked softly. He pushed his face up to her neck and kissed her under the ear. A wave of warmth rippled down her body. He pressed closer, the thick hair of his chest hot against her shoulder.

She told him of her dream from the night before: She had driven to the house on Madoc Bay and found, on the small beach in front of the house, Nebraska standing barefoot, dressed in a flowered smock and one of Vivian's old hats. Around Nebraska stood the children, clapping and singing a ditty she remembered from grade school—"La-di-la, La-di-lo, The mouse danced on the elephant's toe." Enchanted, Vivian moved closer—she was now dressed in a white bathing suit—and began to join in the song. When the children noticed her, they squealed and started to run down the beach, Nebraska leading the way. A sudden wind filled Nebraska's hat and lifted her up. The children clutched at Nebraska's naked feet and rose behind her into the sky.

"Cold pastrami," Edward said, settling back down into the pillows.

"What?"

"Eating cold pastrami before going to bed always gives you crazy dreams. Didn't Sosha ever tell you that?"

"Well, we did eat pastrami, but . . . Edward, maybe I'm letting Nebraska spend too much time with the children. Maybe *I* should be with them all day long, not some . . . outsider."

"But look at all you've been able to accomplish since Nebraska's been working here."

"Accomplish what?"

"Well, there's your acting. And your civic duties, and . . ."

Vivian cut him off. "My acting! That's a joke, a *horrible* joke. And my civic duties . . . What's more civic than taking care of your own children?" Vivian plopped her hands against the mattress and took a deep breath, then exhaled it slowly. "After all these years I can still feel guilty for having Nebraska here."

"Guilty?"

"Guilty, yes. As if it's my fault for slavery or something like that."

Edward rolled over on his back and let out a sharp laugh. "Ishkibibble. That's the most ridiculous thing I've heard in all my life."

"I know," Vivian said. "I know." She started to go on but was interrupted by the sound of somebody scraping along the hallway to the bedroom. Lifting her head, she saw Benjamin shuffling toward the foot of their bed in his house slippers. He looked at her devilishly.

"Why, Benjie, honey, you frightened us!"

"Benjie?" Edward pulled the covers up tight around the two of them, then said briskly, "Cowboy! Come on up here!"

Benjamin put his foot on the rung of the poster bed and hoisted himself up by the blankets. He got caught in a half somersault position until Edward reached down and pulled him all the way over. When he landed with his feet between Vivian and Edward, Edward grabbed his right foot, slowly dragged him forward, and began to tickle him.

Benjamin squealed with laughter. In defense of her son, Vivian reached over and tickled her husband. Edward rolled into a ball and howled, and Benjamin, freed, stood and jumped up and down as if the bed were a trampoline. He fell between them again and the sheets and blankets twisted about them all.

Edward peeled up Benjamin's pajama shirt, pressed his mouth to the boy's belly and blew hard until the skin made a spluttering noise and Benjamin squirmed like an eel and shrieked ecstatically.

"Edward! You're going to make him sick!" Vivian reached over to tickle Edward under the chin, but Edward ducked behind Benjamin, using him like a shield, and Vivian tickled Benjamin by mistake. As her son's eyes grew wide with merriment and he giggled for mercy, she put her ear against his body, heard the laughter coming from inside his chest, and thought how perfectly content she'd be to spend the rest of eternity in this bed with her husband and son, away from the world and its problems, swirled in sheets and laughter.

1961

THE NEWS ABOUT MARGERY BERMAN came one afternoon after
Nebraska had gone to pick up Viv at school. Nebraska had left
the Golds' house as usual about two thirty to take the bus downtown, then crosstown, so that by three o'clock she was in front
of the Booker T. Washington School as Viv came out, books
and papers in arm. By three thirty they were back at the Golds'
house, and all the way there on the bus Viv chattered pre-
cociously about the geography she'd learned in her third-grade
class that day. Sometimes the child went on in such a way about
how the Mississippi River was the longest in the world—next to
the Nile and Amazon—or about how addition and multiplica-
tion worked quite different spells on numbers, that Nebraska felt
her own head swim. It was a joy beyond telling that Viv was, in
the school principal's term, "an uncommonly brilliant child."
But it was also a source of uneasiness from time to time when
she realized that her own child's schooling already rivaled her
own. ("Viv goes on like a little politician," she once remarked to
Mary. "Maybe she'll be president of the United States one day.
Maybe another John Fitzgerald Kennedy!")

On that Wednesday Viv had talked of how some pieces of
stone break down more easily than others, and how the teacher
took a piece of sandstone and a piece of coal and rubbed them
together. Just as she was sitting at the Golds' kitchen table,

showing how the teacher had rubbed the stones, Romaine burst in the back door, her one eye looking about wildly, her blind eye tearing and twitching.

"Miss Gold, Miss Gold," Romaine shouted. "Miss Margery's been . . . been beat up and raped by two colored boys from up at the country club. Said, said . . ." She paused, catching a breath. "Said they was working out back on the boiler system and needed to hitchhike a ride home. She gave 'em a ride an' . . ." She broke into tears, her bad eye knotting. "An' they drove her into the woods and beat her up so bad you can hardly see her face she done swoll up so!"

For seconds no one moved. Nebraska watched Vivian suspended in disbelief, the younger children staring. Rachel put her hands over her face and began to cry. "It sounds *so horrible!*"

Vivian started toward the telephone, but Romaine said, "We been callin' and callin' here but your phone must be out of order." Vivian picked up the phone, let it drop. "Nothing but a busy signal," she affirmed. Then Vivian turned to Nebraska and said, "I can't believe that Margery would pick up two boys like that."

Nebraska shook her head. "No'm, I can't believe it neither," and then saw the calm in Vivian shatter and heard her say, "God dammit! God DAMMIT!"

Vivian groped about in her purse for the car keys and told Benjamin and Viv to go play somewhere, that she and Romaine and Nebraska had business to attend to. "Take care of them, Rachel." Rachel nodded, rubbing her eyes with a table napkin.

Feeling her body beginning to sway, Nebraska followed Vivian and Romaine to the car, and soon they were speeding down the block. "Two colored boys . . . two colored boys . . ." The phrase beat as rhythmically as the car wheels in her mind. A grotesque image of a white woman came before her— someone who looked like Miss Berman, but also resembled Miss Gold. The white woman was thrown down against the seat of an automobile, and one Negro boy held her mouth clamped shut while the other crawled hungrily over her. She imagined herself coming across that automobile and flinging the door open, reaching in and snatching out the boys much as she used to snatch up Todd and Junior when they tussled on the floor. "Don't no colored boys got a right to hit on a white woman!" she shouted in the fantasy. "Don't no colored boys got a right to reflect bad on us all who is colored!" And did not the thought of black flesh meeting white turn her stomach more than anything imaginable? Did not the face of the plantation guard loom over her again, as if she had been Margery Berman and he the black attacker?

The Bermans' house appeared down the block, the modern ranch-style home Nebraska knew so well from Romaine's descriptions of its snaking hallways and three-inch-thick carpets where dirt cantankerously lodged. After they parked in front of the half-constructed carport, they entered. Nebraska, suddenly feeling sheepish, trailed behind.

Margery lay on the den sofa, her feet propped up on the sofa arm. Her husband Izzy—silver-haired and muscled like a boxer—sat on an ottoman next to the sofa, applying compresses to her bruises and speaking gently at her shoulder. While a nurse held Margery's wrist and looked at a wall clock, two policemen paced back and forth, asking questions and jotting notes in a pad.

Romaine snuffled, "Miss Margery. Got Miss Gold here to see you."

Margery's eyes eased open. "Hello, Vivian," she said tremulously. "Hello, how are you?"

"How am I? How are you, poor sweetheart," voiced Vivian as she squatted at the side of her friend.

"How are you, poor sweetheart?"

Vivian, stunned, glanced up at the nurse, who explained, "Miss Gold, she's still in a state of shock, ma'am. She's really not sure what she's saying just yet."

Dr. Schwartz came barreling from the back room, threw out "Hello, Vivian," and bent to Izzy's side. "I think Margery'll be all right, here," Nebraska heard him say. "I've called an ambulance just in case. We . . . we really don't know how much she was abused. God, I'm really sorry, Izzy. This is such a tragic thing to happen."

Izzy looked down at the floor and nodded as in a stupor. "Yes, a tragic thing." He looked up and his voice rose. "A tragic thing! You come in here and tell me it's a tragic thing as if I don't know! It's more than tragic. I'll kill those bastards with my own hands!" He fell silent, sucking deep breaths to steady himself.

Nebraska felt Izzy Berman's eyes cross to her and press against her chest. The eyes were cold and accusing, eyes that made her feel as though she were bearing some burden of guilt. The older of the two policemen broke Izzy's stare when he said with some gruffness, "Mr. Berman, sir, Rick just got a report from headquarters that a Negro male, age sixteen, five nine, was picked up near the River Mill Highway, out by River Mill Country Club. Said he was employed by the Junction Services Company. Found him crashing into the woods like he was running from something—or somebody. The boy was identified as James Lee Smith."

The name of the boy turned around and around inside of Nebraska's head much as a kite spirals wildly before crashing to earth. James Lee Smith, Jimbo Smith, flashed before her standing next to Junior. The two played a game of stretch in the dirt out back of Golden Castles. One threw a knife into the ground in front of the other, who then had to stretch his leg to touch the edge of the knife. The second boy then threw the knife and the first was made to stretch. Whoever made the other fall from stretching won the game. When Nebraska had discovered they were playing with a switchblade honed sharp enough to carve up a man, she'd made Junior stop. Jimbo had looked up at her with an expression more willful and surly than that of any child she had ever known.

But it could *not* have been Jimbo Smith who hitched that ride with Margery. She thought of Jimbo's mother, Dinah, who had worked as a cleaning woman at the state docks for twenty years to get enough money to raise Jimbo and his sisters right. She thought of . . .

Nebraska's reflections were cut off abruptly when Margery started coughing violently. When her coughing subsided, her eyes opened owl-large, scanned the room, and sank like pins into Nebraska. "How'd you get *here!*" Margery exclaimed, lifting her finger toward Nebraska. Her hands suddenly jerked to her face; Izzy pried them away and began kissing her soothingly on the forehead.

Dr. Schwartz left the sofa and motioned to Vivian and Nebraska. "Could you step in here a moment?" He directed them to the dining room, then turned to Nebraska. "Miss Waters, I've known you for a long time and this is hard for me to say. I've known you since you nearly burned up Sarah's feet by accident that day." He laughed, then became serious again. "I've always had great respect for you. The thing of it is . . ."

Nebraska dropped her gaze. Did he know that Junior had once played with Jimbo Smith? Did he, *could* he, suspect that her son was involved? The questions rushed through her mind. She began to pray silently: Jesus Christ Almighty God, Jesus Christ, save my child, save me, save my Junior, save us all, Lord, praise be Thy name, save us all for we have sinned, and save us from these terrible things we are all having said about us, for there are those who would have us sin when we have not. Junior moved above the prayer. He gathered his books and his football equipment for school that day. He kissed her on the cheek. He took the bus to Dexter High and did not take the bus that would lead him as far away as River Mill Road.

"You see," Dr. Schwartz started, after hesitating and hunting for words a long moment. "Margery has undergone a terrible trauma. Sometimes, in a state like this, a woman will be unable to face anyone that reminds her in any way at all of the person, or persons, who've brutalized her." He fidgeted. "Frequently a woman will react to the presence of a strange man, or of a man she might know but not know well. In this case—" He broke off, trying to look at Nebraska, but looking down at the tips of his shoes. "Now, don't get me wrong. This is just a personal theory of mine. Margery seems to be acutely sensitive to the presence of any Negro person, man or woman, except Romaine. You see, Miss Waters, the mind has a way of becoming completely irrational in a state like this. Well, to put it bluntly, it would be better if you were to leave and avoid seeing her for a while. I'm sorry."

"Thank you," Nebraska said, so pleased there had been no mention of her son's name that she wanted to kiss the doctor. Thinking back on her visits to the mental ward at the colored hospital and of seeing the man who did not exist stalking her down the rows of the five-and-ten, she added, "I understand completely and want to do all I can to help."

After Vivian drove Nebraska home and returned to Margery's, where Edward was to meet her, Nebraska started a chicken cooking for the children's supper and ran water for some pots that needed scrubbing. She filled the sink to the top with water and plunged her arms in up to the elbows, letting the heat and steam rise past her elbows into her entire body, soothing her. She lifted out a scouring pad and a skillet, but plunged in her arms again, content to stand still and bathe away the sorrows of the afternoon.

"Beeenjie! Viiivian! Come keep Nebraska company," she called. She heard the children bounding down the steps from the attic. Twisting around, she saw them rumpled and giggling.

"Y'all been playing up in all them ol' boxes and things again? Y'all gonna get hurt playing up there one day. I don't know why Miss Gold don't close it off. You know you'd catch it if she caught you up there."

"Is Mrs. Berman gonna die?" Benjamin asked.

"Hush! What would make you say such a terrible thing as that?"

"Rachel said she's very sick," the boy answered.

"She ain't sick like that," Nebraska said.

"How's she sick?" Viv asked.

"I said for y'all to keep me company, chirren, not drive me crazy with all these questions."

"Are you gonna die, Nebraska?" Benjamin asked.

"Well, of course, sugar, everybody dies one day."

"Even Mrs. Gold?" Viv inquired.

"What'd y'all get into upstairs? Some sort of curiosity potion?"

"Is she?" Viv persisted.

"Yes, of course, Viv. It's the way God intended it to be. We all pass on to another place before long." She plunged her arms into the sink again, started to send the children away, but felt such a sad spot in her heart that she could not bear to be alone. The warmth of the water, subsiding slightly, continued to move along her arms until she felt as though the entire upper part of her body were immersed as well.

"How old are you, Nebraska?" Benjamin spoke with great seriousness.

"Old enough to know you ain't gotta wash dishes in heaven."

"I'm eight," Benjamin said.

"Like me," Viv said.

"Then you old enough, Benjie, to know you never s'posed to ask a woman her age." Nebraska reached up with her left hand and turned on the hot water spigot. Drawing out a large frying pan from the suds, she started to scour it, the sound of the scouring low and constant. She finished, pushed the frying pan back into the suds, brought it up, and scoured again.

"Why isn't Mrs. Berman gonna go to heaven?" Benjamin asked.

"I didn't say she wasn't gonna go to heaven, boy. I said she ain't *died!*" Nebraska held her wrist up to her forehead and let out a long sigh. The scene at the Berman house returned to her. "You don't go to heaven until you die, honey. When the body of this world is cast off, then the soul flies way, way up in the sky." She lifted her right arm up and waved it about, continuing to gather up some forks and spoons on the bottom of the sink with her other hand. "Goes way, way, *way* up."

"What does it do when it gets way up?"

"Y'all don't know that *yet*?" Nebraska glanced behind her. Benjamin and Viv had their right arms up in the air, waving them about as if twirling lariats. "Don't copycat me," she said brusquely. Like toy soldiers they brought their arms immediately to their sides.

Nebraska continued. "When the soul gets way, way, *way* up, it meets with St. Peter, who stands by the gates of heaven to make sure the soul hadn't done too bad on this earth, hadn't robbed or killed or . . ." She searched for the proper expression, but could not find it. "Or done nothin' to hurt nobody like Miss Berman."

Viv began to ask a question about Mrs. Berman, but Nebraska gave her a hard look over her shoulder and kept talking.

"And if it hadn't done too bad, or if it has done bad but repented, then it continues on into heaven itself—and that's where it's more beautiful than all three of us could imagine if we sat right down and talked about it for the next three weeks."

"My teacher told the class that Jesus was in heaven," said Benjamin, "but Daddy said he wasn't."

Viv sang, "Jesus loves me, this I know."

Benjamin chimed in, "For the Bible tells me so."

"Hmm. Don't let your daddy hear you singin' that, Benjie, or he be put out just as sure as I'm standin' here washin' pots and pans."

"That's what we sing in school," came Benjamin. He started to sing a speeded up version. Viv joined in. The tempo, too fast for either of them to pronounce the words, set them giggling.

"You see," Nebraska said quietly, lifting her hands out of the sink and drying them on a dish towel, "your momma and daddy is raised up in a different tradition to me and Abraham and Viv."

"What tradition is Jesus raised up in, Nebraska?" Benjamin looked at her quizzically.

"Jesus?" Nebraska leaned back against the sink, folding her hands in front of her. She cocked her head to one side and looked upward, figuring. "Well, Jesus was raised up in the Jewish tradition, too, but Jesus was also in the Baptist tradition." She intoned, "I am the First and the Last, the Alpha and the Oma."

"Are you gonna be in heaven with Mommy when you and Mommy die?" Benjamin asked.

"Well . . . well, maybe so, sugar. Course we got different bringings up, so we might be in different parts of heaven."

"Like when we go to Woolworth's and you sit in one place and Mommy and I sit in another?"

Nebraska chuckled. "No, no, Benjie. That's a different kind of different."

"There's no Woolworth's in heaven," Viv explained. "I know that 'cause Momma already told me when I asked."

"Other reasons too," Nebraska corrected.

The children looked at her with faces so puzzled that she could not break off the conversation as she would have liked in order to check the chicken and bring in the clothes from the line before Mr. and Mrs. Gold returned.

"Black people and white people just live in different customs, Benjie," she explained. "Live in different places. It wouldn't make no mind to most colored if white and colored sat together at the counter, but would make a lot of difference to most whites. They just fussier about their way of doin' things, I guess." She watched their faces to see if the explanation sufficed, but their expressions registered only minimal change. "But in Jesus' eyes, we are all the same, each and every one, colored and white alike."

"Why can't Mommy be with you in heaven then?"

"Benjie, you ask more questions than a revenuer." Nebraska softened her tone and went on. "The answer is that heaven got nothin' to do with a man's color on this earth, but got everything to do with a man's religion."

"Will there be colored people where Mommy is in heaven?"

"No, no," Nebraska answered. "At least no colored people I knows of. Leastways, no Madoc colored."

"I don't understand," Benjamin followed.

"Me neither," said Viv.

"Well, I don't understand neither," Nebraska practically shouted. "I'm just an ol' washwoman, and y'all ask me questions like I'm Reverend Ray. And even he can't figure out all this Negro and white junk, much less this Baptist, Jewish, Catholic, Presbyterian runaround." She regained her calm. "Just remember that Jesus Christ loves us all—you and Mr. and Miss Gold, too, Benjie. In the end, He'll make sure we all ends up where we needs to be. He don't hold it against no one that they been raised as a Jew, or even a 'Piscopalian."

"Why doesn't he put Woolworth's in Heaven?" Viv asked.

Nebraska stamped her foot hard and the children ran out of the room like banshees. They circled the interior of the house —from the kitchen to the hallway to the living room to the dining room and back to the kitchen—then bounded up the stairs for the attic. "Let's play heaven," Nebraska heard Benjamin call to Viv. "You close your eyes and I'll hide where you can't find me."

Nebraska shouted toward the ceiling, "Quit that! Y'all play right."

The back door flew open. Rachel entered. "Why are you yelling? Why are you yelling? Is something wrong?"

Stunned by her abrupt entrance, Nebraska said nothing.

Rachel came to the table and sank on the bench, twisting at her hands like someone under great strain. "I can't believe what those Negroes did to Mrs. Berman. I can't believe it." She pulled at her hands as if they were made of rags.

"Don't yank at your hands like that, Rachel. You gonna bruise yourself." Nebraska walked back to the sink.

Rachel stopped her short. "Don't tell me what not to do."

"Don't tell me," Nebraska returned, "to not tell you what not to do. I been tellin' you what not to do since you was as high as my knee. These is adult problems and there's no need for someone like you to hurt yourself over somethin' that's more than you can full understand at your age."

"Nebraska, I can fully understand everything—at my age. That's such a dumb remark. You can all be so dumb sometime. I just talked to Mother on the telephone and she said they caught a boy named Jimbo Smith and I've heard you talk about him. You always go on about Jesus Christ and all that other nonsense, but your kind can't even control their own . . ."

Nebraska took two quick steps toward Rachel and shot out her hand. The back of it cracked across Rachel's face and the girl dropped her head straight down, mouth frozen open, then clutched her face where she had been hit. The girl's hand slid down and she leaped up and went running from the room, crying with low, hoarse sounds.

Trembling, Nebraska walked briskly out back, unclipping the sheets and pillowcases from the clothesline, balling up the socks and bunching the shirts into the laundry bag to take inside to iron. She came back to the kitchen and an acrid smell hit her nostrils: grease! She flung open the oven and a small fire danced beneath the chicken.

"Wheeeo!" she cried, watching the flames leap higher. "Benjamin! Vivian! Rachel! Get out of this house right now. There's a fire!"

The phone rang. "Jesus God, why it ain't out of order now," she said frantically, hunting for the baking soda to toss on the flames that licked upward toward the stove top. Rachel, horrified, came and stood at the kitchen door. Her face was long and tear-stained. "I'm sorry, Nebraska. I'm . . ."

Nebraska whirled and shouted, "Get your selfish self up in that attic and get the chirren!"

By the time Rachel left and came back down with Benjamin and Viv in tow, Nebraska had found the baking soda and poured it over the flame, but another flame was now shooting up behind the stove.

She remembered the closet—the fire extinguisher in the closet. Rushing there, she pulled down the cans of dog food and boxes of cereal and meal and found the red cylinder attached to the wall. Yanking out the pin and squeezing the trigger, she shot the foam about wildly. The flames died. She continued to squeeze until her hand ached. When the foam was emptied, she squeezed still, her arm beginning to shake.

She dropped the cylinder, leaned back against the counter, then turned to the sink. She plunged her hands deep into the water that still stood from dishwashing and waited for her body to return to its full balance in this kitchen that seemed suddenly to be in the house of a stranger.

"I'm thinking about quittin' the Golds," Nebraska said one night two weeks later.

It was dusk and she had walked down to the pen where Abraham kept his dogs, finding him there with pieces of bone and scraps in a bag. He dropped these to the three dogs that leaped against the side of the chicken-wire fence, bellowing and snapping. One of the dogs, a yellow-haired, spindly animal whose eyes cast back the rising moon, leaped higher than the others. From time to time Abraham faked throwing a scrap in the direction of that dog, which made it go into a fit of leaping. He threw real scraps to the other two, who tore at the gristle until it looked, at least to Nebraska, as if their teeth would rip out.

"That damn yellow hound is half rabbit," Abraham said with a tone somewhere between frustration and respect.

"I'm thinkin' about quittin' the Golds."

"And when he's out chasing rabbit," Abraham continued, shaking his head disappointedly, "then he won't run or jump. He's half chicken then."

"Abraham! I'm studyin' on quittin' the Golds."

"I heard you."

"Why didn't you answer?"

"You got another job?" returned Abraham. When Nebraska didn't answer, he repeated the question, then leaned over to pull a tick off the brow of one dog standing with its front paws hung over a strand of wire. He worked off the tick and pinched it between his fingers. A clot of blood spread in a brown circle.

"How can I get another job if I still gots this one?" Nebraska asked.

"How you gonna get a letter from the Golds saying you was a good cook if you go on and quit? How you gonna get another job if you don' got no letter?"

"I been with the Golds near 'bout fifteen years and anybody can tell you I been everything a woman could be: cook, nurse, Aunt Jemima come breakfast if I get there early enough. Anything you could ask."

"Well, if you been everything, why quit?"

"That's what I don't know, Abraham. I just feel sometimes they don't 'preciate how I been everything. Specially the chirren. Ooh, if I could tell you 'bout that Rachel, and 'bout how ol' man Berman from the high school looked at me like I was somethin' straight from hell just 'cause I was black. And Miss Gold couldn't a cared less."

"You tol' me yourself, Gardenia, how Benjie trails after you."

"I loves that boy, Abraham, but he probably be like all the rest when he grow up. Just think of me as an ol' colored woman in the kitchen."

"Not if you raise him right."

"Not if Miss Gold raise him right. But she goes off playin' golf or this and that so much I think she ain't gonna have time to raise him like I'm doin'."

A hound arched double, coughed. Abraham reached into his sack and pulled out a half loaf of bread and threw two pieces to the dog. The dog swallowed the bread, coughed once, and settled.

"Abraham! Got that good loaf of bread and feedin' it to the dogs!"

"Hush, hush, Gardenia. You want him to suf'cate on a piece o' bone?"

"Shouldn't be giving a dog a piece of bone anyway."

"Besides," continued Abraham without responding to Nebraska's comment, "I paid for that bread wi' my own money. Earned it down at the union hall."

"Playing cards."

"I earned it. I can spend it like I want." He turned and looked at her menacingly.

"You sound more like Wenda June every day."

"Wenda June Waters don't sound so bad to me."

"What about Nebraska?" asked Nebraska. "How come Nebraska can't spend her money like she wants? How come my money go to the rent and the gas and the food and your money goes to cards or animals?"

Reaching into the bag, Abraham brought out a half loaf of bread and, turning briefly as if to make sure Nebraska was watching, emptied it into the pen. The dogs lit on the bread with stormlike ferocity, pulling chunks of it into the corners, wolfing it down.

"Why did you do that?" Nebraska tried to keep the waver out of her voice.

"Because," said Abraham, still facing the pen, "I felt like it."

Nebraska felt drops come to her eyes. "You think I was born to take care of other people? To take care of you and everybody else?" The drops became full tears. "What about me? Who takes care of me, Abraham Waters?"

He answered sullenly, "Jesus take care of you."

"Don't—don't make fun of Jesus. He'll strike you dead."

"Shut up, woman."

"Don't tell me"—she could hardly get out the words for the building tears—"don't tell me to shut up!"

"I said shut up!"

Abraham opened the door of the pen and strode into the area where the dogs were. As they bounded at his side, he reached out and kicked one in the shin and it ran yelping to a small house. The other two backed off. The yellow one slunk toward him, wagging its tail, but Abraham picked up a stick and lashed it across the shoulder. "Don't no one dispute me," he raged above the mewling of the yellow hound.

Nebraska clasped a hand over her eyes, unable to bear what she saw. She took her hand away and challenged loudly, "You're not even half a man, actin' cruel to a bunch of helpless dogs."

"Why don't you talk like that to Mr. Gold?" Abraham swaggered about the pen, waving his stick, saying, "You gotta twist up your soul in knots to say anything bad to him, but to me you go on like a wild bitch."

"That ain't true."

"'Tis true," Abraham retorted. "Just 'cause he pay you twenty dollars a week, you too afraid to speak your mind."

"I wish somebody'd give you twenty dollars a week."

"No one wants a nigger who can't read or write," said Abraham bitterly. "Niggers is the first to get laid off the construction group. And folks like me who don' got no skills but diggin' and carryin' get laid off first anyways."

"That's no excuse for riding me into the dirt, Abraham."

Nebraska's tears, stemmed by her anger, returned. She saw her husband, as if imprisoned by the faltering light, kick another dog. But then he changed his expression, bent over, and began stroking the dog's ear. The other two dogs came up to him and started to lick him on the face.

"At least somebody 'preciates me." He stared up at her.

"Leave me be," Nebraska said. She turned and headed for the house.

With feet aching, she kicked off her shoes, took them in her hand, and did something she had not done in years: run. She lumbered past the ditch and turned at the hermit's house, her feet padding with great pain over the stones and clumps of weed and grass on the path. A gnat flew into her nose. She snorted to clear it. More gnats swirled about her eyes, and waving her hand to disperse them, she almost lost her balance.

The housing project loomed dark and ghostly beyond the woods. A sheet, hanging to air from a top window like a small wing sewn to the building, rippled and flapped. The neat, regular apartments that had seemed so shiny, so full of dreams and promise ten years ago, became cramped boxes in which lives circled and fidgeted, hunted for some way to walk out a door, board a bus, travel off to a land where the world was still shiny.

Though her pace accelerated, she could not escape the howling of the dogs. The sound stayed at her back until she reached the porch of her apartment and, finding Viv there, lifted her and held her close as she sat hard in the porch rocker.

∽

"Dear Mr. and Miss Gold, I can't stay with you anny . . . any longer. I want to tan . . . to thank you for . . ."

Nebraska tore up the note and started another one. She could check her spelling with no one who usually helped her with writing—Rachel, Wenda June, Junior. Least of all could she check it with Vivian, since the note was to announce her "retirement" from the Golds' home.

She had decided to quit the Golds as the talk built, day after day, about the alleged rapist, Jimbo Smith. Setting out plates on the Golds' dinner table was close to unbearable while Vivian and Edward sat in the next room denouncing the Smith boy or talking to Izzy Berman on the telephone, saying, "Yes, it's terrible, Izzy" and continuing in whispers: "Nebraska knows the family."

Then—and she heard this from Mary, who knew Dinah Smith quite well—Jimbo jumped bail. The bail had been put up by his sister in the Air Force, and it was the second day out on that bail when Jimbo stole a car, drove across the Mississippi state line at two in the morning, and disappeared without a trace near Hattiesburg. "But he weren't guilty," Mary had assured Nebraska. "He was jes' runnin' into the woods that day on some fool chase with a buddy o' his. Dinah tol' me so, and Dinah is as good a Christian as you ever wanna meet."

When Nebraska had related this story to the Golds, they had simply looked at her coldly. Gravely, Edward spoke: "Nebraska, it's up to the courts to decide. A man is innocent until proven guilty in this country, but if he jumps bail he practically points the finger at himself."

"Maybe he was just frightened," Vivian had suggested, then turned to Nebraska and back to Edward, indicating she was caught between believing her husband and wanting to appear sympathetic to Nebraska. "Of course," she went on, "I know Mary sometimes has a habit of, shall I say, distorting the truth for her own purposes."

Was that what did it, finally made Nebraska realize that Vivian did not fully appreciate her worth as a human being? The accusation against Mary of "distorting the truth" was one accusation too many on top of the accusations against the Smith boy. It was Nebraska they were accusing. Hence, her note flowed: "Dear Mr. and Miss Gold, I cat stay . . . can't stay with you any longer. . . ."

The note was folded once and folded again, then folded yet again until it looked like a thin scoop used at the pharmacist's office to guide poison into a vial. The note was placed into the pouch in the back of her purse, where she also kept a picture of Viv and Benjamin, a lucky dollar, and, now brittle and the color of autumn, the clipping of Vivian Gold from the Madoc newspaper, two clippings of Vivian's theater work from a county newspaper, and one that read: "Vivian Gold, Long-Standing Star of Madoc Players, Retires From Stage."

She held the note for a week after writing it before daring to lay it on the table on Tuesday afternoon, only to pick it up hastily when she thought she heard Vivian turning into the driveway. When she realized it was Marsha Weinacker, the next-door neighbor, who'd driven in, she placed the note on the table again. Envisioning Vivian coming home and finding the note, she decided the message wasn't substantial enough. She picked it back up, took it home, and reworked it all evening, but then realized Benjamin would arrive home the next day before Vivian and might see it first. She held the note until Friday, but since Friday was payday, decided to wait until Monday, and then, on Saturday, began to wonder if she should quit at all.

On Sunday afternoon, during the silent prayer, she decided it was most fitting to call Vivian and tell her she would not be returning to work. She called but could only say, "I'm not feeling too good, Miss Gold, and I'll come in on Tuesday."

A few minutes after talking with Vivian the phone rang; it was Mary, and the decision was made for her. Jimbo had been killed in a bar in Memphis. That was all the news: Jimbo was dead, from a fight that broke out in a bar.

On Monday she talked to Mary eight times on the phone, three times to Dinah, and once to Romaine, who squeezed out of her what little information she had. The rest of the day she lay in bed, looking out the window, or at the shade drawn down over the window. She told no one about the note.

On Tuesday, as she walked in a daze from the bus stop toward the Golds' home, the note, jammed down in her uniform pocket, burned against her hip. The magnolia trees, the mailbox on the corner, the houses she had walked by thousands of times —all the places turned and wavered before her. She made a mental picture of the block, realizing she would never walk down it again as housekeeper of the Golds.

She caught sight of a car parked in the Golds' driveway. As she walked closer to the house, she saw the insignia—MADOC POLICE DEPARTMENT—and grew afraid. She spotted Viv playing in the front yard. "Viv?" she nervously questioned herself. "Shouldn't she be at school?"

Half expecting to see Jimbo walk from the front door followed by Junior and Mary, Nebraska saw Vivian's face appear instead and heard her shout back into the house: "Here comes Nebraska now!" When Vivian stuck her head outside the house again she called to Nebraska and beckoned with her arm.

"Oh, God, what's wrong now?" Nebraska spoke to the still air. "Is it Mr. Gold? Is it my Abraham?"

A picture came to her from years before: a silver butter knife engraved with B. That picture was followed by others over the years: a cigarette lighter, cake forks, even a silver platter. "Wenda June?" she could barely say, recalling how Wenda June had secretly returned item after item as Nebraska discovered them and had sworn ten times over she'd never steal from the Brookses again. "Is it my Wenda June?"

Scurrying along the driveway to the back door, she entered, dropped her bag, and headed for the living room, where two police officers sat. Her heart, already heavy, began to crack in two. On the couch were Mr. and Mrs. Gold and Babs. In the corner, legs tucked under her dress where she sat on a lounge chair, was Wenda June.

Viv came running in from the yard, piping, "Wenda and me was in Woolworth's and I didn't have to go to school 'cause these men brought us here. Can I stay here all day?"

"What?"

Vivian, coming to Nebraska's side, put her hand on her shoulder. "Dear, something odd has happened."

"Ma'am?"

"Wenda June . . . Wenda June was arrested, sort of, for protesting."

"What?" Nebraska asked again, suddenly feeling like she was drunk, or crazy. She headed for her daughter. "Baby, my baby!"

"We did it, Momma," Wenda June said triumphantly. "Sat right down at the white counter. Wasn't three folks in there that time of morning, but the cook called the manager and the manager called the police. And the newspaper came too! We're gonna have our pictures in the *Madoc Register* this time tomorrow! You'll have some fine shots to fill up your photo album now!"

Edward rose and strode over to Nebraska. "Nebraska," he began judiciously, "I'd like you to meet Officer Pettibone and Officer Duncan. They were gentlemanly enough to call me after the arrest. Well, it wasn't really a *formal* arrest. It was more like"—he smiled benignly—"more like an eviction."

Babs giggled.

"How do, ma'am," said Officer Pettibone, holding out his hand to Nebraska and smiling broadly from his six foot plus height. "I had heard about your daughter's problem"—he lowered his voice—"you know, her being sick and all"—"so I figured she wasn't really responsible. I just got in touch with Mr. Gold and he asked us to bring her here."

Babs broke in. "They knew about Wenda June 'cause I've known Squirrel, I mean Officer Pettibone, since high school—wh-why he was such a cutup then!—and Squirrel drops by Aunt Sosha's for a cup of coffee now and then, after I'm home, of course, and—"

"Babs, please!" Vivian said. "Not now!"

The other policeman stepped forward and nodded "How do" to Nebraska, but did not extend his hand. "We ain't even gonna file no report on your daughter, Mrs. Waters," he said, "unless, of course, the newspaper insists on running that there picture. We're askin' 'em real nice not to. Even Mr. Gold gave 'em a call and put in a few good words for Wenda. We just had to grill her a little to make sure it wasn't part of no national conspiracy or nothin'."

Wenda June burst out: "We just sat down like it was nobody's business!"

"Nobody's but the law's," snapped the second policeman.

"And one day this whole city's gonna blow up too," Wenda June said at the same enthusiastic pitch.

"Blow away?" Vivian said loudly and sweetly, standing between Wenda June and the policemen. "Why, we haven't had a hurricane since Evelyn back in '53." After offering the men a cup of coffee or tea, which they refused, she finished: "What harm, really, does it do for people to sit down wherever they like?"

"No harm, ma'am," Officer Pettibone said politely. "I don't make the law, though. I just enforce it."

"This ain't the law," Babs commented, "this is just family."

"*Mazel tov*," Vivian said.

"Amen," Nebraska responded quietly, unable to take her eyes off her daughter. Finding the note in her pocket, she secretly crumpled it up.

1963

Why do they all wear these damn sunglasses? Vivian wondered as she sat in her car and looked into the dark, convex frames of the state guardsman's. She saw only herself, frantic and perplexed, reflected back.

"I'm sorry, ma'am," the guardsman said. "The University of Alabama campus is off limits except to summer school students and authorized personnel."

Vivian glanced down the street—at the yellow barricades set up alongside the university grounds, at the state troopers and state guardsmen lined up in their round blue helmets, their sunglasses like the masks printed over the eyes of criminal suspects in the *Madoc Register*.

She thought back on her early morning call from Nebraska, the call not two hours ago that had shot through the house of her Randomville relatives, where she was visiting for a few days: "Miss Gold, Rachel called me late last night and said she's gonna march for integration today at the university. She told me she hoped I'd be proud, but I told her I was nothin' but frightened. I'd have called Mr. Gold, but you know how he is. He'd have driven up and snatched her out of school altogether, what with all the hell been goin' on up in Birmingham. And I knew if I told him I was gonna call you, he'd pitch a fit. Go on to Tuscaloosa and look after Rachel, ma'am, but don't tell Mr. Gold I asked you. And God be with y'all both up there."

Vivian started to drive away from the guardsman but had a thought: If I could only see his eyes!

Vivian spoke sweetly, coolly. "Don't I know you, sir?"

"Me?" The guardsman shook his head. "Don't think so, ma'am."

"Yes, I do," Vivian persisted, lengthening out her drawl, picking out the biggest city in Alabama and making her guess. "You've got relatives in Birmingham, don't you? Good-lookin' relatives!"

Vivian waited anxiously. Slowly the man grinned. "Yas'm," he said gently.

"But I can't see your face," Vivian lamented.

The man took off his sunglasses; his eyes were blue, like swimming pools. Suddenly he seemed no older than eighteen.

"Now I know which relative of yours you remind me of," Vivian went on, diving straight down into those blue pools, "the *handsome* one."

"Probably my uncle, Hiram Jones," the guardsman said, adding sultrily, "He *is* a right good-looker."

Vivian nodded. "Ol' Hiram. That rascal!"

"Yes, ma'am. Yes, ma'am!" the guardsman said, laughing, putting his glasses back on. He looked to both sides, then glanced over his shoulder. "Well, ma'am, I'll tell you what." He leaned over so close, Vivian thought he was going to kiss her. "This ain't allowed, but . . ." He reached into his pocket and pulled out a special pass and gave it to her.

"Oh, one thing," the guardsman said before Vivian could drive on. "What's your daughter's name?"

"Candy Simmons," Vivian answered craftily.

"Candy Simmons . . ." The man rolled the name around deliciously on his tongue. "Well, tell Candy that ol' Billy Walker's gonna look her up one day real soon."

Vivian drove on to Rachel's dormitory. The June morning was cloudless, the temperature already in the nineties. Groups of men and women wearing journalist's tags trudged through the heat; male students in light slacks and short-sleeved white shirts milled about beneath trees, wolfishly eyeing the smartly dressed big-city women who carried reporter's pads and microphones; helmeted young men chomping on gum or tobacco stood in front of buildings everywhere, sunglasses turning back and forth.

In front of Rachel's dorm, Vivian parked her car and got out. "What on earth?" she asked out loud as she looked up at the building and saw, in a fourth floor window, an enormous sign: WELCOME, VIVIAN! She hurried to the dormitory entrance. Had Nebraska called Rachel and told her she was driving up? She was puzzled as to why Rachel had not simply written WELCOME, MOTHER! but then realized WELCOME, VIVIAN! high above a campus was really more personal.

"I'm Vivian Gold, Rachel Gold's mother," Vivian said to a blue-haired woman at the front desk.

Clicking her dentures, the woman answered with annoyance, "Is that your girl who's got that damn sign up in the window?"

Vivian blushed.

"Is it?"

"Yes, I believe it is," Vivian answered. "You shouldn't be angry with her, though. That's just Rachel's way of being thoughtful and affectionate."

"Affectionate!" The woman's dentures clicked soundly. "I don't care how much of a nigger lover she is, this dorm's no place for a sign like that."

"What?"

"We asked her to take it down, but she said she'd tell the newspapers, and we all know they'd surely puff it up as big as a mile-high pie. As it is, every Yankee TV camera in the United States will probably broadcast that sign right up to Bobby Kennedy, who'll say it's proof all the students are really for her."

"For who?" Vivian asked, bewildered.

"For who?" The woman's dentures practically rattled in her mouth. "Where'd you come from lady, the moon? For that colored girl, Vivian Malone!"

❦

On the fourth floor of the dormitory Vivian talked to a long-legged girl in a bathrobe, a blue-eyed beauty in hair curlers, and a slender barefoot girl in a gym outfit—but no one knew, or seemed to care, where Rachel was. She knocked on Rachel's door five different times, surveyed the showers, and walked to the end of the hallway. Out the window she saw the auditorium where the crowd gathered. Behind her a Johnny Mathis record began playing; she thought how odd that thousands of white students in Alabama's segregated schools had come of age necking to the tones of black crooners.

"Mrs. Gold," a voice came at her shoulder.

Turning around, she saw a wispy redhead in a shirtwaist dress. "Are you looking for Rachel?"

"Yes, I am. Do you know where she is?"

The girl nodded and stepped closer, dropping her voice. "Everybody knows, but some of the girls are afraid you're a policewoman."

"A police—"

The girl held her finger to her mouth, saying "shhh," and continuing. "I know you're really Rachel's mom. You're both, you know, kind of European-looking." She paused and went on hesitantly: "Rachel's escaped."

"*Escaped!* From what?" Vivian's heart knocked.

"Escaped from the dorm." The girl answered so quietly, Vivian had to bend over to catch all she said. "They won't let us out of here until this thing's blown over." She dropped her voice even lower. "The Klan burned crosses last night."

Vivian touched the girl on the shoulder, whispered "Thank you," and hurried toward the lobby. The elevator seemingly took hours—no, *days*—to descend the floors. As the elevator chain clanked and rattled and the mechanism heaved one floor lower,

Vivian began to wish desperately for Edward to be there. "He'd know what to do now," she said to herself. "He'd know what to do!" Then she thought of Nebraska, strolling into the Golds' home about now, lingering over coffee, and praying for her and Rachel to the accompaniment of a radio gospel show. "Damn her! Why'd I let her talk me into not calling Edward!"

The blue-haired woman sat sentinel at the dorm desk. "Well?" she inquired. "Did you get her to take down that sign?"

"Change," Vivian requested, laying a dollar bill on the counter.

"Did you?"

"Change, please!"

The woman reached into a cigar box and slapped the nickels and dimes on the desk.

Vivian called Edward's office from the phone booth near the desk. The line was busy. She went to the door, squinted in the sharply angled sunlight, and went back to the phone. Busy still.

Starting to sweat profusely, she turned to the Coke machine next to the phone booth and dropped in a nickel. The coin thunked down to the return slot. She dropped it in again; it rattled down.

"You're a day late!" the dorm attendant said with grim satisfaction. "Just last night the soft drink folks came around with a deputy and removed all the bottles. Bottles can crack open people's heads, don't you know? You think they're gonna let this place turn into another Oxford?"

Not wanting to believe the woman, Vivian went nervously to the phone a third time and the call went through. "Gold's Real Estate." Babs's voice chimed through the line. "Hello? Hello? Gold's Real Estate! Wh-what's goin' on? GOLD'S REAL ESTATE!"

As Babs's voice became shrill through the wire, Vivian anticipated Edward's response: "Call the police, Vivian! There's not a damn thing I can do all the way down here in Madoc. Don't you have sense enough just to call the police?" Imagining a hundred Billy Walkers stalking her daughter, she hung up, giving Babs no word.

Seconds later she was out the door, not knowing where she was going exactly, but heading toward the spot where everyone else was headed. "This is all Nebraska's fault," she said to herself as she moved by the buildings that looked dark red and hot as ovens in the pounding sun. *If Nebraska had only called Edward last night!*

A state trooper stopped her. Vivian saw herself, nervous, birdlike, in the vast black lenses over his eyes. She fumbled with her excuse for being on campus, then, remembering the security pass, offered it sheepishly. He waved her through.

Another trooper stopped her and she flashed the card officiously. He simply nodded.

Then she saw him: his gubernatorial chest puffed out, his dimpled chin up, his black hair slicked down. Governor Wallace stood on the auditorium steps, pompous as that day at the Old Dixie. But more guards crowded around him now, and cameras and microphones pushed up at him as though he were some exotic, alien being.

About thirty yards to the right of Wallace she saw her daughter. "Rachel!" she yelled over the noise of the crowd. Rachel turned, spotted her mother, and her dark, curly head disappeared behind the shoulders of a man in a white shirt. The man stepped to one side, but Rachel had vanished completely.

Something glinted on a rooftop and Vivian looked up. "Are they carrying rifles?" she whispered. A man with a carbine slung over his shoulder walked closer to a rooftop edge, scanning the crowd with binoculars. He seemed to fix on the spot Rachel had vanished.

Vivian saw Rachel's head pop out from behind another white shirt, then disappear, pop out, then disappear again. "RACHEL!"

Vivian started for the corner of the auditorium where Rachel was, but an arm cut down in front of her. "Off limits, ma'am."

She flashed her security pass and started off again.

"Off limits," the voice above the arm said brusquely.

"But . . ."

"This is as far as that pass'll take anyone but high-level security."

"Yes, but, Mr. Walker, Barney Walker, Johnny Walker, whatever his name is, told me I could—"

The hand touched her collarbone and shoved her gently back.

"But, my daughter—"

"NO!" boomed the voice. Vivian wilted.

She became dimly aware of some activity on the auditorium steps. Governor Wallace stood behind a lectern, tucked into the shade, saying something Vivian could not quite make out because of a glitch in the public address system. Standing in the fierce sunlight in front of Wallace was a balding man, as large and bearish as a wrestler. When Wallace finished speaking, the large man started responding, speaking slowly, rocking slightly as he talked like a Jew *daven*ing before an ark. It seemed, to Vivian, much like a religious ritual: serious, formal, discreet.

Vivian glimpsed Rachel as a security guard came up behind the girl and said something. Rachel flew.

At the instant Vivian began dashing to her child, a camera locked on the side of her face, its shutter snapping, film whirring. "Please, don't," she said to the man whose face was hidden behind it. "I can't let anybody find out I've been here! Please, stop!" A young man crossed in front of Vivian, snatched the photographer's camera, and yanked out the film.

A man materialized on the rooftop next to the man with the rifle and binoculars. He clutched a walkie-talkie and pointed to where Rachel was.

Rachel broke from the crowd into an open area about thirty yards off to the left of Governor Wallace. Three security guards closed around her like football tackles. One blocked her in front while another grabbed her shoulder, paralyzing her with his massive hand. He dropped his hand, made her lift her arms, and the third guard began frisking her; he slapped his hands along her shoulders, ribs, hips, and legs.

"Leave her alone!" Vivian cried, arriving where they stood.

Ignoring Vivian, the man began frisking Rachel again, this time whacking the sides of her breasts.

"You bastard," Vivian shouted, "get your hands off her!"

The man dropped his hands and, with the other two men, disappeared back into the crowd.

"Rachel, are you all right? Honey, are you *all right?*"

"I'm okay," Rachel answered, out of breath, seeming more stunned than anything. "I'm . . ." She gulped a breath. "I'm okay." She looked up quizzically at her mother. "What are you *doing* here?"

Before Vivian could answer, another voice, loud and clear, broke over the crowd: the bearish man standing before Wallace asked the governor if he would stand aside and allow the entrance of James Hood and Vivian Malone.

Wallace's eyes flickered over the crowd and suddenly, Vivian was sure, fixed on her standing with Rachel in the open area where the guards had left them. She caught a glimmer of recognition—a twitch in one eye, as though he were marking one person more he was about to spite. Then, with a hint of religiosity, he stepped back from the lectern into the doorway of the auditorium, pushed his chin into the air, and did not say yes, no, or maybe. He simply became rigid, like part of the building itself.

"Nebraska sent you," Rachel said, with a touch of bitterness.

Vivian, watching the impassive governor, did not answer.

"Nebraska sent you, didn't she?"

"Rachel, you knew we'd both be worried sick!"

Rachel took off back to the crowd.

Vivian started to latch onto her, to say "Please, don't," but hesitated, watching, with a touch of awe, Rachel's slender body moving quickly, determinedly, toward the mass of white-shirted men.

Governor Wallace lurched away from the doorway and, flanked by guards, walked down the steps and got into a car. More guards pushed back the crowd and the car rolled slowly across the campus. People clapped and cheered.

"I'm going to look after you whether you like it or not," Vivian called at her daughter's back, then added: "Don't ever let your father know about any of this. You hear me? You HEAR ME?"

Rachel angled toward a group of young people holding signs. There were only four signs in all, two reading INTEGRATION YES; the other two, NOW OR NEVER. The small group seemed lost in the larger crowd, swallowed up by the applauding, whistling numbers, by the cameras and microphones.

Rachel stopped next to a man carrying one of the signs and Vivian came up alongside. The car eased by where they stood, and beyond the barricade of uniformed men Vivian caught the outline of Governor Wallace's head behind the windshield; he turned, he nodded.

A deep, low noise rose around her and she saw Rachel and the others in the group with their hands cupped to their mouths. "Boo . . ." their voices sounded. "Booooo . . ."

As the car rolled by, Vivian felt the low noise rising up through her own chest. She began to boo quietly, cautiously, then more loudly, then more loudly still.

1965

From the fourth rung up on the folding ladder, Nebraska regarded the dishes on the second shelf of the cabinet that needed to be moved to the top shelf in order to make room for new dishes. She had already cleared out the old dishes from the top shelf, but catching sight of a bit of cobweb way in the back, decided to clean the shelf thoroughly. Vivian and Edward had taken off to a cocktail party and dinner for the evening, and before long Sosha and Babs would come by to pick up Benjamin and to drive her home with her daughter. She glanced down at the kitchen table where Benjamin sat with Viv.

"Look, Momma." Viv faced Nebraska. She had clipped on an old pair of Rachel's Spanish earrings and was waving an aluminum-foil-covered scepter.

Nebraska shook her head disapprovingly. "I'm only letting you make up 'cause it's a play," she said.

"I'm King Ahasuerus," Benjamin pronounced, "and this is my bride, Queen Esther!" He thumped his chest and turned back and forth before the doorway into the living room, as though he were addressing an audience.

Viv put the scepter down and began to smear on lipstick.

"No lipstick!" Nebraska said sternly.

"She's *got* to wear lipstick," Benjamin said.

Nebraska turned back to cleaning the shelf. "Since you

started preparin' for your *Bar Mitzva* next year, can't nobody tell you nothin'."

"Come on, Nebraska. I have to practice the *Purim* play. Viv's just helping me."

He placed an aluminum foil crown on his own head, picked out some pages of the script, and handed one page to Viv. He also handed her a silver eye mask, which she donned, making her look, Nebraska thought, more like a clown than a queen.

"Nebraska," Benjamin said coaxingly, "could you do us a *huge* favor?"

"I'm not making you up too."

"No, no, don't worry." He paused. "Could you be Haman?"

"What?"

"Haman's the bad guy. He's the one everybody wants to play the part of."

"I ain't a guy. I'm a woman."

"But Haman can't be a woman."

Nebraska went back to cleaning the shelf.

"Okay," Benjamin conceded. "You win. You can be Miss Haman. Here's the part."

"I'm not playing any part, Bop," Nebraska answered, using the nickname she had coined for Benjamin the summer before, when he had followed Rachel around chanting bop-di-bop after his sister had played him some 1950s records that had belonged to Sarah.

"Just read it out loud. *Please.*"

Nebraska declined.

"*Please,* Momma," Viv said. "It's a lot of fun." She lifted the scepter and waved it at her mother. "Poof! You're Haman."

"Give me the paper," Nebraska said, and muttered, "Whoever heard of a job that asks for readin' on top of cleanin'!"

Benjamin stood and handed Nebraska the paper. She started to descend the ladder, but seeing as how it was tiring enough to climb it once, held her position.

Benjamin cleared his throat noisily. "I'll read the introduction. Many years ago there was a king named Ahasuerus, who reigned from India to Ethiopia. Ahasuerus was unhappy with his wife, Vashti, so he banished her and took a new wife, whose name was Esther. Esther was young, and Esther was beautiful."

Viv stood and curtsied. "At your service, my king."

"In the town where Ahasuerus lived, called Shushan," Benjamin continued, "there lived a man named Haman, an adviser much in favor with the king. Haman hated Mordecai, a Jew who was Esther's cousin and guardian, because Mordecai did not bow his head when Haman passed. To get even with Mordecai, Haman plotted to have all the Jews killed."

"You expect me to act like somebody like that!" Nebraska protested. "Here, take your ol' paper." She started to fling down the script, but was stopped by the sight of Babs peeking through the back door.

"Wh-why, what's goin' on," Babs exclaimed, entering, followed by Sosha. "Are y'all havin' Mardi Gras without us?"

"I'm practicing a *Purim* play," explained Benjamin. "I'm the king, Viv's Esther, Nebraska's gonna read the part of Haman."

"Look who came along," Sosha said.

Wenda June trailed in slowly, looking around like she was lost. "Hey, Momma."

"We figured we'd give all y'all a ride at the same time," Babs said.

Benjamin sighed heavily. "They have to help me practice first."

"Miss Brooks, I was only readin' 'cause Benjie asked. I gots work to do. You read it, ma'am." Nebraska held out her script.

"Me?" Sosha huffed. "I don't have my glasses."

"Me neither," Babs added quickly. "Besides, Vivian's done enough acting for me and Aunt Sosha combined."

Benjamin nodded to Viv. "Start."

Viv tapped her scepter on the table to get the king's attention. "O my lord and master, Haman is here to see you. I beg of you, my husband and king, heed his words with great caution."

"Cut!" Benjamin said, then nodded to Nebraska. "Okay, Haman, you're on."

Nebraska's throat constricted with stage fright. "King Ah —Ah—"

"Ahasuerus," Benjamin filled in.

"King," Nebraska continued, "there . . . there are many Jews in your king—kingdom who do not fo-follow your laws." The words came slowly from her lips. "The Jews are cre—" She knew the word clearly, but had trouble reading it aloud, laboring over syllables that looked odd and out of place.

"Creating," Benjamin said.

"Thank you."

"Haman doesn't say thank you."

"Don't get smart, Bop."

"Please, Nebraska, who's directing this play?"

Nebraska brushed off Benjamin's question. "The Jews are creating trouble and should be ex-ex-excited."

"Excited?" Benjamin leaped up from the table and spoke with great irritation. "The word is *executed!*"

"Don't talk to Momma like that," Wenda June said with a low fierceness.

"Wenda, this is a play. If Nebraska doesn't get the lines right, how can I practice my part?"

Nebraska drew a breath and plunged ahead. "Executed . . ." She stumbled to another word, but all the words began to feel liquid and unmanageable in her mouth. "I think . . ." Nebraska hesitated and looked down. Everyone was quiet, waiting for her to continue. "Walks forward."

"No!" Benjamin cried. "That's just the stage direction! That's what Haman does, not what he says!"

Nebraska blurted out the next line: "I think we should kill all the Jews!" She bit her lip. "I can't say that."

"It's just a play," Benjamin moaned.

"Don't talk to her in that tone," warned Wenda June.

"Quiet now, all of you," Sosha said.

Benjamin shook his head. "This is ridiculous. You try to have a play with people who can't read and . . ."

Before he could finish his sentence, Wenda June shouted, "I'll play Haman!" and lunged for Benjamin, grabbing him by the neck and yanking him toward the door. He shook loose, crying for Nebraska to help.

"Y'all stop that," Nebraska yelled, moving down a step, while Sosha beseeched Babs to contain Wenda June.

Wenda June spun around and spat her words out at Sosha. "I'm quitting. I can't stand this anymore. I'm sick of being treated like an animal."

"Calm down," Babs cried. "You'll go crazy again if you keep carrying on like this."

"Go to hell!" Wenda's words, directed at Babs, burned into Nebraska. She watched her daughter crack Queen Esther's scepter in two and throw it at the feet of Sosha, who stood impassively, hands on hips.

Sosha spoke briskly. "Babs! Call the police this instant and tell them Wenda June's a thief."

"A thief?" Benjamin asked.

"A thief. A *gonif*." Sosha lowered her gaze at Wenda June. "I've seen you stealing."

"She . . ." Nebraska tried to keep herself from saying the words, but could not. "She always returned what she stole! I know, 'cause I searched our house top to bottom and found what she took and made her take it back. She hasn't kept nothin', Miss Brooks. And she don't know no better."

"She does, too, know better. And whether she returned things or not is beside the point. Some things she sold to a pawn shop because Lewis Meltzer called me to ask why my favorite brooch was at his window."

Nebraska looked away in embarrassment, tears starting to run down her cheeks. "I couldn't let her lose her job."

"I don't need this job, Momma. I don't need to be a Tom."

"Call the police," repeated Sosha bitterly. "I always knew you couldn't trust *shvartzeh*."

"Speak English, you old bitch Jew. Say you can't trust niggers!"

Babs stepped forward. "Don't you talk like that to Aunt Sosha!"

Nebraska started to hurry down from the ladder to wrest Wenda June into the other room, to scold her and at the same time comfort her. Her left foot felt for a lower step of the ladder, but found only the edge of the step and slipped. As she fell, she pushed her right foot behind her to catch herself and landed hard. Her foot twisted and fire ran along her shin and up to her hip.

With her back against the floor, Nebraska watched the faces gathering quickly over her but did not see Wenda June's. Out of the corner of her eye she glimpsed her daughter running out the back door. Next to that sight, the pain in her ankle felt small.

୭〜

"If you were a horse, they'd shoot you," joked Todd two weeks later as Nebraska sat on her front porch, her broken ankle in its cast on the railing of the porch.

"My, my, it's so good to see you, honey."

She could hardly take her eyes off her son, who sat on the railing next to her foot. His lean, smiling face, bearded with a goatee, turned in the light as he surveyed the area in front of the project. "How's the radio, sugar?"

He smiled more broadly. "I've got good news, Momma. I've been promoted to full-fledged disc jockey."

To Nebraska the words were better than silver. Since Wenda June had locked herself in her room, Junior had decided to join up with the army and go to Vietnam, and the cost of the doctor's bills for her ankle was mounting sky high. Todd's announcement was the best news she'd heard since the *Purim* play accident. She patted her hands together. "Why, Todd, that's wonderful. Abraham! ABRAHAM!"

"He's down to the dog pen," Todd said, stroking his bearded chin and beaming. He assumed his announcer's voice: "This is W.H.O.P., Nordham, Pennsylvania's, whoppin' 'n' hoppin' station of soul. I'd like to play a Clarence Carter song now for my mother, Nebraska Waters of Madoc, Alabama." He held out his hands and pretended to set down a needle on a spinning disc. He started to hum the song.

Overhead a window slammed. "Sounds like Wenda." Nebraska bowed her head a brief moment, saying a silent prayer for her daughter.

"She'll be all right, Mother," Todd assured her.

Nebraska nodded. "I guess it's just God's way."

"A disc jockey! Can you imagine?" Her son drummed his hands against his knee as though beating out time.

"The army was good for you, wasn't it. Learned all 'bout radios."

"All kinds of communications—short wave, telegraph. Yas'm. The army was very good to me."

"Why in heaven's name does Junior want to go over to Vietnam?"

"Momma, you know how frustrated Junior feels here in Madoc. Ever since Jimbo was killed, Junior tells me he's been afraid a white man could accuse a black man of *anything* and get away with it." Todd shook his head. "Junior'd be at that big march comin' up in Selma if Jimbo hadn't got killed."

"Why should that stop him?"

"Because of you, Momma. He told me, 'Momma don't need nothin' else to make her sad like that.'"

Nebraska groaned quietly, thinking of Junior, who was working for a few weeks on a pogy boat somewhere in the Gulf of Mexico. "Then don't he know I don't want him to go over to Vietnam and get hisself killed!"

"It's different, Momma," Todd argued gently. "In Vietnam, it's not your color but how you shoot."

"Stop it, honey. You gonna make me sadder about Junior goin' away." She hesitated, then conceded: "I think I do understand." She went on, shifting her foot on the railing an inch or two. "Todd, is there really any difference up North?"

"Yes and no," he said, sliding down from the railing and squatting beside her.

"How do you mean?"

"It's different in that you can go anywhere and eat sitting next to anybody and vote, but . . . well, it's like when they killed President Kennedy. Things might seem different on the surface, but people still feel the same way. They still don't want to let anybody, black or white, really speak up for freedom. It's just that there are more black people down here, so you hear more about injustice in the South and see more about it on television. Truth is, I'd rather live right here in Golden Castles than Harlem any day of the week."

Nebraska's ankle healed slowly. The difficulty of walking, combined with the difficulty of living in the same house with Wenda June, drove her spirits down. In her mind she walked in the march out of Selma. There were two marches—the first one turned back by state troopers with tear gas and billy sticks, the second one a triumphant walk to the state capital—and Nebraska marched in the second. As she watched films of the march on the evening news she saw herself standing next to Martin Luther King, holding his hand, striding forward. Time and again as his face came over the television, she placed herself there, singing softly, walking defiantly. Her right ankle, swollen by the fracture, and her feet, swollen by the heat, were miraculously healed as she clutched the hand of the Montgomery preacher who had stood on the steps of the capitol at Washington, D.C., two years earlier." Other civil rights leaders walked alongside. There were white people too—one a reverend, another a rabbi. American flags waved everywhere.

The Madoc rabbi—the new one who had come down from Cincinnati to replace the drawling Texan, who had long ago given up the rabbinate to try making it with a folk-singing act in Atlanta—had publicly endorsed the march and suggested that every freedom-loving Madoc citizen, white and black, support the Movement. The public response had been vehement. When Nebraska talked to Vivian on the telephone to discuss when her ankle would be healed enough for her to return, Vivian told her, "Nebraska, the Temple has received three bomb threats, and a half-dozen families in the congregation have been threatened at their homes. Edward's so afraid every time the phone rings."

Then the furor died down. It soon seemed that the march, like the riots in Birmingham, like the speeches in Washington, were enveloped in the indolent air of the Madoc summer, and the concerns returned to how much so-and-so was earning in his new job at the docks or who was expecting relatives down from Michigan.

Nebraska's fantasies of walking next to Martin Luther King changed back to the old fantasies: of Abraham's taking up religion and helping to pay the rent, of Wenda June's recovering, of her feet no longer aching.

When Nebraska realized how her fantasies had returned to what they had always been, she figured they were better ones to have anyway. The new fantasy—the one of walking to Montgomery—really had no point. When she got right down to it, as good as the thought of marching and singing felt, as stirred-up as the hope of casting a voting ballot made her feel, she really did not know what just walking would do.

"And then, just as I was startin' to step down this ladder, Benjie, he said . . . Mary? Mary!"

Mary's breathing was so labored that Nebraska stopped her narrative in mid-sentence and walked a step closer to her friend. Mary's eyes had a faraway glimmer, as if she were thinking of something else, or simply not thinking at all. Nebraska reached out and touched her forehead, pulled out another Kleenex, and wiped off the beads of perspiration.

"Come on, sugar," she said sweetly to the elderly woman. "You'll feel better when this heat passes."

"It gets so hot every summer. I's plenty used to it by now."

The woman's words, halting and weak, reassured Nebraska. "Well, I thought you was plenty bored of hearing me talk about my troubles."

"Carry on, child."

"Anyways, he got put out because of how I had trouble saying all the words right. And when he got put out, my, you shoulda seen Wenda June. 'My mother's a lady,' she shouted, and then near 'bout broke his head. My two chirren fightin' over me. Ain't that somethin'?

"And then, well, Miss Babs started goin' this way, and Grandma Brooks was headin' that way, and . . . well, I'm so confusin' on it now. What happened was, lickety-split, the whole room started goin' like a storm, and the next thing I knowed I was tumbling. My, you wouldn't believe tumbling, I mean like you never seen. Tumbling *down*, Mary. Way, *way* down, and the ceiling just flip-flopping overhead above me. Mary? Mary! Don't close your eyes likes that, sugar. Don't you want to look at me? It'd be real nice if you'd look at me."

Nebraska took a washcloth from the foot of the bed and dipped it into a pan of tepid water she had set out for the express purpose of swabbing Mary's face and chest. But Mary's throat, which had never fully healed from the operation to remove the tumor, she did not touch. She swabbed around it, circling, feinting with the cloth so that it seemed she were cleaning the most delicate china.

The woman's eyes flew open. "Carry on, Neb—"

"You be all right, Mary. This heat is all that's got you down. So, as I was saying." She paused. "Did I ever tell you about the time I was over at Madoc Bay with all the Golds and

. . . well, this heat reminds me of it . . . was over the bay at the summer house of theirs and one by one the chirren came in the back room where I was and said, 'Nebraska, it's such a puuurty day outside. Why don't you come on in swimmin'.' Now, Mary, you know how much I hate water—not water for cookin' or bathing or drinking—but, you know, water for swimmin' in."

Mary smiled perceptibly. Nebraska, pleased that the tale was distracting the woman, took heart to continue.

"So I said, 'Me? Go in swimmin'? Why, I'd sink like the *Titanic!*', and Rachel said, 'We'll hold on to you Nebuba,' since even though she was old enough to call me Nebraska right she still held onto Nebuba, kind of like some people call me Gardenia and I call Benjie Bop.

"So I said I'd go, but only in wadin', and then only if Mr. Gold took my pitcher so I could show it to everyone and not have to go wadin' again just to prove to anybody that asked that I had really done it. Well, I'll tell you . . . Mary? Mary?"

Nebraska sat on the edge of the bed and leaned closer to her friend. "Can I get you somethin'?"

"A little root beer, please."

Nebraska trudged into the kitchen, found the soda, and poured it, all the while thinking how peculiar it was Mary always drank root beer and never Coke or ginger ale. She started back to the room. At the doorway she was struck by the sharp, hard odor of a person too old to clean herself, do for herself, even ask for herself. Mary, without a husband for more than thirty years and with one child who had died from sickle-cell anemia, seemed alone in that smell. Determined, Nebraska pushed her way into the room as if breaking through the wall of isolation slowly building around the woman.

She poured the root beer and spoke in a voice full of life and good cheer. "Yes, yes, where was I? Of course, at the bay. So, Mary, they latched onto me and said, 'Go put on a pair of shorts,' and when I said, 'Who's got shorts big enough for this big ol' thing?' they laughed and said they had bought some. But rather than be offended, or angry, I jes' figure they was joking.

So I hiked up my white uniform and made it tight by clippin' the hem with clothespins. Slipped off my shoes. Slipped off my socks. And we walked.

"Walked to the edge of the water, then started to wade. Well, Mary, I'll tell you, people was comin' from up and down the shoreline callin' 'Ol' Nebraska Waters gonna go in swimmin',' and I didn't have to worry that Mr. Gold would take my pitcher 'cause three other neighbors come running out with cameras and started snappin'. I felt like a beauty queen, Mary! Can you believe it, big ol' me felt like a Junior Miss America!

"Then—and the cameras was a-snappin'—we waded out deeper. And the sand? The sand felt good, Mary, and here and there, where weeds and things was on the bottom, it made me start at first, but then I got used to it. Just me wadin' along happy as could be, the cameras snappin', Rachel and Benjie holdin' on, Sarah and that sissy Reginald from next door walkin' alongside beatin' the water to frighten away crabs and stingarees like the one Todd caught out there how many years ago. Ooh, those stingarees are ugly! Worse than an old man who act like he smell somethin' bad." Nebraska stopped herself, afraid she may have offended Mary by this comment, but the woman, breathing peacefully now, did not flinch.

"Anyway," she continued, leaning over and pouring some more root beer in Mary's glass and waiting for the foam to settle before adding to her tale, "the water got deeper and deeper, and I thought to myself, What would it be like to be underneath the water and nothin' but darkness; what would it be like to feel like a big ol' whale—which I am anyway—swimmin' in the ocean for just a minute? After we waded out some more, I said, 'Hold onto me, chirren, 'cause I'm gonna plunge on,' and took a deep breath and went under! Mary, wasn't nothin' but pitch black, blacker than Abraham's neck, blacker than all of us put together. Couldn't see a thing. And then somethin' flicked by me like a shot of silver and I thought this is Jesus Christ, sure enough, comin' like a fish as they used to symbol him in olden times. And whop! I lifted up my head, shakin', and who was it but Benjie, that rascal, who had jumped in front of me!

"I started to chase him, wading fast now, and he scampered up the stairs at the end of the dock. I scampered, too, bugaloo, up the first stair, with Rachel and Sarah pushin' behind me, and then to the second. Mr. Gold was up above, takin' pitchers, and I felt someone else pushin' and turned around, and who was it but Miss Gold, who had dove in to hope me some. You know that story 'bout the train goin' up the hill? Well, I wasn't named from a train side for nothin'. That train was me goin' 'I think I can, I think I can,' just like Rachel used to say when she was little. We got on up to the third step and kaboom! I fell back like the *Titanic* and what they called the Himbimburg Blimp combined. They drugged me up, and I was so frightened. But I was laughing so much I couldn't a sunk if . . . Mary? Mary!"

She reached across and touched her friend's brow. Mary opened her eyes, sallow and distant. Nebraska went on in a voice quieter and more cautious. "I couldn't a sunk if . . . well, that's what it was like when I fell from that ladder in Benjie's *Purim* play, but I wasn't laughing then."

Nebraska dipped the rag again and pressed it to Mary's brow, then took the edge of a towel, dipped it in the water, and pressed it to her own brow.

"You really loves them peoples, don't you?" Mary whispered.

"The Golds is all I knows. Ever since that day when I bumped into you right out here."

"You know what the worstest feelin' in the whole world is, Nebraska?"

"To be sick, I reckon."

"No, dear heart, the worstest feelin' is to be without anybody when it comes time to die."

Nebraska swallowed hard. "How . . . how would you know such a thing, Mary?"

" 'Cause . . ." The woman smiled wanly, the skin around her lips seeming to crinkle. " 'Cause I jes' know is all."

"Well," Nebraska responded, emboldening her speech in order to pick up Mary's spirits, "I guess I won't be that way. I'll have Wenda June fussin' over somethin' in one corner, Abraham makin' over his dogs in another, and . . ."

Mary raised her hand to silence Nebraska. "It don't matter, dear. What counts is y'all stay together. When heaven comes we all will be happy. But here in this life it's those who gots somebody to hold on to."

"You gots me, Mary." Nebraska, voice choked, moved closer and took her friend's hands in her own, rubbing them hard as if trying to rub up life.

"I knows I do," whispered the woman, her fingers straightening and trembling so that they seemed to Nebraska to have a vitality of their own before curling back up. The pink splotches on Mary's face appeared to grow larger, as if another face were moving there.

"Have some more root beer."

Mary waved it off.

"Come closer," Mary said. Nebraska bent so close that the odor of the woman nearly drove her back. A thin hand rose and came behind her neck and pulled her closer still. "I loves you, Nebraska. God be with you. And God be with everyone you loves. Now let me be, 'cause Jesus is gathering me up in His arms this very minute."

As she took Mary's hand off her neck and folded it across the chest that became still as stone, she felt the soul rising from her friend's body into the gathering arms.

1967

Vivian stood on the porch of Margery Berman's house. Before ringing the doorbell, she hesitated a long moment. She looked around and saw the cracked paint on the front wall of the house, a lantern next to the front walk askew, and leaves spilling over the drainage gutters. It all had the look of abandonment.

Izzy had left Margery ten months before, in August, just before the start of the new school term. He had run off with a young woman from Demopolis, Alabama, who had started teaching in the social studies department. Missy Thomas, a former Junior Miss America contestant, had literally "stole Margery blind," as Nebraska put it. Izzy had disappeared for three days before calling Edward from Florida, remorseful that he had taken off with Missy, but saying he was unable to give her up.

After Izzy had returned with Missy in September and resumed his position as principal, the social repercussions started: the Jewish community's outrage at Izzy's abandonment of his wife in the aftermath of her rape; the public school parents' outrage that a principal of Lafayette could debase himself while acting as a model for young students. It was Margery's suggestion, though, that for more than ten years things had not been good between her and Izzy that ran like a tornado through the channels of gossip and more or less "took Izzy off the hook," according to Edna Solomon, who sat at the crossroads of all gossip, monumental or otherwise, in Madoc. Edna had told Vivian and Edward, "It seems that if Margery had not been abused by those colored boys, she and Izzy would have split up that very year! It's best we keep it hushed as much as we can now, or people will be saying it was what you'd expect from a member of the tribe."

Then, somehow, by the time the gossip about Margery and Izzy found its way home, Margery was under the impression Vivian had set going "the hideous rumors." When Vivian had objected, saying she had been horrified by Izzy's actions, Margery had responded snidely: "Since you've often been Izzy's leading lady, I'm sure you feel, oh, *so* upset." Edward had stepped in, telling Margery that Izzy had called *him* from Florida, not Vivian. Even Nebraska and Romaine had gotten involved, relaying phony messages to each other's employers: "Miss Gold feels real bad about what happened" or "Miss Margery says why don't you give her a call."

Screwing up her courage now, Vivian rang the doorbell and waited nervously. She rang again, heard a peephole cover open, then a lock being turned.

The door opened to reveal Romaine in the dark foyer, blinking like a mole at the bright sunshine. "Miss Gold, Miss Gold! It's good to see you!"

"Good to see you, Romaine."

"Miss Margery's asleep, I believe, but I can wake her."

Vivian saw her way out. "Well, I don't want to disturb her nap," and began to back up toward the walk. "Please tell her I dropped by and . . ."

"No'm, she ain't nappin'. She's *sleepin'*!"

"You mean she hasn't gotten up at all yet? Why, it's already three."

Romaine shrugged. "You know how it's been since . . . Well, all of us understands. Now, you take this friend of mine Isabel. Isabel was married to a man who met this little tart who called herself Maybelline, and it wasn't three weeks later but Isabel's husband had disappeared with this man-trap over in New Orleans." Romaine paused.

"Romaine! ROMAINE!" Margery's voice sailed from down the hall. "Who are you gabbing to?"

"Miss Vivian Gold's come to cheer us all up some, ma'am." Romaine waved Vivian in and showed her to Izzy's leather reading chair in the den. "She's up now, ma'am. I'm sure she'll be glad to see you." Romaine winked with her one good eye, then hurried off into the house.

৩৴

"Well, well!" Margery stood at the entrance to the den. Her robe hung open around her nightgown and her hair was pulled back, but wisps of it stuck out like broomstraws. She walked through the den, drew the curtains open in front of the glass doors, and pushed open the doors. "Bloody mary?" she asked, stepping into the backyard.

Like a genie, Romaine appeared with a tray of tomato juice, vodka, Tabasco, glasses, and swizzle sticks.

"Or do you want a Virgin Mary?" Margery asked. "You sort of think of yourself like that, don't you?"

Vivian's instinct was to leave, but she stood and walked into the backyard and took a seat at the lawn table.

"So, how's Broadway," Margery started, pouring herself a double shot of vodka and splashing some tomato juice over it. "Your career goes so *fast*, I can never keep up with it!" She swallowed the drink slowly, eyeing Vivian over the rim of the glass, then turned away to look at Romaine, who was fighting a knot in the garden hose. The knot resolved itself and the hose skeeted water toward the table.

"Sorry, Miss Gold and Miss Margery." Romaine grinned and aimed the nozzle at the monkey grass near the fence.

"That fence looks worse than me," Margery said. "You'd think Izzy could have had the courtesy to paint it before running off like he did."

"Are you going to sell bulbs for the council this spring?" Vivian hoped her question would distract Margery from the subject of Izzy. "Are you?"

"Hell no." Margery laughed. "I don't have time for charitable causes anymore. Nobody's around to take care of *me*. Except Romaine, of course, that ol' fool."

"But we could sell them together. It would be fun. The council has always . . ."

"Missy Thomas—you know Missy Thomas, don't you— Missy Thomas never gave two hoots for a charitable cause. They stood her up there like a mannikin during the Junior Miss America Pageant and she twirled a baton and sang 'Stars Fell on Alabama.' When she didn't win the damn crown she wept buckets for three days. Charitable cause! You think my husband was a charitable cause?"

Vivian leaned forward and placed her hand on Margery's wrist. "Don't make it so hard on yourself, Margery."

"I don't make it hard on myself. I don't need to. Other people do it for me." Margery wrested her arm away and reached for the vodka. "By the way, I hear your son's going to Madoc Military Academy this fall."

"Yes. Where'd you hear it?"

"Where do you think? Edna Solomon. You know . . ." Margery sloshed some vodka into her glass. "It's funny, what with you and Edward being such big liberals and all, how Benjamin's going to an all-white private academy just as soon as integration's hitting the public schools."

"We'd be happy for Benjamin to go to Lafayette, but he doesn't want to go there. He'd rather go to a private school, and Madoc Military's the only one around. Of course, he'll just be there as a day student. Benjamin says he's tired of the classes in his public school being chewed up with discipline problems. He's also tired of all the kids going crazy with talk of next year's fraternity and sorority bids when the damn clubs don't even invite the few Jewish students to be in them."

Margery lit a cigarette. "Benjamin certainly doesn't mind

going to the Old Dixie Country Club!" She dragged on the cigarette and puffed the smoke toward Vivian. "Of course, I don't blame anybody for not wanting to attend Lafayette High. I can't even see why the colored want to go there. It's nothin' but a broken down ol' hole. And the teachers have been there so long they've got cobwebs in their hair."

The garden hose caught in a knot again and Romaine bent over and twisted it like she was trying to kill a snake.

"Very good," Margery called, applauding.

Romaine laughed and continued battling the hose.

"More vodka?" Margery asked, motioning to Vivian, then answering the question herself by saying "thank you" and refilling her own glass.

"Margery . . ." Vivian heard the shakiness in her voice as she started to make her confession. "Margery, dear, Izzy's asked me to be . . . to be a special drama director at Lafayette High. . . . I've discussed it with Edward, and thought and thought . . ."

"And said yes?" Margery concluded.

Vivian nodded, quietly saying "Yes."

Margery shaded her eyes with one hand and snapped, "Romaine, can't you even squirt a hose!"

Romaine turned and smirked.

"It's a good chance for me," Vivian went on gently. "It may be my last chance to really do something in the theater."

"You've *never* had a chance, Vivian!" Margery stood and walked toward the monkey grass, speaking with her back to Vivian. "A little talent is required, don't you realize?"

"You used to think I had a lot of talent," Vivian responded with sudden meekness.

"I used to think a lot of things." Margery bent over and plucked out some weeds and muttered something to Romaine.

"Margery, please don't make me feel awful about this."

Margery continued to pull weeds.

"This doesn't mean I think what Izzy did was right," Vivian went on. "Don't you believe me?"

Margery tossed the weeds toward a trash bin and started to pull more.

"Well," Vivian said, determined to keep her composure, "you know, Viv's starting at Lafayette next fall too. *Oklahoma!* is the first play I'm scheduling, and I'm hoping she'll try out."

Margery looked up. "Do they get that much sun out West?"

Romaine glanced up from her watering then looked back down.

"Are you going to cast Izzy in one of your plays too? Maybe he could play the oldest, most broken down Romeo of all time! Maybe Missy Thomas could play Juliet. Maybe you could!"

"Margery, that's not fair at all!"

"Romaine," Margery snapped, "I think those shrubs near the patio desperately need water."

Romaine dutifully wheeled about and walked several steps forward, but hesitated with the hose.

"Romaine!"

Romaine lifted the hose and sent the stream toward the shrubs, which were only a couple of feet from where Vivian stood. When splashing water began to prickle her legs, Vivian said good-bye.

The black students clung together in the vast white campus. These students were from the "freedom of choice" zones, neighborhoods bordering two school districts that allowed residents to attend either a black school like Dexter High or a white school like Lafayette. According to what one white politician termed "Madoc's ideal zoning," though, only a handful of black neighborhoods qualified as "freedom of choice." A modest percentage of students from these neighborhoods chose to go to white high schools (frequently at the insistence of their parents). No white neighborhoods were designated "freedom of choice"—the white students had no option but to attend white schools. When a federal judge in Montgomery complained that Madoc's desegregation plan was "a pitiful sham," a local school board member stated on the Madoc news that "Washington and all its local hit men should shut up, give us our tax dollars, and take the mudslinging up north where it's really needed."

Lafayette High, the largest school, white or black, in Madoc, was a seemingly endless formation of yellowish stucco buildings in the Mexican adobe style that had been the rage in Madoc in the 1920s. The school, as many a student of American History 101 cracked, "looked like Alabama's commemoration of the Alamo."

Vivian was distressed by the way the first influx of black students bunched up and gossiped among themselves and drove off in their cars together. Heartsick, she remembered scattered images of Tuscaloosa, the ones she had never related to Edward: the men with rifles walking rooftops, the governor's twitching eye, the security guard pounding Rachel's body.

"After all these years of turmoil, it's not right for colored and white to attend the same school and *still* not mix," she told Edward. He advised her not to make a fuss or she'd find herself without a directing job. When she did start to make a fuss, exclaiming to a gym coach that "it's a shame the colored students feel they have to stick together," the man shrugged, spat out a wad of tobacco, and remarked: "Who else you 'speck to hang out with a bunch o' coons?"

Comments like that didn't hurt her nearly as much, though, as the way Viv Waters—her namesake, her godchild, her only family at Lafayette—went by her as if she did not exist. Daily, on the sound of the last bell, the black students came out in small pockets; in one of those pockets Viv was tucked away, her face turned to the side when passing the theater building. "Hey, Viv!" Vivian had called out the first three times she had spotted her. Ostensibly engaged in a conversation, Viv walked on as if she hadn't noticed.

During Vivian's fourth week at Lafayette, when tryouts for the play were rolling, she walked out from the theater when the bell rang and waited for Viv's group to pass by. The entire group hesitated at the flagpole near the theater building. In what Vivian was convinced was a subterfuge, the group then splintered into smaller groups and Viv, obscured in one of them, disappeared.

The next day Vivian followed the girl closely, going with her as far as the street. Viv broke away from the group and headed to a beat-up old Chevrolet by the curb. Upon getting closer, Vivian recognized Junior sitting inside, his face cocked against the window, nodding as if to a radio. She walked up to the car soon after Viv got in. "Hello, Junior. How you feeling, honey?"

As she asked the question she remembered the day a year earlier when Junior had returned home from Vietnam, his left leg shot off below the knee. The evening news had shown him walking across the lobby of the Madoc airport, limping awkwardly on his new artificial leg and pointing to a giant medal pinned to his shirt. Since then he had replaced the leg twice, both times developing a rash from the ill-fitting prosthetic device.

Junior, large and sad as a buffalo, looked up and smiled. "Hello, Mrs. Gold." He opened the door and climbed out; he was not wearing his leg. "It's a pretty day, ma'am. My momma said you was teaching here part-time. That's nice."

"Hi, Viv." Vivian bent over and waved at Viv in the front seat.

Viv waved back without turning to face her.

"You know," said Junior, "Viv can't wait to get her learner's permit for driving. Yes, ma'am. Even now I let her drive some around the stadium parking lot. I can't wait till she gets that permit."

"Is it—it a problem for you with—I mean . . ."

"My leg? Oh, no, ma'am. My leg don't matter. If it was a gear shift, then it'd be hard." Junior chuckled. "But this automatic transmission, well, heck, I could probably drive it if I'd lost both of my legs and a couple o' fingers too!" He leaned back against the hood and laughed softly. "The reason I can't wait till

Viv gets her learner's permit is she wants to drive so bad now that she's driving me nuts!"

"Junior?" Viv's voice from inside the car was insistent. "Junior, it's gettin' late."

Vivian started to bend over to speak to Viv again, but found herself suddenly staring at the tip of Junior's amputated leg, which peeked out from under the end of his cut-off pants leg. The stump, pink and folded into itself like a clenched fist, drew back in as Junior shifted position where he leaned. "We got a new leg ordered," he said, more it seemed to keep the chatter going than to allay Vivian's shock.

"Junior!" Viv scooted over to the driver's side and looked up at Vivian. "Sorry, Mrs. Gold, but we gotta run an errand for my mother." She scooted back to the other side of the front seat.

Junior lowered his head and twisted toward the still-open door, saying something under his breath to Viv.

"We gotta go, Mrs. Gold," he said, smiling apologetically.

"I really wanted to talk to Viv."

"Yes, well . . ." He hesitated. "Momma wants us to pick up some paint out at the shopping center so she can fix up the bathroom tonight."

"Aw, you're gonna make your momma paint after working so hard all day?" As Vivian spoke, the word *momma* sounded strange in her ears, as if she were talking about someone other than Nebraska.

"Well, I hold the ladder so she don't fall."

"Junior, come *on!*" Viv whined.

Junior continued. "The preacher once said Momma had a case of the falling sickness—falling off ladders, falling down the open heater like she did that time at your house—so we watch out for her good."

The horn beeped.

"I guess Viv's anxious to get movin' so we'll have time to let her practice-drive." Nodding good-day, Junior climbed slowly back into the car and cranked it up. He smiled sweetly through the windshield, but then the sadness seemed to cross his face again. The car roared away.

◦～◦

The following afternoon, before leaving for play practice at Lafayette, Vivian sat with Nebraska in the kitchen. They had been talking about Wenda June's new apartment: a one-bedroom residence in a new apartment complex near the state docks called Misty Hill, even though, as Junior had pointed out, there were no hills around for twenty miles. When Wenda had quit Sosha's after the *Purim* play fight, she had found work cleaning up in a Greek bakery. Six months later, announcing that "Madoc seems as good as any place to live if you have some money" and that she had saved "plenty of money" (she had contributed only a pittance to the upkeep of the Waters clan), she plunked down her first deposit at Misty Hill.

As Vivian helped to peel onions, wondering if Wenda June really did think Madoc was "as good as any place," a thought occurred to her. "How did the painting go last night?" she asked.

"Paintin'?" Nebraska slid the knife blade along the top of the onion, slicing it just about all the way through before turning it to the side to do the same.

"When I saw Junior yesterday he told me he was going to get some paint for you to fix up your bathroom."

"Told you what?" Nebraska looked up.

"That's what he said."

"I don't know nothin' 'bout no paintin'."

"Well." Vivian shrugged. "That's what he told me all right."

Nebraska sniffed, reached up and rubbed her right eye with the back of her wrist, and coughed. "I don't know what's gettin' into my chirren. Viv hardly speaks to me. Junior has become her idol. I mean idol! The two of them just go around like nobody's business. Even Wenda June feels jealous sometime."

"Fourteen's a funny age, Nebraska. Look at Benjamin. He

plays like he belongs to another family sometimes. Adolescence is always like that."

Nebraska wiped her left eye this time, then continued cutting and dicing. "Things is changin' odd these days, Miss Gold. It wasn't like this when Todd and Sarah was comin' along. It was just startin' with Junior and"—she paused, glanced up, then glanced back down—"and Rachel." She shook her head. "This Vietnam mess and this civil rights mess got everybody confusin'."

Vivian searched Nebraska's face. "They're just teen-agers. I think they're a little young to be worrying about politics."

"You right, ma'am. They ain't studyin' on no politics. It's something else, some kind o' funny change goin' about."

"Nebraska." Vivian reached out and stilled the woman's chopping. Bringing a Kleenex to her eyes, Nebraska dried a tear and coughed. Vivian's eyes began to water too. "Nebraska. Answer me honestly. Is Viv . . ." She did not know how to phrase the question, so backed into it: "Does Viv not have the fullest respect for what you do?"

"Miss Gold," Nebraska immediately answered, her eyes tearing from what Vivian hoped was only the onion, "if you want to know the truth, Viv don't want nobody to know her momma works in some white lady's house."

The next day Vivian arrived early at Lafayette and asked a favor of Izzy Berman. Izzy complied, sending a note to Viv's teacher indicating Viv should see Mrs. Gold at once in the theater. Viv arrived at the theater running, coming to a halt in the doorway, asking, wide-eyed with fear, "Has something happened to Momma?" Vivian, sitting on the stage, beckoned her in, answering, "No. No, nobody's sick or hurt. I'm sorry if I frightened you. I just wanted . . . wanted to talk."

Viv's face dropped. She looked around as though to leave, but seemed resigned to the visit. She walked in angrily, her shoes clacking loudly in the empty auditorium. As she got closer to the stage, Vivian watched her face moving in and out of the pools of light that came from the upper windows.

"Up this way, dear."

"What are those funny lights?" Viv asked, stalling, and pointed to a set of red, green, yellow, and white spots that half rose from the floor.

"Those are stagelights. They can be controlled from up there." She pointed to a box above the back of the auditorium.

"Don't people trip on them?"

Vivian stood. She walked toward Viv, holding out her hand when she arrived at the top of the ladder. "No, the actors learn quickly that they've got to watch out for them. Besides, no one should come this close to the edge of the stage during a play." Unable to coax Viv up, Vivian walked down the ladder and found an auditorium seat within the edge of a pool of light. As she sat, the chair creaked and wheezed.

"If a chair sounds like that, this must be an old place," Viv remarked.

"Well, I wouldn't know exactly how old," Vivian said. "This is only my first month here. But I do remember—if you won't tell anybody—that the building was being put up when I was a student at Lafayette."

"When *you* were here?"

"I'm not *that* old," said Vivian, laughing softly. "Thirty's not too old for a woman. Is it?"

Viv bunched her features. "You and Momma are just alike. Always lyin' about age."

"Do you really think your momma and I are just alike?"

"No," the girl said quickly. "Look, Mrs. Gold, I've really got to go. Miss Phillips will murder me."

"It's all right to be here. Principal Berman cleared it."

From where she still stood at the foot of the ladder, Viv looked about as if trapped, then walked up the aisle toward Vivian and sat in another creaking, wheezing chair within the same pool. She shaded her eyes with her hand. "What do you want from me?"

"I want," Vivian said, "to know why you've been treating me like I don't exist. Like I'm invisible."

Looking down at the edge of the seat, Viv started to toy with her shoestrings.

"Why?" Vivian persisted.

"I don't know what you're talking about."

"Are you unhappy at being at Lafayette instead of Dexter High?"

"No."

"Viv, dear, I've known you for a long time. I watched you grow up in my house many afternoons like one of my own. Now you treat me like a stranger. Or like a criminal."

"I know who you are."

"Well, why do you act like you don't?"

Viv crossed her legs and began fiddling with the hem of her dress.

"How's school coming?" Vivian asked, thinking how fragile her voice sounded in the empty auditorium.

"Fine."

"How're the new people you've met?"

"Fine."

"How's science class?"

The girl looked up, face brightening momentarily. "I like science a lot. We're studying electromagnetism now. I think Lafayette's got better science than Dexter."

"You know, Viv, I've always wanted the best for you." Vivian heard her own voice getting thicker in her throat. "Your mother is very, *very* special to us, and we've always tried to do whatever we could to help her out. It makes me so happy when I see her children doing well. It makes me feel . . . feel proud."

"Yas'm. Is that all?"

Vivian threw up her hands and slapped them down on the arms of the chair. "Is that all? Yes, I guess so."

Viv did not move.

"Viv, don't make me feel like I'm mean because your mother works for me. And don't feel your mother's not as fine as anybody on the face of this earth because she cooks and cleans. It's a good job. It's not a strain. And it's a whole lot better than working in some big office building where people hardly say hello, much less know what your name is."

"Yas'm."

"Don't 'yas'm' me. Tell me what you're thinking, Viv. Speak up like your mother would."

Uneasily the girl shifted in her seat, crossed her leg the other way, and then, as though having used up the possibilities of sitting positions, stood and leaned against another row of seats. Looking straight down at the floor she spoke: "Ricky and Lorraine told me my momma's a Tom."

"What?"

"Yes."

"But . . . but what do you mean?"

"Ricky and Lorraine told me if my momma works for a white family then she's a Tom."

"You mean an Uncle Tom."

"Yes."

"Who are Ricky and Lorraine?"

Viv glanced up, looked back down. "Friends. They came from Dexter too. Lorraine's daddy sells insurance. Ricky's does construction, like mine."

"And their mothers?"

"One worked for Mrs. Grenoble, but she quit. The other says she'd starve before she'd work for anybody."

"The one whose husband sells insurance."

"Yes, I think so."

"Well," Vivian responded patiently, drawing a deep breath and letting it out to steady her comments, "first of all I'm not Mrs. Grenoble. Take my word for it. And second of all, the fact is, Viv, your father is not an insurance salesman. Your family can use a second income."

"Yes. Is that all?"

"Fine." Vivian stifled a sudden urge to cry. "Fine. Have it your way. Just remember, your mother, honestly and truly, is like one of us. We consider you all like part of the family. You can make it hard on me, Viv, but please don't make it hard on Nebraska."

"Yas'm." The girl eased from the row of seats. "Can I go now?"

"Yes. Yes, you can go."

∽

A week later two of the girls in the chorus of *Oklahoma!* dropped out when they were elected cheerleader alternates. Vivian had Izzy make an announcement over the loudspeaker that auditions would be held to fill the two empty parts. She could not have been more startled when Viv walked into the auditorium after the final bell, signed her name on a sheet of paper for tryouts, and went to take a seat with the other girls who had come to audition. "Hello, Viv," Vivian said pertly. Silently, Viv nodded back.

As soon as Viv sat, the girl sitting to the right of her stood abruptly and made her way out. Sandy Grenoble, Maxine Grenoble's daughter, who had a large role in the play and had volunteered to help with auditions, looked at Vivian anxiously. "Anybody who wants to leave can now do so," Vivian said firmly. A girl to the left of Viv stood, said "Excuse me," and pushed her way from the row to the aisle. A consideration struck Vivian: were they leaving because Viv was there?

"Mrs. Gold," Sandy Grenoble said, "can I talk with you a minute?" Vivian waved her away.

"Anybody else?" Vivian's heart sank as three more girls stood and started to walk off.

More students showed up at the door of the auditorium—a black cluster who took seats in the far left corner, and a white cluster who took seats in the opposite corner. The white cluster, mostly boys, lit up cigarettes. "No smoking in here," Vivian snapped. Three cigarettes, ground out quickly, were flipped in the general direction of where she stood.

"Thank you." She smiled graciously, hoping to mask her uneasiness.

Someone in the white group whistled shrilly, then clapped.

"This is not a ball game." Vivian spoke forcefully. "If you're not here to audition but want to watch, feel free to do so. But do not, I repeat, do *not* disturb those who are here to try out."

The boy whom Vivian suspected of whistling now stood, snapped to attention, and saluted. "Yes, Mrs. Gold," he barked. When he sat back down the group giggled wildly, then stilled.

"I mean it. If you can't be quiet, I'll close the auditions to visitors, which I hate to do because I believe you can learn something just by watching."

For a moment she could have heard paper clips drop. Thinking she had gained control, she continued with the audition. Another girl rose and began to leave. "Young lady, where are you going?"

The girl sidled off, speechless, then hesitated.

"I'm sorry. It's too late to leave. It's not fair to the others." As Vivian spoke she could not help but glance at Viv, who was balled up in her seat like a wounded child. "We'll start," she added vigorously. "As a matter of fact"—she nodded in the direction of the girl who had sidled off but stopped—"as a matter of fact, you can begin."

The piano player, round and bespectacled, rummaged through the sheet music on top of the piano and turned up selections from *Guys and Dolls, Oklahoma!*, and *Flower Drum Song*. "Which one you want her to do?" the piano player asked.

"Are you familiar with *Oklahoma!*?"

"No, ma'am," answered the girl, now at the stage.

"*Flower Drum Song?*"

"Yes, ma'am."

"Try that one, Joey. Give her the music to, oh, how 'bout 'I Enjoy Being a Girl!'" Vivian took a few steps toward the stage. She read the name on the sheet. "Lori, the chorus part is simple, but requires a bit of voice and a bit of dancing. I'll just have you run through this once, then do some steps, and that'll be fine for the moment."

The piano player started. Lori, holding the sheet music, began to sing:

When I have a brand new hairdo

A spluttering noise erupted from the corner where the white students sat. Glancing around, Vivian saw the same boy who whistled (it must have been him) making a liquid sound into his hands. "Sorry," he said with mock sheepishness. "I couldn't hold it."

"Keep going, Lori, you're doing fine," Vivian encouraged.

With my eyelashes all in curl,
I float as the clouds on air do,
I enjoy being a girl!

"Next," Vivian said after Lori was finished. When she turned around she saw three more girls had left. Only Viv and three other girls remained. Sandy Grenoble tugged on her sleeve and whispered, "Mrs. Gold, you know who's here? Mindy. She's the daughter of Hattie, a woman who used to work for us. Hattie quit last year. Mindy's a convict, Mrs. Gold. She once told me she robbed a thousand dollars from the bank."

"I think she was probably kidding."

"No, ma'am. Mother told me that's why Hattie could afford to quit."

"Well, we'll let the police tend to it, then. Why don't we continue with the auditions."

"Y'all talkin' about me?" A lean girl in a red blazer stood from the group of black students. "Y'all say something about me?"

"I beg your pardon," Vivian answered.

"I'm Mindy. I heard my name."

"Hi, Mindy," Sandy called out. "I just said I was hoping you'd try out."

"Bull," came back the girl.

Vivian saw a familiar figure in the doorway. An arm summoned her. She hurried out and found Izzy standing there, flushed, rubbing his hands. "Vivian . . ." He rubbed his hands faster. "What in hell's going on here?"

"What do you mean?"

"I've gotten calls from the mothers of three girls who say they came to the audition but that you'd already picked who you want."

Vivian stepped back in puzzlement. "I don't understand."

"They say . . . well . . . Oh, this integration thing's not easy, you know. We have to go very, *very* delicately. Why on earth would you have your cook's daughter—of *all* people—come to tryouts."

"What difference does it make? It surely doesn't mean she's got the part automatically."

"Vivian—Viv—look, dear. I'm sorry this whole thing's turned into a big *megillah*, but . . ."

"What whole thing? What *megillah*?"

"This integration thing." Izzy paused, lowering his voice. "Look, I just made up the complaint. The mothers of the girls called to tell me they weren't going to let their daughters on the same stage with any quote nigger s.o.b. unquote. You understand the position I'm in."

"You mean with Missy Thomas, don't you?" Vivian snapped. "You mean because you ran off and left one of my best friends for some tart that you can't afford bad publicity? Isn't that it?"

"Women! Jesus! Women are all the same! Can't you understand politics? POLITICS!"

"Can't you understand *people*? Believe me, Izzy, it's far more important to this fourteen-year-old girl that she be able to get up on that stage and audition for a part like anybody else than it is for the mothers of those girls to fear their daughters'll contract a disease from somebody's complexion."

"I knew it was a mistake to take you on."

"Take that back, Izzy. Take it back!"

"I take it back," he said quickly, rubbing his hands together furiously, shaking his head. "I knew I should have retired when I saw this colored stuff heading like a tornado for Lafayette. And it's going to get even worse!"

"I have no more time to talk." Vivian turned to go. "I have an audition to finish."

When she entered the auditorium she found the white students strung down one side of the seats and the black down the other. The two groups paced back and forth like opposing combat lines waiting for the signal to start war. "Children." Vivian clapped her hands sharply. "Principal Berman is going to sit in." The students scrambled to their seats and fell quiet. Izzy came reluctantly in and settled into a back row.

"Viv Waters," Vivian called. "Your turn to audition." The girl sat fast in her seat. "Viv!"

In a fluster, Viv stood and hurried to the stage. The piano player handed her the part and started the introduction to "I Enjoy Being a Girl." The song began. Viv failed to sing.

"Just relax, Viv." Vivian came closer to the stage and spoke soothingly. "I know you sing in the choir at church. It's really no different."

"Listen to Mrs. Gold," one of the black students called from the back.

"Hush," Vivian said, then nodded her head to the pianist. "Start the music again, please."

Viv's voice rose, wavering but melodic.

> When I have a brand new hairdo
> With my . . .

A voice from the white students' corner cut across the singing. "Mrs. Gold, there's flies in here."

"Quiet," Izzy said, rising. "The next one to talk gets detention duty."

"But, Principal Berman, sir." Vivian asked the piano player and Viv to halt and looked around to see the whistler, tall and with peach-colored hair, standing up and addressing the principal with mock formality. "I can't watch it with so many flies, sir. I think they're coming around because they smell"—he hesitated, almost backing off from the stunt—"because they smell Neeegro puuussy."

As the whistler came down on the last syllable, a black boy, large and fierce, leaped from his seat and seemed to tightrope the backs of the chair leading to the white group. His arm shot out, fist catching the whistler on the shoulder while another white student, a girl, leaped up and brought out an object from her purse.

Turning, Vivian saw Viv, crying and shaking her head; she turned back, starting toward the melee, and saw the object from the white girl's purse flicker in a stream of sunlight: *knife*. The word, like the object, flashed through her mind and turned to a flame as she hurried to the group of eight, now ten, students, black and white, grappling and tumbling over the auditorium seats.

Vivian heard a shriek and saw the whistler clutching his arm; blood soaked his sleeve. "Everybody stop!" she yelled, working her way frantically into the shouting, grappling bodies. "EVERYBODY STOP!"

A fist smacked her on the jaw and she reeled back, grabbing onto the arm of a chair. The auditorium rocked around her.

Looking up, she saw Izzy at the door, his chest heaving, the gym coach standing next to him, and a gang of football players bursting from the door behind them. The players charged down the aisles, whooping, yawping, seizing students, throwing headlocks and full nelsons on the biggest ones. One fat white boy resisted and a football player clamped him hard around the chest. A black girl, running to a back exit, was stopped by a player who latched onto her wrists.

On rubber legs Vivian walked out of the auditorium and leaned against a cast-iron lamp pole at the side of the steps. The sun caught her squarely on the forehead like a hot bar of metal.

She closed her eyes tightly, then opened them to see the first students being shoved outside.

She waited until she made it to the parking lot, and threw up behind the back of her car.

❦

It took all evening for Vivian to persuade Edward she should return to Lafayette High. Izzy called twice to make sure she was all right, and Nebraska called, too, confused by reports of what had actually gone on. After each call Edward became more adamant, saying "It's not safe," and finally, "Enough talk, Vivian, you're *not* going back." Despite Edward's objections Vivian turned to him and firmly said, "This job, more than anything else in the world right now, is important to me."

When she showed up at the auditorium the next day, it was locked. She jiggled the door hard, then pounded. "Hello," she called, "is somebody in there? *I think you've locked me out by mistake!*"

"It's no mistake," came a voice, and she turned to see Izzy, standing at the bottom of the steps, hands in pockets, looking a little to one side. "Vivian . . ."

"Vivian what?" she asked.

"It's just not going to work out."

"The play?"

"The play'll work out, I've just had to postpone it until things cool down. It's . . . well, I'm going to have to get somebody else to do the productions."

"Why?"

"*I* adore you, Vivian, I always have, you know that. But the *pressure* on me is too great. I've gotten calls all day from parents, white and colored. The story's all over town."

"You could stick up for me!"

"I have, and will, as a friend. But as principal of this school . . ." He looked off to the side, keeping his head low. "Sorry, Vivian, it just wasn't meant to be."

1968

THE PHONE CALL CAME in the early evening. "Nebraska, Nebraska, this is Sarah. Nebraska, I'm so upset. He meant so much to me, so much to so many of us."

"Sarah? Are you okay, sugar? What on earth's wrong?"

Nebraska heard a catch in Sarah's breath, a sharp drawing in, unmistakable even as far away as Boston, where her oldest Gold child now managed a drama group, where she raised a boy and a girl, where she sometimes called from in the early evening like this to ask Nebraska's advice about disciplining a child or about how much fatback to stir into collard greens. The catch came again, and then the voice spoke as though it were twelve years old again and at Madoc Bay, wrought up with some private failing or loss. "Nebraska? You haven't heard that King's been shot?"

"No," Nebraska answered hesitantly. "King?"

"Martin Luther King." Static wavered on the phone then faded.

"Oh, Lord."

"Yes, in Memphis. I heard it from a girlfriend who just called. She's down there with a reporter she's engaged to who was covering a story."

"Was it—was it a white man?"

"Yes."

"Oh, honey. God willing, he'll live."

"God willing," Sarah's voice came over the distance.

Nebraska hunted for something more to say, but words wouldn't come. Why was it that tragedy always came in the early evening like this, at the time when the sun was setting in such a way as to cast its sad red light over the roofs of the housing project? Other calls came back to her, calls that had ripped her up inside: Vivian's voice saying "Saul Gold passed away this evening, Nebraska"; a later year, with even greater sorrow, "Rivka Gold passed away this evening, Nebraska"; and only recently, the most tragic news—"Nebraska, dear, Rachel's child was stillborn." Every time the call came the light seemed to grow redder and deeper, and as she would wander about the apartment, figuring on how she would get to work especially early the next day so that she could help out as everyone got prepared to go to the house of other relatives, or to the mortuary, or to the funeral, the light would turn and spill over the backs of the chairs, over the television, over the sofa, so that the light became like the light that filtered through the Japanese magnolia in spring next to the Golds' den window. But this light was deeper and sadder, like blood that had once passed out of her body into a stream.

"I'm sorry I had to be the one to tell you, Nebraska."

"Sarah, sweetheart. That's all right. Better to hear tragedy from family than read it in the papers."

"Yes. Of course."

Nebraska cleared her throat. She tried to envision the face of the man she had seen on television and in the newspapers and in her fantasies of walking. Once, as well, she had seen that face in a dream. The man had been standing out by the pen with Abraham, saying he wasn't Martin Luther King but rather Abraham's brother come to give them enough money to buy an airplane and fly away to the Promised Land.

"How're the chirren, Sarah? How're Jeffrey and Rivka?"

"They're fine. Call me if you want to, Nebraska. Reverse the charges. I know this comes as a shock."

"Yes, dear." Suddenly she simply wanted to be alone. "I have to go, honey," she said quickly.

She tried to conjure the face of King again but could not. After all, she had not known him, had not talked with him or shaken his hand. Why, then, should she be so upset? Why the dampness that came to her eyes as she sat hard on the couch and felt the weariness of another day settle through her body? "Todd. Will he be okay?" She envisioned her son walking down a street in Newark, New Jersey, on the way to the radio station where he had just gotten a new job. Then Junior—perhaps he was visiting over at Wenda June's. Then Viv—where was Viv? Why had she not come back yet from the downtown, where she had gone to purchase curtain rods for the upstairs bedroom? Why had the note been lying on the table when she arrived home after Mr. Gold had dropped her off about six thirty, the note reading, "Dear Momma, be back before 7," and she was not yet back?

The face of the man came to her more clearly of a sudden. It rose like an apparition, the large eyes, the smile that made her think he must have been a dashing, gay young man, the features gathering together and hammering out a point, an argument. Was it only just now evident to her that Martin Luther King resembled her own father?

Her father's face was even harder to recall. She had lost him before she turned five. He just disappeared, they told her. But the aunt who'd raised her on the Randomville plantation after her mother died when she was eleven said to her, "Nebraska, your father is still alive. He works in Birmingham." When she had gone with her aunt to Birmingham soon after, the woman took her to a general mercantile store owned by Jews named Bloom and stood at the window, pointing to a well-built black man with wide, strong features who was pushing a broom listlessly at the back of the store; then her aunt said, "Look at him good, Nebraska, 'cause I can't walk in and introduce you. He don' want nothin' to do with none of us'n no more." Nebraska had not believed the man was really her father, but when she would wake up crying for her father when she was twelve and thirteen, it was the broom pusher she cried for.

That face had grown alongside her mother's face as the years passed and she grieved for them both. She mourned for them whenever the trains passed because she had been named from a train side—though a friend of Mrs. Gold's told her that "Nebraska" was not a name written on a train side ever, and that the man who had told her mother it said "Nebraska" had been playing a joke or concealing his own illiteracy, one (but Nebraska refused to believe this explanation, saying if it were true then she still did not want to know). And when the trains used to pass close to the Madoc Lumber Company when she and Abraham and the children lived in the shack, that humming, wailing, and chugging of the boxcars made her yearn to run and leap into an empty car, riding it back to Randomville, where her mother and father might miraculously appear.

But it had been months, no, years, since the broom pusher's face had returned to her as clearly as it now did.

Rising, she walked to the window and drew back the curtains; light grew deeper and redder. Faces, long and silhouetted, appeared in windows. Doors began to open. Neighbors stepped out, down, bent toward one another gossiping, turning up radios that seemed to take over Golden Castles with an incessant and mournful blare. Had they heard too?

She sat back down and was startled by a flock of starlings swooping low over the bloodied rooftops across the way. A rap came at the door. The screen door jiggled and the rap came again. "Cooomin'!" she called, and got up heavily from the sofa. When she opened the door she saw Viv standing and smiling sheepishly, saying, "I'm sorry I'm late, Momma, but Mr. Gold and Benjamin saw me walking home and offered me a ride. We went and got some ice cream."

"She was in good hands, Nebraska," Edward said. Benjamin, taller than his father, his short hair jet-black and curly, was still finishing a cone.

"Mr. Gold," Nebraska said as calmly as she was able,

"thank you, sir. But this is no good time for you and my Benjie to be standin' on the porch of no colored."

By the time Edward and Benjamin had come in to call Vivian on the phone, waited several minutes because the line was busy, and decided to go on without calling, the atmosphere of Golden Castles had begun to transform. No longer was it just another balmy April evening in southern Alabama, the smell of cooking and the clink of silverware gradually fading into the hum of televisions and clack of checkers and children's voices. It was suddenly an evening that crackled with an unusual, nervous energy: people came from doors faster, heads bent together more quickly, radios were turned up louder. A next-door neighbor, whose apartment shared the porch with Nebraska's, pushed open her door and walked in front of Nebraska's window, leaning on the railing. "What's goin' on?" she yelled. A teen-age girl called back, "Luther King's been killed."

"Killed?" A terror ran through Nebraska's body. "He done died so quick?"

The woman on the porch called back to the girl, "What's all this fuss about? He ain't from round here."

"Luther King's been killed by a white man," the girl shouted.

The woman on the porch waved a handkerchief as if to dismiss the issue, tucked it into her sleeve, and returned to her house.

"She just moved in," Nebraska explained to Mr. Gold and Benjamin, carefully watching their expressions. "She's from up the country whereabouts I used to be. She don't know nothin' 'bout nothin'."

"Some say ignorance is bliss," Edward said, his voice edged with sarcasm. "Well . . ." He looked straight at Nebraska. "Now what?"

"Just wait a minute. Wait a few minutes. It'll pass over. This is sad, sad, Mr. Gold, but it's no reason for black to hit on white. Before you knows it, those folks'll be back eatin' supper and watching *I Love Lucy.*" Nebraska tried to sound convincing. "Really, Mr. Gold."

Benjamin started toward the door. "I'm ready to leave," he said impetuously. "Nobody's going to bother us. Don't they know we're friends of Nebraska?"

"Benjamin," Edward commanded, "get away from that door."

Benjamin flopped down on the sofa. "This is *ridiculous!*"

"Listen to your daddy," Nebraska said sternly. "He know."

Edward turned on the television. An announcer said "critical condition" as a camera panned a motel's second-floor balcony where the shooting had taken place.

"Nebraska, he didn't die," Edward said with an odd note of jubilance in his voice.

Nebraska sat on the couch next to Benjamin, folded her hands and began to pray. "You know, Benjie"—she looked up—"Reverend King reminded me a little bit of my own daddy."

"I thought he died when you were too little to remember." Benjamin turned to her. "Isn't that what you told us?"

As she started to explain, her prayer continuing in part of her mind, the phone rang and shattered whatever composure she had been able to maintain. She lifted the receiver, her heart thumping. "Yes? Yes? Junior, where are you? Get home right now."

She was distracted by someone running past her window followed by a band of youngsters. She craned her neck. The band disappeared down the street.

"Mr. Gold and Benjie are over here," she said into the phone, almost forgetting whom she was talking to. "They dropped off Viv."

The voice in the receiver rose a notch and the facts were made clear: there was a stir at the Misty Hill apartments and other new apartment complexes near the docks; somebody had heard that black communities in other cities were beginning to have standoffs with police; a fire had been lit in New York City's Harlem—the news came to somebody with a ham radio; Wenda June had closed herself in the bathroom; Mr. Gold and Benjie should get home—fast.

The facts stacked up in Nebraska's mind and fused into one. After she put the receiver down all she could say was, "Mr. Gold, why don't you let me and Viv ride with y'all over to where Junior's visiting Wenda June. We'll pick him up and ride on to Magnolia Court and drop y'all off. No, I gots a better idea. Junior can ride behind us in his car and bring us back. It's better that way, Mr. Gold. I love Benjie too much to worry 'bout y'all making it home perfectly safe."

Benjamin protested. "Nothin's gonna happen, Nebraska."

"Sugar, there's crazy people black and white in this world." Nebraska stood and slipped on her shoes.

"I think it'll blow over myself." Edward paused. "You know, Madoc's had far better race relations than any town in Alabama. It's just a question of whether folks see this as something we're responsible for, something that's our fault as opposed to some lunatic madman who just got hold of a rifle. If they try to pin this on *every* white person, well, that is plumb crazy."

" 'Zactly," Nebraska added, then hunted for some other reassurance but simply trailed off.

She looked out the window. A van eased down the street, avoiding the project residents milling about. Four or five residents made a barricade of bodies and stopped the van. A window rolled down slowly and a friendly, bearded young man with shoulder-length blond hair leaned out, smiling. Seemingly out of nowhere a rock as large as a softball banged against the van's sideview mirror only a foot from the smiling youth's temple. With a look of shock and disbelief crossing his face, the young man cranked up the window madly. Another rock slapped against the glass and sent a web of cracks spreading in every direction.

A large woman in a housecoat—Nebraska recognized her

from a neighboring church—hustled from her porch and grabbed the child who had thrown the second rock. She whipped him on the calf with a stick and shouted so loudly that Nebraska could hear her words through the windows of her own house: "Let those boys through. They ain't ever done nothin' to you!" The barricade parted and off the van spun.

Another woman came to the first woman's defense. "Listen to Mamie! Y'all fools or somethin'?" Another woman, this one only a girl of sixteen, shouted back, "Jesus said, 'An eye for an eye.'"

Nebraska shook her head. "Jesus said? That was Samson, Mr. Gold."

"I wish he hadn't." Edward paced nervously, looking over Nebraska's shoulder at the commotion outside. "Lord God, help us."

Benjamin stood to look. Edward signaled him back. "Dad," the boy implored.

"Stay put, please, Benjie. We've got enough as it is without your hanging out the window."

"I wasn't hanging out the window."

"Please, son!"

"Oh, Mr. Gold, look there." Nebraska pointed to the ice cream truck coming down the street, its bell ting-tinging and a gray-bearded, portly man hanging from the open window, waving. "That's Mr. Lucky—what everybody call him—the ice cream man. He come round everyday 'bout early evening."

There was a hesitation in the group of residents on the street. One resident, a boy no older than fifteen, waved Mr. Lucky on, then another boy, older, his hair in cornrows, reached up and opened the door of the truck. Mr. Lucky tried to close it. The boy opened it again. Somebody reached for the freezer door at the back of the truck, unlatched it, and began to yank out boxes of ice cream and Popsicles, turning them bottom upwards. Children ("They so young," said Nebraska, "they don't even know what they doin'") scampered to pick up the treats from the ground. Mr. Lucky flung open the door of the truck, climbed down ceremoniously, and went and stood in front of the dumped-out boxes.

A fist swung out and caught the man in the belly, doubling him over. "God dammit," Edward said, "I'm going out there." He started toward the door but Nebraska stopped him by putting her foot down on the threshold.

"What's goin' on?" a voice came from the back of the apartment, and Abraham appeared, the back porch screen slamming a second after he entered.

"Let me pass," Edward said. "Let me out the door. That man is employed by a friend of mine. Am I going to let him get . . . get killed?"

Nebraska threw Abraham a glance, saw his frightened, puzzled look, and marked the street scene: two boys tall enough to be basketball players strode into the crowd and grabbed the teen-ager who had socked Mr. Lucky. One threw him to the ground. The other lifted up Mr. Lucky under the arms and hoisted him back into the cab of the ice cream truck, closed the door, climbed up the other side, then started the truck up himself.

"Where are the police?" Edward turned to Abraham, then to Nebraska, then back to watching the street. "Where are—"

"It'll blow over," commented Abraham, who now took a seat in the kitchen. "Just a bunch o' wild kids wi' nothin' better to do."

A siren started in the distance. Another joined it. They became a wail.

"The TV said King's died!" someone shouted. Nebraska reached over and turned up the set. An advertisement for margarine sent dancing yellow sticks up a mountain of bread. She changed the channel. Walter Cronkite's face danced through the heavy waves of static. Dead. Yes, dead.

Nebraska looked up to see the crowd outdoors startled into a moment of silence; a plume of smoke began to rise from one of the buildings close by. The reddish sky, gone to deep purple and indigo, changed from sadness to agony. The smoke filled the sky, bringing darkness permanently.

Was she dreaming?

The crowd broke into clumps of three and four and moved quickly, in random patterns, toward the direction of smoke. Another plume rose from another project.

Abraham came into the living room and leaned against the sill. "A bunch o' fools." He coughed. "They burnin' up their own homes?"

"Must be an arsonist," said Edward, leaning against the sill next to Abraham a moment before turning and walking back to the couch. He wiped his face with the back of his hand as if he were wiping off soot. "An arsonist—just some maniac starting fires."

"Yes, I know what one is," Abraham returned snidely.

Nebraska, folding her arms, patted her heart with her right hand. "God, tell me it ain't true. Tell me." Benjamin scooted closer to her on the couch and put his arm around her, saying, "Aw, Nebraska, there's nothing to be worried about."

"I'm more worried 'bout you than me, Bop." She kissed her hand and touched it to his forehead.

Sirens screamed in the air, sweeping up the blaring radios and shouting voices into a whirling lariat of alarm.

Viv appeared from upstairs, drying her eyes. "He's dead, Momma." She ran into Nebraska's free arm, the arm not wrapped around Benjie. "Daddy? What's going on outside?"

"Niggers is burnin' up Madoc is what," answered Abraham. "Gonna burn up themselves next 'cause some politician's been shot. Ain't that stupid? My dogs could do better than that."

"Let's go, Nebraska." Edward spoke abruptly, and this time as he moved toward the door Nebraska did not stop him but said, "Let's go, Viv, you and me gonna part the waters for family."

Viv hesitated.

"Come on, Viv!"

"Who's gonna stay with Daddy?"

"What do you mean, 'stay with Daddy'?" Nebraska was stopped in her tracks. "I think Abraham'll be just fine, don't you?"

"Maybe the Golds will be plenty fine too," Abraham suggested.

Nebraska turned to her husband. "Am I losing my hearing? You want Mr. Gold and Benjie—the only two white faces in Golden Castles right this moment—to walk into an insane asylum?"

"And what 'bout my Viv?" Abraham countered. "You want her to walk into a sane asylum too?"

"He's right, Nebraska," Edward agreed. "Leave Viv here. Matter of fact, you stay here as well. The cops'll be here any minute. They'll see us out fine."

Nebraska flung open the door and stood her ground. She looked hard at Viv. "Act right. Act right, girl I done raised from day one."

Viv edged toward the door.

Abraham backed away, speaking angrily. "Shit, Nebraska. You think you a pastor who's always got to save!" He turned and went to the kitchen.

Viv whirled and fixed her father with a stare of contempt. "Don't talk like that in front of Benjie, Daddy. Why do you always want to run Momma down? She's trying to act right, to act Christian, and you're making her seem like a hardhearted nobody."

"Whoever's going, let's just go!" Edward said.

Nebraska went out first, trying to march with her chin up but making a point to look out on every side of the small group of Waterses and Golds that walked from the apartment. The night, growing darker, gathered close about them, and the crowd was distracted by the fire that leaped into the sky over the projects. For a moment Nebraska forgot why the fires were burning, forgot the call from Sarah that had come when the sky was still glowing red from what was only the sun.

When they reached Edward's car they got in. A police car roared past them of a sudden and came to an abrupt halt fifty feet away. Four policemen, helmeted, leaped from the car and began to chase a young man. Through the windshield Nebraska spied the man they were chasing as he doubled behind another car—he was about twenty, black, and carried a portable television set. Another young man, who could have been the first one's brother by his looks, raced in the opposite direction and hurled a bottle at one of the police. Another policeman in the group, broad and dark as a tank, barreled toward the culprit with the TV set. Caught in the glare of the cop car headlight, the policeman wielded his billy stick. In the skirmish that followed, Nebraska could barely sort out the action: the youth threw the television set at the policeman; the billy club cut through the air and crashed down on the boy's neck; the other youth raced back again with another bottle but tumbled as a second policeman's stick caught him between the shoulder blades.

Project residents amassed around the police while a truck loaded with more cops moaned through the street. The new units leaped down dressed in riot gear—overcoats, helmets, boots, gas masks—and three German shepherds appeared, snarling and straining on leashes.

It was the savagery of those dogs—their mouths frozen open, their teeth glaring and frothing over in the headlights and the revolving red of the sirens—that snatched Nebraska from the almost dreamlike state she had been in since the telephone call and thrust her back into the stark edges of reality. She was not in a room, behind a window, watching a television personality say that a great man had been shot; no, she was on her own street, in a car with people who meant the world's riches to her, and her neighbors were setting fire to their own dwellings as in some crazed group suicide, and a real attack dog was hurtling toward a man's leg at this very moment, its teeth cutting deep into the muscle as the man fell and screamed and the dog strained to slash again as it was dragged back by the leash.

The scene before her revolved away as Edward started the car and swung about in a circle in the middle of the street, rolling over the curb, back into the street, and then taking off in the other direction.

"The police would help us," Benjamin said.

"The hell with the police." Edward pressed the accelerator and the car bore around a curve.

"Wenda June's is that way," said Nebraska anxiously, but Edward did not turn where she pointed. "Mr. Gold, please, I gots to go see 'bout Wenda June and Junior. And it's best if Junior comes with us, 'cause . . ."

"I'm sorry," Edward said firmly.

"That's not fair," Benjamin dissented.

"What's fair is what's safest for us," Edward snapped. "I'm sorry. That's just the way it is."

Nebraska put her palms up to her forehead and spoke through tears. "I'm worried 'bout mine on both sides, Mr. Gold. Don't you understand?"

Benjamin leaned forward. "Daddy, listen to her."

"Listen to me!" Edward returned. "We don't have time to run off on any damn excursion."

"But . . ."

"You want to be noble, Benjamin? You want to get a bullet in your head?"

"Mr. Gold!" Nebraska implored. "I understands how you feel. It's just that Junior told me Wenda June went near 'bout crazy when she heard about King. It's just . . ." The project buildings became a blur in the darkness. The brick units changed to wooden houses where black families wandered out of backyards and side yards onto the walks, gathering, passing on the news. "I don't want her to go off into the street. I don't want her . . . to go . . ." The tears started streaming, but she recalled them, squeezing her temples with her fingers. Her head began to ache.

Some unseen object bumped against the front of the car. A dog sent piercing yelps into the air.

"You hit a puppy!" Viv shouted. "You hit a puppy dog!"

"Hush," said Nebraska, who continued to draw back the tears until they seemed to pound in some locked-up place behind her eyes. "Don't never cry over some animal."

"You hit a puppy dog!"

Edward slowed, swung the car around, and started down the street leading to Wenda June's. The vehicle raced through the smoky air, coming to Misty Hill.

Nebraska pointed the way to the drive and scoured the premises for sight of the car. Where was Junior's car? Could he have gone off in it and left Wenda by herself?

Leaning over, she pressed the horn three times in the Gold family signal that had become the Waterses' signal as well. Nobody appeared at the door at the top of the stairs. "Wenda June," she called, starting out of the car onto the bottom step. Junior came out of the door, his face long and ghostly in the yellow porch light.

"She's not here, Momma," he said frantically. "I don't know where she's gone. She just lit up and stole the car and took off. Said she was going into the town."

"The town? O Jesus, help us."

Her son began to make his way down the stairs by holding on to the banister with one hand and his crutches with another, hopping step by step.

"I need to call Vivian," Edward said, pushing up the stairs past Junior. He entered the apartment and returned a moment later, his face ashen. "She's—she's not there. A neighbor answered the phone and said he was supposed to tell me—tell me that Vivian had gone off with Babs. They went to . . ." He blinked rapidly, nervously, continuing as though stunned. "They went to Gold's Western Wear."

"Gold's Western Wear?" Nebraska could hardly say the words. "They drove into the downtown tonight? Why, Gold's Western ain't even open past five."

"He said the police had called Babs to tell her it had been looted." Breaking off in mid-sentence he bounded down the stairs and into the car, cranking it up and squealing out of the drive almost before Junior had a good chance to finish getting in.

The downtown loomed larger as the car turned and accelerated, flew through smoke, hung close on curves leading to the street where Gold's Western Wear sat in a row of small stores and shops, many of them now hung with the signs For Sale or This Space For Rent.

Whirring siren lights came into view and beyond them the lights of a firetruck flashed. Nebraska let her tears begin to flow. Through them she watched flames leap from rooftop to rooftop. She spotted Babs's car on the curb across from Gold's Western Wear. Next to it was a police car. In front of it and a little out in the street . . . Junior's car? "It *is* Junior's car," she said aloud.

"There's Wenda June," Viv yelled, pointing to her sister standing near the police car.

"I see Vivian," Edward said half in relief and half in fear. He slammed to a halt several yards before reaching the cars, turned up on the curb across from Gold's Western Wear, and threw the car into neutral.

"Wh-what are ya'll doin' here?" Babs asked as they quickly got out of the car. She pursed her lips and tapped her striped blouse at the chest. "Can you believe it? Wenda June Waters is burnin' up this city! Burnin' it up!"

"Wenda June," Nebraska wailed, seeing her daughter standing next to the policeman, her wrists handcuffed in front of her. "What you gone and done, child? What you gone and done?"

Wenda June turned her head. "Go away, Momma."

"Baby, what you gone and done!"

"We knew who she was this time," the policeman said. "Try to get her off on a nut charge now!" Nebraska recognized him as the man who had stood so kindly in the Golds' living room that day when Wenda had been arrested. His voice, once gentle, was hard and sharp.

"I didn't want you to see me here, Momma. This ain't against *you!*"

"Oh, my baby, let me hold you!"

Before Nebraska could reach her daughter, Wenda June broke from the policeman's reach, her handcuffs knocking against her legs, and headed for her mother. Nebraska opened her arms wide, but Wenda veered around her at the last second, raced by Babs and Benjamin, and leaped into Edward's still idling car.

"Wh-what in God's name?" Babs yelled.

Nebraska turned to see her daughter lean over and grab the automatic transmission stick. She shifted the car into forward, then grasped the wheel with her cuffed hands, her palms turned upward flashing like those of a drowned man bobbing up through water. The car veered past Vivian and Edward and lurched into the middle of the street. The policeman dropped to his haunches, lifted his gun, fired once, twice; the left front tire blew.

Nebraska screamed "Wenda June!" and saw her daughter, face contorted, shouting something back as the car smashed into the flaming doorway of a building, exploded, and became a burning coffin.

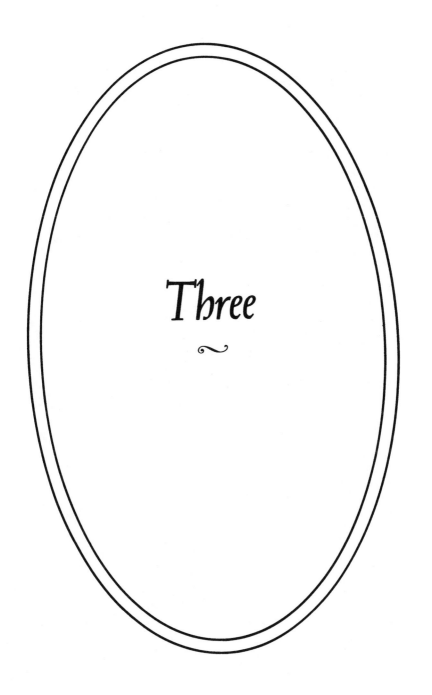

Three

1971

"C'MON, BOP, let's dance."

"I don't wanna."

"Bop!"

"Nebraska!"

"Benjamin," Vivian said from the living room couch, "listen to Nebraska. How're you going to go to college if you don't know how to dance?"

"I can dance fine."

"Put on the music, Miss Gold."

Vivian stood and walked over to the radio. The strains of "Moon River" filled the room. Nebraska moved closer to where Benjamin lay on the floor, his arms out, looking up at the ceiling. Nebraska held out her arms and started to sway. "This is how they do it on Lawrence Welk. I knows you knows how 'cause we watched him many a Saturday night." She swayed faster and started to turn.

Benjamin put his hands over his eyes. "Blaaah! That's not how people dance anymore."

"That's how Edward and I dance," Vivian said, turning up the radio and watching Nebraska change directions as she turned. "I will admit, though, that Nebraska's doing a variation I'm *not* familiar with."

"Called the feelin' good step, Miss Gold."

"It's about time somebody felt good around here!" Vivian

walked toward Nebraska, repeating "the feelin' good step" and thinking there was once a time when she never thought she'd hear Nebraska say those words.

That time had been more than three years ago, when Wenda June Waters had jumped from the guard of Officer Pettibone, leaped into Edward's car, and spun off directly at her and Edward. As Vivian had watched the car bear down on them, her life rushed before her: not as images of childhood and family (as she'd always been told happened), but as a strong, quick light, like heat lightning. When the car turned away, the heat lightning became the flames of the buildings, and she closed her eyes against them. Then she'd heard the gunfire, Wenda June's shouting back to Nebraska, and the sound of the car ramming into the building.

Would Wenda June have run into the building if Officer Pettibone had not shot out the tire? Vivian wondered. And, further back in her mind, she asked what she dared never mention to anyone: Had Wenda *meant* to threaten Edward and her? These questions had racked her until she could not sleep.

She and Nebraska had never discussed these questions outright. For the first two months after Wenda's death, Nebraska had not been able to come to work at all. By the time the fall had rolled around, she was working full time, but went about the Golds' house quietly, listlessly, as though she were moving behind other sets of walls. Then, as the weeks wore on, when she washed dishes she began to sing her sad, slow gospel songs, stopping in the middle of nearly every one and sobbing for her lost child.

After more than a year had passed, Vivian and Nebraska and Edward had been able to talk about the night of Wenda June's death. Even then, they talked only about the moment Wenda June had shouted back to her mother. Edward had heard her shout, "I'm sorry!" Vivian had heard "Momma!" For Nebraska, as the months passed, the words "I love you!" were remembered more and more clearly.

The questions, whether asked or not, quieted. The sorrow

quieted, too, but never lay entirely still—it simply became submerged beneath the small events of each day. A month earlier Nebraska had even begun to sing through whole songs standing at the sink without having to pause and lay her head against her wrist. To Vivian's delight, Nebraska had even come in with a new wig one recent day, a beautiful curled reddish-tinted piece that she said looked " 'zactly like one Edna Solomon wore." When she had put her face up to the mirror, stating "no more gray hair creeping round for Nebraska," Vivian not only noted a surprising brightness in the woman's face but also noted that the sorrow, for the moment, seemed like a bad dream shaken off.

As Vivian turned up the music even louder, turning her head from side to side and limbering up her wrists, "Moon River" changed to a slow rumba, "La Vida." Vivian sang along. "What is life abouuut?" She came closer to Nebraska and started to whirl too.

"I'll tell you what it's all 'bout," Nebraska answered. "It's 'bout feelin' good"—she paused to spin around once—"or 'bout feelin' sad."

"Hm, mm," Vivian agreed, dance-stepping toward Benjamin, who now rolled over and pressed his face into the carpet and threw his arms over his head. "You know what we need, Miss Nebraska? We need a little drink."

Vivian danced lightly toward the bar in the den, brought down a bottle of sherry, and poured some into a glass. After taking a sip she smacked her lips. "Try some."

"What would Reverend Thompson say?" Nebraska eased toward Vivian, shaking her head slowly, and leaned over and took a sip. "Wheeeooo!"

"Nebraska! Are you a riot!" Vivian shook her head as well and beckoned her son. Benjamin refused, nodding his head and pressing deeper into the carpet and moaning. "What're you moaning about, Benjie?"

"Benjie acts like he's in love," said Nebraska, who now danced over to the radio and changed the station. "Need somethin' faster. Somethin' we can really *dance* to." A fast-paced song took over the room. "That's my man," Nebraska shouted. "Mr. James Brown!"

Benjamin rolled over on his back and exhaled noisily. "This is dumb," he remarked. "I can't believe I'm lying here with my own mother and Nebraska dancing like it's a rock concert or something."

"It is a rock concert," Vivian said matter-of-factly, sipping the sherry and handing it to Nebraska.

"I was just *kidding*, Mother. You don't really think this is like a rock concert."

"What's he singing about? What's he saying?" Vivian stopped dancing a minute to listen.

> I got something that makes me want to shout
> I got something that tells me what it's all about
> I got soul—I'm super bad

"Super*baaad*," Nebraska growled, wiggling her rump and sticking her chin out like a gobbler.

"If he's got soul, then why doesn't he feel good?"

"Miss Gold, when you got soul, feelin' bad means you feelin' good."

> Sometimes I feel so nice
> I jump back I wanta kiss myself

"Did he just say he wanted to kiss himself?"

Nebraska laughed. "Yas'm. And he oughta kiss hisself. 'Member when he sang up in Washington and the chirren stopped fightin' and went back to school?"

Vivian sang, "I feel *superbad*." She started to shake her rear end. Looking over, she saw Nebraska slipping off her shoes and sliding her feet back and forth over the carpet.

"That's how he does it, but faster." Nebraska leaned back and looked up at the ceiling. "Course, he don't got to clean the carpet when he's finished."

"Sure doesn't," Vivian said, imitating Nebraska's movements then moving closer. She bumped her rear end against Nebraska's and the woman nearly shrieked. "What kind o' dance you call that, Miss Gold?"

"Called the booty dance."

"The booty dance? Where on earth did you learn such a thing?"

"Nebraska, sweetheart," she responded wickedly, "there's some things I know that even you don't."

"I guess you's right!"

"Have I ever showed you the banana dance?"

"The banana dance? In front of your own son?"

Benjamin lifted his arms toward the ceiling, yawned loudly, and brought his arms down slowly until he was spread in a T-shape on the floor. "Believe me, Nebraska," he cracked, "my mother's hardly gonna shock you. I don't even think she's able."

Vivian danced to the bar again, refilled the glass with sherry, sipped, and handed the glass to Nebraska. "You'd shock me if you got up off the floor and let us teach you how to dance." She moved lightly around her son's left arm.

"Well," Nebraska said, touching the glass to her lips, "I done sinned once already today, so I might as well go on and sin twice."

"That's the spirit."

James Brown spun to a close and the radio announcer said the summer weather would be hot and damp. Another record started. Vivian stood still, resting, arms akimbo, cocking her ear to catch the lyrics:

> See, See See Rider
> Oh see what you gone and done.
> Oh see, yes, see Rider,
> Lord see, what you gone and done.
> You made me love you hard,
> Now your other gal's done come.

Nebraska spun away to a corner of the room, lost in the music altogether. Her body moved lightly as a feather, floating

here and there on the stream of air conditioning that moved
through the air. She moved as if she had never broken an ankle,
never had swollen feet. She held her arms far out, as though
trying to touch something that moved there, then closed her
fingers tight and started spinning around.

"Nebraska's got the spirit! That's what you've got to do,
Benjamin, just git down on it!"

> I'm goin' far away tomorrow,
> And won't be back 'til Fall.
> I'm leavin' on the first train,
> The 'Bama Cannonball.
> I might just find me a good man,
> So don' 'speck me back at all.

"Don' 'speck me back at all," Nebraska echoed.

"Edward and Abraham gotta remember this song," Vivian
said. Laughing, she began to do a dance step of her own, a
sort of solitary fox-trot. Putting her left foot far out, she brought
her right foot up to it, did the same by leading with her right
foot, and went round and round in a swoon. "More sherry," she
cried. She sipped and handed the glass to Nebraska, who also
sipped.

Nebraska danced a circle around Benjamin, chanting his
name to the beat of "See See Rider": "Bop, Bop, Bop Bop Bop
Bop, oh, Bop Bop what you have Bopped."

"Okay. Okay!" Grudgingly, Benjamin got up from the
floor and stretched, moaning histrionically, but beginning to
show a few signs of rhythmic life. Vivian watched his head loll
around once and his left foot go out and jiggle like a boy's effort
to wake up sleeping toes. Nebraska sipped the sherry again,
took the liberty of refilling the glass, and handed it back to
Vivian, who took something closer to a swig.

"Oh, if Mr. Gold could see us now." Nebraska put her
hand to her mouth and laughed loudly, the laughter seeming to
rustle the lampshades as her leg brushed against a table and two
small lamps shook. Taking another sip of sherry, she handed the

glass back to Vivian, smacking her lips. Suddenly, she turned serious. "Don't ever tell nobody you saw Nebraska drink like this." She took the glass from Vivian, sipped again, and broke into a smile.

> See, See See Rider
> Oh see, what you gone and done.

Benjamin began to strut across the floor like a drugged chicken, his long limbs catching the music. Vivian, charting his movements, came toward him sideways and tried to imitate his step.

Nebraska faced them both and patted her stomach to the beat. "We got to *learn* him, Miss Gold."

Vivian moved around in front of her son and grabbed his right hand, placing her left hand behind his back and struggling to lead a dance. The two of them blended into a step that was a cross between a tango and a two-step, fighting each other about the room. Nebraska tapped Vivian's shoulder, broke in, took one of Benjamin's hands, and announced, "This is called the apple."

"The apple!"

The three of them looked to see where the exclamation had come from. Standing in the kitchen, dressed blue as a jaybird, a sheaf of papers under her arm, was Babs.

"Cousin," Vivian called. "What are you doing here in the middle of the afternoon?"

"Wh-what am I doing? What are *y'all* doing? I came by to drop off some zoning plans for Edward. But that don't explain wh-what—"

"We're just waitin' for you," Vivian returned, summoning her in, continuing to sway to the music that now drew to a close.

"Well," came Babs quickly, "I can't dance to race music. Specially when I should be at the office."

"Race music!" Nebraska howled. "Where we racin' to?"

"Take another sip," Vivian said, downing the last of her

sherry and quickly filling the glass again, handing it to Nebraska. "Babs," she called, "get your tush in here and shake it!"

With a scowl, Babs eased toward the living room. Vivian eyed her closely, waiting for the look of anxiety, of distrust, that crossed her cousin's face whenever she came into Nebraska's presence. Vivian watched for the same expression on Nebraska's face. Neither woman registered more than good humor, though. Neither woman flinched or turned away with the recognitions that had passed between them so many times: Wenda June had once turned on Sosha, had derided her; Wenda June had been killed, possibly as the result of a bullet fired by an old high school friend of Babs's.

But the grudges, like the sorrow, seemed to spin away in the summer afternoon, and as Vivian took yet another sip of sherry, the room began to swing about gently. She reached over and tousled Benjamin's hair, turned off the radio, and went to the piano. Feeling as if she were on stage again, she pounded the keys and sang:

> *When it gets too hot for comfort,*
> *And you can't get ice cream cones,*
> *'Tain't no sin, to take off your skin,*
> *And dance around in your bones!*

Nebraska joined in. Benjamin, not knowing the words, whistled. He then grabbed Babs and started the half two-step, half tango that he had danced with his mother. "You learned him, Miss Gold," Nebraska conceded, "but *what* did you learn him?"

> *Just be like those Bamboo Babies,*
> *In the South Sea tropic zones,*
> *'Tain't no sin, to take off your skin,*
> *And dance around in your bones!*

Babs blushed. "I wouldn't even take off my skirt, much less my skin!" Benjamin spun her out and brought her back to him.

"That boy can dance!" Nebraska exclaimed. "He gonna

make it at college sure 'nough, now." She did the half two-step, half tango herself.

Vivian sang another chorus of the song, watching Babs, Nebraska, and Benjamin turning about in the living room. She repeated the refrain, her hands banging the keyboard, feet working the pedals.

"Oh, 'tain't no sin, to take off your skin, and dance around in your bones! 'Tain't no sin, to take off your skin, and . . ."

The singing buoyed up Vivian powerfully, mixing with the sherry and the summer afternoon. As she played the song once more, she regained a belief she had not been able to hold in a long time: the world was a pretty good place after all.

❧

It was not quite a week later that Vivian helped Benjamin pack. They sat in his room with the overhead light casting a glow on the small mounds of underwear, socks, shirts, and books. Jeans, khaki pants, and polyester slacks were hung in a travel case. Vivian sorted through the socks, making sure each one had a match, then balled them up as Nebraska had balled them up earlier in the day after taking them from the dryer.

Starting to rearrange the socks again, she was cut off by Benjamin. "Really, Mom, I think the socks'll be okay."

"You don't even have name tags on them. How're you going to keep track of them at the dorm?"

"I haven't needed name tags since camp."

"I'm just looking out after your own good." Vivian looked about the room. "Are you going to take your baseball mitt?"

"Nah. I'm not into being a jock anymore."

"But it's such a great mitt. And you used to play baseball for hours with Edward and—"

"I don't want to, you see!" Benjamin stood and gathered the socks and hurled them into the suitcase. He tossed in the underwear with equal brusqueness.

"Don't get mad with me, Benjie. I'm just trying to help. You asked me to help you pack, so don't throw a tantrum."

"A *tantrum?*" Benjamin sat back down on the edge of the bed. "Mom, you're acting like a real Jewish mother right now. I'm not going off to war. I'm just going off to college. And Atlanta's only eight hours by car."

"Eight hours is a long way." Vivian tried not to get flustered or angry. "Besides, Atlanta is a big city. It's not like Madoc. It's not like you can trust everybody."

"Yes, yes. Is that all?"

"No, it's not all. You know I dislike the expression 'Jewish mother.' A Jewish mother is a stereotype who nags and makes chicken soup. I don't do either."

"You're right," answered Benjamin, standing again and sorting through his shirts, picking out the knits and folding them into a plastic bag before laying them in the suitcase. "Nebraska's the real Jewish mother around here. All day long she's gone on: 'Benjie, remember your toothbrush. Benjie, make sure to write. Benjie, eat this and eat that.' My God, what an incredible nag she's become. Is she getting senile or something?"

"You're impossible tonight, son. You know it's only that Nebraska loves you a great deal."

"Why does everybody have to love me? Why can't someone hate me for a change?"

Vivian walked toward the door of the room and looked out the window. She spoke with her back turned to her son: "If you keep acting like this, I'm sure there'll be plenty of people in the world who'll do just that."

"Mother—Mom—I'm sorry. It's just the going-off-to-school number's got me uptight. I admit it."

Still facing out the window, Vivian watched the trees down the block trembling in an evening breeze. The streetlight threw yellow pools over the darkened sidewalks. "Do you think you'll look up Viv at Atlanta Technical?"

"Maybe."

Vivian recalled the acceptance Viv had received from Atlanta Technical, one of the South's finest black private universities. She could again hear Nebraska telling the Golds excitedly about the acceptance, then hesitantly confessing, "But Mr. Gold, the bank loan is so high in what they want you to pay." Edward, without the smallest prodding from Vivian, had immediately said he would make the loan personally to Nebraska, and that she could pay back the loan with no interest whatsoever. Then a scholarship had come through the next week, and then Todd—now a station manager in West Virginia—had sent Nebraska a check for twenty-five hundred dollars to help his sister off to a solid start.

Viv's acceptance at Atlanta Technical was not only a joyous occasion, though; it was also an ironic one. Benjamin, accepted at Morton University, one of the South's finest white private universities, would be studying within five miles of Viv. "It's funny," Vivian had remarked to Edward, "how Viv held out at Lafayette High only to turn around and go to a black college, and how Benjamin ended up at a college no farther away than his high school had been from Viv's." Edward (who had deplored Lafayette since the *Oklahoma!* incident and who had not talked to Izzy Berman since Vivian had been let go as theater director) had simply answered: "It's not surprising Viv's going to a Negro college. After this whole state's been in an uproar over integration, over bussing, over civil rights, now the Negroes decide they were better off not mixing with the whites. Can you blame them?" And he continued: "Of course, if you could see the way some of the colored handle my rental property . . . Jesus, you'd think they'd never received any education at all—in a colored *or* white school."

Even Vivian would admit that some of Edward's rental tenants had been bad, so bad that she dared not fully enumerate the damages when she was with her golf-playing friends for fear of sounding as though she were making a veiled argument for "shipping 'em back to Africa," as Cissy Vance would say. Smashed appliances, ripped-out fixtures, scarred floors—the damages were nearly obscene.

"Have you seen my snakeskin belt?"

Vivian, taken from her thoughts, turned to see her son

rifling through a drawer. He was looking for the rattler-covered belt he had bought on a trip to Dallas to visit Rachel, who worked part-time as a substitute teacher and was married to a percussionist in the Dallas Symphony.

"I thought you didn't need help."

"Of course I need help," Benjamin erupted, then went on softly: "Don't mind me. I'm just . . . just a little wired is all."

Vivian went immediately to a drawer, opened it, and drew out the belt, letting it dangle like a live snake before flipping it toward the suitcase. "It was never one of my favorites." She wrinkled her nose.

Benjamin picked up what looked like a collage of rags. "Guess what. It's time for these blue jeans to go."

"I don't believe it, don't *believe* it," said Vivian melodramatically. "My son might—just might—not dress like a bum in college after all."

Rolling his eyes, Benjamin grinned and shrugged his shoulders.

"Well," Vivian went on, as though her train of thought had never been broken, "it would be nice if you'd look up Viv at least once before Christmas. She doesn't know a soul in Atlanta, and not knowing a soul in Atlanta is almost as bad as not knowing a soul in New York."

Benjamin's voice rose with an edge: "Mother, don't you realize that Viv and I live in different worlds? She doesn't want me to visit her. And I don't particularly want to visit her myself. This is not 1950. It's not 1960. Black kids do their own thing now. White kids do their own thing. What am I gonna do? Ride over to visit Viv and walk into a completely black classroom and say, 'Hi, my name is Benjamin Gold. Viv Waters's mom is our cook. I just wanted to come over and say hi y'all'?"

"Viv Waters's Mom is not your *cook*. She's . . . an aunt. Yes, an aunt."

"Great," Benjamin retorted. "That's even better. I'll just walk in and say 'Viv Waters's mom is my aunt.' I'm sure that'll go over big with the Black Muslims in the class."

"What do you care about a bunch of Black Muslims? Nebraska still helped raise you."

"I don't believe you, Mother. It's not—"

"You know," interrupted Vivian, "Nebraska and I were calculating the number of years we'd been raising children. We figured it was about a hundred and fifty. That's a lot of raising."

Benjamin answered coldly, "Did it ever occur to y'all that you didn't do it for us but that you did it for yourselves?"

"Oh, you're so intelligent, Benjamin," Vivian returned. "But you're still so young. Even if I, even if *we*, did do it for ourselves, don't you think it's a natural instinct, and that you'll do the same when you're a parent?"

"I'm never going to be a parent."

"Honey . . ." Vivian sat on the edge of the bed next to her son and pushed back a lock of his hair with her fingers. "Just let us miss you, okay? Is there any harm in missing you? Even if you don't miss us?"

"I'll miss you, I'll *miss* you, for Christ's sake."

"And you'll write?" Vivian tried to make a mental snapshot of her son sitting there during his last night as a full-time resident of Magnolia Court. The snapshot blurred, though, and she resigned herself to what she might remember.

"Yes, I'll write, I'll write," said Benjamin smiling, as though he had allowed himself, with some pleasure, to be defeated. "And you can come and visit and bring Rachel, and Sarah, and my nieces and nephews, and Babs, and even Nebraska."

৫৴৲

The Greyhound bus for Atlanta pulled out early the next morning. Edward drove Benjamin down before going to work. At the house, Vivian had thrown her arms around him, kissing him on the cheeks and forehead and only laughing and squeezing more tightly when he squirmed in her embrace. She had then slipped a twenty-dollar bill in his hand, said it was "mad money," and told him to have a good meal and a beer out on the town the first week of school and to do so for her.

Not an hour after Edward had driven away, the house seemed changed. She went about the kitchen, putting away the breakfast dishes, then climbed the stairs to Benjie's room, noting with a little perturbation that he had failed to pack one pair of socks. She put the socks away, stripped the sheets from the bed to take downstairs so that Nebraska would not have to walk up, and pushed a few books flush against others on the shelf. Before she started back down the stairs, she stopped at the window, seeing the trees down the block from the night before now flooded with sunshine. A thought whirled through her: the time elapsed between last night and this morning seemed no shorter or longer than the time elapsed between her giving birth to Benjamin and his leaving home for college. She closed her eyes, opened them. The trees were still there. "Of course," she said to herself. "Why wouldn't they still be?"

Heading down the stairs, she had a sharp sensation of her feet on the staircase and her hand on the railing. At the bottom of the stairs she came to a mirror above a chest of drawers. She looked at herself.

Here and there across the face that was well into its fifties —but looked not over forty, maybe forty-one or two—the skin was drawn from lack of sleep. *Was* it lack of sleep? Or was it the years? The eyes, as deep and dark as they had always been ("Eyes never change," Rivka Gold had once said), stared back at themselves, stared through themselves at the consciousness that watched back from the brain. Had she really given birth to a son? Had she really given birth at all? Had there really been some force behind those eyes in the mirror that carried the capacity to create a life, to make it spring up as God had sprung up Adam?

She raised a hand and watched it move back and forth over the face in the mirror, lightly brushing the drawn places on the skin. While she felt the hand, she imagined it was someone else's, maybe her father's, maybe Edward's, touching her softly.

She imagined a linkage of bodies stretching back to the

first day of creation, for had not that hand been formed in another body just as Benjamin's had been formed in her own? She imagined herself dead. It was easy to do so. But she could not imagine her children dead. She could think of them in no way other than breathing, laughing, growing, going their rounds in Texas, and Georgia, and Massachusetts.

Had Benjamin really left just that morning?

The back door jiggled and a voice lifted through the house: "He phoned me from the bus station." Nebraska dropped her packages, slipped off her walking shoes, and continued, "He called me from the Greyhound just to say good-bye, Nebraska, and you know, I just up and boohooed for nearly half an hour. Viv's gone. Benjie's gone. Well," she said, taking off her wig and storing it neatly in the closet, "it's just you and me now, Miss Gold. Just you and me."

"Oh, Nebraska," Vivian said with a forced pluckiness, "I think we'll survive. Don't you?" She tried to shake the image of herself in the mirror as she came into the kitchen.

Nebraska scooted into the breakfast nook and poured a cup of coffee. "Yas'm, we'll survive, you and me." She added, "Yas'm, we'll survive anything," shaking so much Sweet'n Low into her coffee Vivian realized she was unaware of what she was doing.

Six weeks later the envelope came from Atlanta. Long and plump, it was addressed in Benjamin's familiar scrawl to Vivian Gold. Eagerly Vivian opened it, her eyes skimming the accompanying note: "Dear Mom, Sarah, and Rachel, I'm sending you all copies of this essay that my freshman English Comp. teacher thought was really good. I thought I'd let you show it to Dad yourselves as I know he sometimes takes these kinds of things the wrong way—like an attack on the family—he's so sensitive and all. The teacher has suggested I submit it to the Morton literary journal. What do you think? Love, Benjie."

A REAL JEWISH MOTHER

I grew up with two mothers. My real mother was like a friend and confidant, a buddy, a sister. We played together when I was a child, talked about sex frankly when I became a teen-ager, and discussed love, the world, and the way people are put together—and the way they sometimes come apart—as I matured into a young adult. My other mother wasn't my mother in the actual sense, but in the metaphorical. She was a black woman named Nebraska, a classic "Mammy" figure who read with difficulty, wrote with difficulty, and never believed for a minute that astronauts really went up in space. Her wisdom was of the earthy kind (no pun intended)—she could draw out a bee sting with wet tobacco, for instance—and she fed all of us with the best fried chicken, black-eyed peas, and collards this side of Yoknapatawpha. She mended our socks and sweaters, and sometimes even our hearts.

In many ways, Nebraska was the real Jewish mother of the family, though, ironically, my real mother is Jewish herself and comes from a long line of sock menders, endearing fussbudgets, and chicken soup makers. I think Nebraska loved us as hard as my real mother, though not as deeply. Nebraska might have *thought* she loved us as deeply, but I've come to realize that what seems to be the thin line between nurturing and blood bond is sometimes a great divide. Nebraska—the Jewish mother—nurtured us with her hands, her food, her needle and thread, her simple ethics: "Act right," and "Don't wash your hands in the sink." My real mother seemed to attend to the interior needs: giving us insight and a kind of love that can only seem to grow out of the supreme identification of one person—a parent—with another person—a child.

It is clear that Madoc, my hometown, as well as the South, and probably a great deal of the United States, owes a debt to Nebraska. I've seen women like her in Texas and Massachusetts, who leave their own children in the morning and do not return to them until night, spending most of their waking hours feeding and doing for their "white children" in the "other part of town." Perhaps it is the case that when many of these white children grow up to hurl insults at black people, to vote for politicians who preach white supremacy, and to hire new Nebraskas to wash their dishes and press their children's clothes, they are unconsciously reacting to the Jewish mother of their youth, battling her by hurling the insults at anonymous black people, resenting her by voting for racist politicians, and then asking her back by hiring someone strange who nevertheless looks like her, talks like her. In fact, the white children never really grow up in relation to their Nebraskas. Held in a perpetual state of adolescence—as the relationship between a child and a Jewish mother can never develop beyond interdependence, beyond the child's needing the mother for physical nurturing and the mother's needing the child to nurture—the white adults are really teen-agers reacting to a parent figure. When George Wallace stood in the doorway of the University of Alabama, maybe he was secretly thumbing his nose at the black Jewish mother who had once coddled him on her bosom.

It is all so complex, isn't it? Frequently people from the North, or from places like England, accuse families like mine of being racists because there's a black woman employed in the house. Were she called an *au pair* or governess, or were she Dutch or German, would they still call us racists? Admittedly, for many years I accused my real mother of keeping a "Negro in bondage" until my sister Sarah, who lives in Boston and once felt that way but then became sympathetic to my mother's viewpoint, explained to me that household employment (that's the term she used) was not only respectable but necessary. If the Nebraskas of the world were not hired to do the job, then the wives of the house-owning husbands should be reimbursed for the work themselves! Also, she told me that my mother was sensitive about my accusations, and that she had always acted out of what she thought was love, whether I was mature enough to appreciate it or not.

All of this discussion brings me to the final and overwhelming consideration: if a woman like Nebraska can be my second mother, can her children be my stepbrothers and sisters?

For a long time I was close to Nebraska's youngest daughter, Viv, who now attends Atlanta Technical. One day, at my mother's request, I paid her a visit. Each of us felt awkward about being seen together on either her campus or mine, so we met in a park. I told her that I was thinking about writing an essay about Nebraska's being the real Jewish mother in my family, and she told me that she thought a real Jewish mother was someone more like my real mother—Viv's second mother: a mother who employed a black cook and treated her with respect, who believed in integration, and gave hand-me-down clothes to her employees instead of to the Salvation Army. Then we each had a revelation. I confessed to Viv that I had always wished my mother were more like her mother. She confessed she had long wished her mother were more like mine. In that moment, I believe, we felt more alone yet more connected to each other than any two people in all of Atlanta.

Vivian started to read the essay again, noting the comments of the professor at the bottom of the page. Unable to do so, she folded the pages and put them in her purse.

When Edward came home that evening and found an envelope addressed to Vivian from Benjamin in the trash barrel, he enthusiastically asked if there had been a letter from his son. "Oh," answered Vivian casually, "he sent me some clippings from the Atlanta paper about drama groups in Georgia. That's all. I've already filed them away."

When Vivian received a special delivery letter from Sarah the next day saying she had written to Benjamin and asked him *not* to publish the essay in the Morton literary journal, Vivian immediately dropped her a note, writing simply, "Dear Sarah, Thank you. Love, Mother."

1973

Sosha Brooks's decline was a rapid one. Like Mary, whose years did not seem to drag her down until the very end, when suddenly they all took their toll at once, Sosha's eighty-plus years brought the gradual symptoms of aging—stiffening joints, bad hearing, decreasing energy—but not until the final months did those years bring the woman down with a terrible and unremitting force. Nebraska was jolted by the rapidity of Sosha Brooks's decline, not only because she had affection for the woman, but also because she could more easily recall Wenda June when in her presence. Painful as it was to recollect that day Wenda had turned bitterly on Sosha, the memory also enabled Nebraska to imagine comforting her daughter again, to conjure up with almost perfect clarity the lines of her troubled child's face.

Sosha's passing away also meant that one more cornerstone was dragged from Vivian's life. When Nebraska and Vivian had sat at the kitchen table not long after Sosha's death, Vivian had said, seemingly out of the blue, "You know, before long Sarah's and Rachel's children will see me like Sarah and Rachel used to see Mother. I'll just be an old grandmother sittin' off in the distance, getting fussier and more crotchety as the days roll by."

To that statement Nebraska had answered, "Well, in that

case, I guess Todd's and Junior's chirren will probably see me the same way. At least you and I will have somethin' more in common to talk about. But you know, I bet they'll respect us, too, just the way your chirren respected your momma and Mr. Gold's momma and the way my chirren would have respected their grandmommas if they had ever had the chance to know them."

Nebraska could well understand Vivian's anguish at losing her mother, but she could not understand Vivian's anxiety about getting older. "We been gettin' older all our lives," she said to Viv on a long distance call to Atlanta one night. "To me, it's just somethin' you gots to accept. No use cryin'. Miss Gold would make you think she didn't start havin' birthdays till Benjie left for college, though." When Viv explained to her that the more comfortable a person's life has been, then the harder it is to face reality, and that white people on the whole had a harder time getting old than blacks because a lot of them had had comfortable lives, Nebraska said nothing but agreed sweetly. Later, when she had hung up, she thought to herself: Bless my 'telligent Viv's heart, but she do have more fixed ideas about white people than most whites have about colored.

Nebraska could agree with one comment of Vivian's: they *were* both getting fussier. Whether that fussiness was due to age, or the seemingly hotter summers, or the yellowness of the moon, Nebraska had no idea. Nebraska only knew that she got ticked off easily about incidents she used to let pass, like Miss Gold's insisting she change the yard sprinkler from one corner of the lawn to another when the first corner wasn't fully watered yet; and that Miss Gold got hot about incidents that *she* used to let pass, like Nebraska's leaving her shoes in the middle of the living room just as company was arriving.

It was Abraham who put his finger on the problem. Since Wenda June's death Abraham had taken to spending more time with his dogs, but he had also stopped drinking. He had even begun to develop a habit of coming in at night and sitting next to Nebraska, watching TV with her, and saying things that made more sense than what Nebraska had ever heard him say. One night, when they were watching *Star Trek*, listening to crickets while looking at space men transported by beam to awesome craggy planets, Abraham had turned to her and said gently, "You knows what I think, Gardenia? I think you and Miss Gold been fussin' after your chillun for so long that now when they ain't around, y'all don't have nothin' to fuss 'bout but each other. All that civil rights stuff was just one more commotion to keep y'all agitated over the young'uns. I think you and Miss Gold gots to learn how to be different with each other now."

Nebraska had nodded, keeping watch on a three-legged monster walking toward her on the flickering screen. And when Abraham leaned over, putting his arm around her and leaning his head on her shoulder, she turned and kissed him strongly, remembering what it was like to be understood by a man she still loved so deeply.

∽

Before long, Babs moved out of the house that had been Sosha's. She rented an apartment out by the new shopping mall, an area that, in Nebraska's opinion, didn't look like Madoc at all but like a picture out of a magazine or movie, one. There were long, sweeping fields with signs implanted at the boundaries: CLOUDVILLE MALL APARTMENTS. TO BE FULLY COMPLETED 1975. There were silvery interstate highways that turned and twisted into cloverleafs before snaking their ways off to Montgomery or New Orleans. There were gasoline stations with signposts which stretched nearly to the first level of clouds and shone all night long. There was every manner of hamburger and barbecue and fish fillet restaurant, all of which were plugged along the sides of the interstate highways like green and red plastic Monopoly houses.

Despite the fact that Cloudville Mall and the area around it looked like someplace that should be somewhere other than Madoc, there was a certain novel quality about it all that attracted Nebraska as well as friends of hers from the Golden Castles project. Downtown Madoc, now practically an all-Negro area except for the banks, the courthouses, and a few remaining white offices like Edward Gold's, had become so run-down that Nebraska did not like to shop there. All the good stores were moving to Cloudville Mall. Romaine explained her own reasons for preferring the new shopping center to downtown: "Nebraska, Nebraska, yes I likes it out there so much. It's so cool with all that air conditioning, and I loves to just sit and watch all them baby carriages be pushed along. I wisht I had me a little baby, don't you, Nebraska? I'd stroll it out at the Cloudville Mall, wouldn't you?"

To Romaine's comments on the mall, Nebraska had answered: "Oh, yes, Romaine . . ." but before she could finish, the woman was looking off in another direction and discussing the possibility of a thunderstorm the next day.

During one of Nebraska's Thursday afternoon excursions to the mall, she nearly ran right into Babs, who was busily shopping for curtains for her new apartment. "Wh-what are you doing way out here, Nebraska?"

"Oh," Nebraska responded, "just come to stroll about. Romaine told me she might be out here. She likes to sit at the open-front coffee shop and drink milk shakes and watch all the little babies. Sometimes I admit I do get a little weary of hearing Romaine carry on, but she do keep me company just to have a Coke."

"A Coke? A Coke with Romaine?" Bundling her packages up in her short arms, Babs looked up at Nebraska. Nebraska could detect the watery reflection of her contact lenses, lenses Babs had bought at Vivian's insistence to "make yourself attractive before it's too late altogether to catch a man." While rubbing one of her eyes, Babs sniffed and spoke: "You ain't ever gonna see Romaine again in your life."

"I don't understand."

"Don't understand? Doesn't Vivian pass on the gossip about Margery Berman anymore?" Babs finished rubbing. "Wh-

why, just three days ago Romaine and Margery ran off together to Miami, Florida."

"What do you mean runned off?"

"Ran off! Just like I said."

"You make it sound like they done eloped or somethin'."

"Just about." Babs drew a deep breath and went on excitedly. "Margery was seeing this man she met over at the Temple. He was named Finkle or Winkle or some name like that, and first thing she knew he had forgot her and taken up with this young girl who was studying out at one of the colleges but used to drive in to services at the Temple now and then. Well, Nebraska, I'll tell you, Margery said she was washin' her hands good of men and was heading to Miami, Florida, where she could live off what Izzy paid her in alimony and maybe take a part-time job teaching French. Of course, between you and me, Margery Berman spoke about as much French as a poodle!"

"But you said Romaine . . ."

"Yes, I said Romaine ran off with her. It's a fact sure as we're standin' in Cloudville Mall. Romaine, so we all hear, said 'Miss Margery Berman is all the family I gots,' and Margery said, 'Romaine is all the family I got.' So durned but they up and left together."

"I can hardly believe it."

"Yes, Nebraska. And that's not all!" Babs sniffed again. "The *real* story, at least as rumor has it—and that comes from Edna Solomon, who says if it's not true she'll lay down and die from embarrassment, and if it is true she'll lay down and die from shock—the real story is that, well, you know."

"You can tell me anything," Nebraska encouraged, leaning so close to Babs that she could smell baby powder.

"The rumor is"—Babs dropped her voice—"the rumor is that the reason Margery had so much trouble holding on to a man when she got one was that, was that . . ."

"Was what?"

"Shhh."

"I'm sorry." Nebraska whispered. "Was what?"

"Was that Margery was kind of . . ."

"Kind of what?"

"Funny!"

"FUNNY?"

"And some people suspected Romaine was a little funny too!"

"Miss Babs!"

"Course, both Margery and Romaine had husbands and children and all, but there was just something about the way they acted, *especially* when they were together. You know, kind of *peculiar*."

"Miss Babs, Romaine might have been odd, but she wasn't *funny*. She was a Christian, ma'am."

"So what?" Babs retorted. "Margery was a Jew. That don't mean a thing more than being Christian these days. The world's gone crazy, Nebraska—children taking drugs and burnin' up their eyeballs, men runnin' off with men, women goin' off with women. I used to say Madoc's never gonna change. Now I wish I'd been right, 'cause now that it's changing, it's changing crazy."

"But Romaine? And Margery Berman?"

Babs hoisted her packages higher on her chest. "You come with me to my apartment, help me put up my curtains, and I'll tell you things about Madoc you'd never believe even if I told them to you, which, of course, I will."

Still dazed, still expecting Romaine to show up at the coffee shop ordering her milk shake, Nebraska followed Babs to her apartment: a middling-sized living room, bedroom, and kitchen with windows that overlooked Cloudville Mall. Beneath the windows in the living room the mall looked like a giant egg carton, oblong and pale; far beyond the mall Nebraska could see the neighborhood where the Golds lived much as she had once seen that same neighborhood so many years ago from the window of the colored hospital.

"From up here the Golds' neighborhood look like it got so many trees!" she exclaimed. "Ain't it beautiful! Sometime you just gotta stand far back from somethin' to know how beautiful it is."

"Wh-what? Beautiful?" Babs said. "It's the ugliest neighborhood in this whole state."

"That ain't true, Miss Babs. I would a thought you'd want to live there yourself even. Give you a chance to be close to what family you still got."

"Hah!" Babs fussed about with her packages, drew out the curtains, and lifted them. "These are my favorites, just like the ones Aunt Sosha had."

Nebraska continued to look out the window, hunting for the street where the Golds' house was. "How do you find living alone, Miss Babs?"

"I don't mind it." Babs brought out curtain rods from another package. "I never really had nobody noways, at least not a husband. Of course, Aunt Sosha was the best there was, even though Vivian never appreciated her. Yes, indeed. And since I only go into Edward's office every other day now that he's got an apprentice, I'm used to spending time alone. I like it, in fact."

"Yas'm." Nebraska tried to sound as if she truly believed this. "I think I see the Golds' house!" she said.

Babs lengthened a rod, opened a drawer, and brought out a hammer and nails. "Now, Nebraska, if you'd just hold that ladder there a minute . . . don't *you* climb up on it because we know what happened when you climbed on a ladder when Wenda June was . . . oh, I'm sorry, I didn't mean to bring up Wenda June."

Nebraska, turned directly toward Babs now, started to talk, but hesitated. She cleared her throat and proceeded slowly: "That's—that's all right, Miss Babs."

Babs stepped toward her, placing a hand on her shoulder and speaking gently. "You don't have to 'Miss Babs' me. Really, dear, call me Babs, just like any full-fledged human being."

Nebraska turned so Babs wouldn't see she'd hurt her feelings and looked out the window again. The Golds' neighborhood wavered before her. Far beyond the neighborhood she tried to envision Miami, Florida, though all she knew of it were postcards the Golds had brought her and a slide show Edward Gold had given of parrot jungles and boardwalks and gleaming hotels. She imagined Margery and Romaine together at Miami Beach—somehow, ludicrous as the image was of the two women, it did not repel her. The image of Romaine with Margery was dreamy and improbable. Besides, weren't they already related in some manner of speaking?

"Nebraska," came Babs anxiously, "would you stop searchin' out a house that ain't worth searchin' out to start with and just hold this ladder for me?" Babs climbed the ladder and started tapping in nails for the rods. "You know, a person can strain their eyes easy when they start getting older. And from what Vivian tells me, you're gettin' older like the rest of us."

"Yas'm. I mean, *yes*."

Babs banged in a nail. "It's a shame life had to turn out like it did. It's too bad you couldn't a worked for me and Sosha, and Wenda June couldn't a worked for Vivian and Edward."

Nebraska stared blankly at the squarish pink-clad rear end of the woman, wondering what on earth possessed her to say such a thing.

Babs fished out another nail from her pocket. "It's just that if Wenda June had worked for Vivian and Edward, she might be alive to this day. If you had worked for me and Aunt Sosha, then you might be appreciated now that we're all gettin' too on in years to do everything we used to do." She put her hand to the small of her back, as if to dramatize advancing age.

Nebraska's hands went limp on the ladder.

Babs's voice went faster: "Wh-what I figured was that Wenda June was confused. She thought you had it so much better than she did 'cause you worked over at the Golds'. She was just jealous of—"

Nebraska's hands tightened again. "Don't talk about my daughter like that. Don't—"

"Nebraska! I'm trying to *tell* you things, like I promised I would."

Letting go of the ladder, Nebraska stepped back. "My daughter was the finest human that ever walked on God's earth. She might have been sick, but it weren't her fault."

"May I finish? *May I?*" Babs descended the ladder and pointed with the butt of the hammer to emphasize her comments. "Aunt Sosha and I always liked you. We would have taken care of you still, maybe even let you have that ol' house, 'cause I sure wasn't gonna stay there by my lonesome."

"I don't believe you." The words tumbled from Nebraska's mouth. "I don't believe you, Miss Babs, or Babs, or whatever your name is. You're a child and always have been. My Wenda June'd a been better if she had stayed up in Detroit and had never come south, 'cause other than Mr. and Mrs. Gold's, there ain't a white house in Madoc fit to work for."

Babs erupted. "So if th-they're so fit to work for, then wh-why did Vivian go and hire a young colored girl to get the bay house ready this summer? Wh-why? I asked Vivian why she didn't use you, and she—she said there was too much liftin' and carryin'. Did she tell you that? Did she? If she's so nice to work for, why did she pay somebody else to—to do the work you've always done?" Her voice became a single, shrill note. "Wh-why?"

"I don't believe you," Nebraska returned heatedly. "Miss Gold told me it was still fixed up so good from last summer that it didn't need no fixin' this summer! And they don't spend time over there like they used to, noways. And I don't believe for a minute that Margery and Romaine are . . . are . . . you know . . ."

"Don't believe me?" Babs's face turned red as a match tip. "Wh-why don't you just ask Vivian, then? Ask her if she didn't hire another Nebraska to come in and do what she didn't think you could do lively enough." Babs was trembling. She turned to walk up the ladder again, but sat down on one of the rungs instead and began to breathe noisily.

"Well, it don't matter!" Nebraska went on harshly. "Sometimes I work for *another* family on my days off, and they want me for *every* special occasion. Yas'm, I works there on my days off so I can make enough extra money to buy meat instead of slop, and I just say the word, they'll pay me a thousand dollars a month, yas'm, a thousand dollars a month just to fix them dinner!"

❧

There was a trick Nebraska had used five hundred times on Vivian Gold, a trick she had learned one day twenty-five years earlier, when they had sat at this same kitchen table and she had wrangled out the confession of the miscarriage. It was the trick of sidestepping into matters of importance. She had learned its subtleties from Vivian herself, who used it in conversations with Edward, talking about one topic while secretly zeroing in on another, whether it be the news that Sarah and her husband were taking separate vacations because "that's the modern thing to do," or the hint that Benjamin did not want to come home after his first year was over in college and wanted "Dad to bankroll a trip to Europe."

"Miss Gold," Nebraska said, initiating the trick, "did you know Miss Babs likes it over at Madoc Bay a whole lot?"

"Babs?" Vivian answered. "Well, I never thought about it. What makes you say that?"

"I bumped into her out at Cloudville Mall. She said that she'd even had a mind to move over there, and knew if she did I could help her to fix up her place, just like I always helped y'all to fix up yours."

"Well, that was sweet of her to say."

"Yas'm. She said she'd have me go along just to get started. I guess it'd be like Miss Margery taking Romaine down to Miami to get started, now that Miss Margery's got a job teachin' some French talk to people in Florida."

"Nebraska!" Vivian gave a quick, caustic laugh. "Babs doesn't know anything about what's going on in Madoc. She hardly even knows Margery. The word from Edna Solomon is that Margery just plain and simply was fed up with Madoc. And Romaine? Well, I don't know, maybe she wanted to find herself a nice Cuban man or something. Whatever, I would have told it all to you myself if Edward hadn't made me swear never to pass on any story about Margery again in this house."

Nebraska, taken aback because her trick had uncovered a revelation she had not expected to find (and not knowing whether to believe Babs's Edna Solomon or Vivian's Edna Solomon) proceeded with the climax of her trick. "Well, if you had a mind to go down to Florida to set up for a while, you know you'd take me to help fix your house up. I could do all the liftin' and carryin'."

"Nebraska, what on earth are you talking about? I have no intention of going to Florida to 'set up.'"

The trick had worked! Had not Vivian admitted so round-aboutly that she would *not* take Nebraska? Had not she ad-mitted that someone else would be needed to lift and carry?

Still hoping she had misunderstood Vivian's hemming and hawing, Nebraska blew her cover and asked outright: "You mean you hired somebody else to fix up the bay house this summer 'cause you didn't think I was strong as an ox no more?" She braced her feet firmly, a lover waiting to hear her partner admit to having an affair.

"Nebraska, if I had hired somebody else to come in, it would only have been to give you the rest you so well deserve."

Nebraska fumbled to change the topic, leaving the matter unresolved, as were so many matters between her and Miss Gold.

On a cool fall night, soon after the discussion with Vivian about Miami, the bay house, and betrayal, Edward called from the office to say the Madoc Real Estate Association was having a surprise dinner for a retiring officer and that Babs had forgotten to give him the message until just then. Vivian told him that she and Nebraska would just eat in the kitchen and she could then drive her home. When Edward objected to his wife's driving into colored Madoc, Vivian remarked, "You've been driving her home all these years, it's time I did so once. Needn't worry. The civil rights commotion's way behind us. Nobody'll bother me 'cause I'm white."

When dinner was finished, Vivian backed out the car and Nebraska scurried out best she could, but said "Wait a minute," and scurried back in. Her feet, aching, turned the scurry into a motion more like a graceful hobble as she went to the telephone, dialed her home, and said to Abraham, "Miss Gold's gonna drop me home. Meet us at the curb. And straighten up the living room just in case she can see through the screen when she's driving off."

Back in the car with Vivian, Nebraska watched the city slide by. The neatly trimmed neighborhood of Magnolia Court changed to the wide, tree-canopied thoroughfare of Governor Street, and soon became the bruised edges of the downtown. Most stores were closed at that hour. Many of those that were had bars over the windows and doorfronts. Those that weren't closed had armed guards out front, telling the entering shoppers "Only ten more minutes, please." Vivian parked outside an open five-and-ten, and Nebraska entered, buying some stockings, counting out the change in her pocket, and wondering how she'd have enough at the end of the month to pay the electric bill. She then decided to figure the electric bill when the time came to pay it, and she blew her remaining two dollars on some polish and dust cloths and window cleaner for her apartment.

In the car again, she watched the downtown roll by: the Baptist church, the street next to Gold's Western Wear (she said a prayer for Wenda June), then Dauphine Square with its fountain lapping water into the air, then the new office building where Edward Gold's office had moved (the storefront where his old office was had been turned into a cafeteria).

Certainly, Nebraska thought, Madoc was the same town she had seen on how many bus rides to and from the Golds' house, and on how many trips home with Edward driving, but for some reason the city now seemed different, as though the presence of Vivian in the car changed the atmosphere. The stores looked more heavily barred, the streets dingier, the sidewalks more menacing. When they arrived at the boundary of Golden Castles, the red-brick housing units looked shabbier than Nebraska had ever thought them.

"This'll be fine, ma'am. You can let me off here."

"I'll drive you right to your doorstep."

"Really, Miss Gold."

"Not another word on it," Vivian insisted.

As the Waterses' doorfront came into view, Nebraska looked for Abraham but did not spot him. "Thank you. See you tomorrow, Miss Gold."

"You know," Vivian cut in, "I think I'd like to come in and visit."

"But . . ." Nebraska could not figure out why she grew nervous suddenly. "It's better if I go on in and you head home."

Vivian slowed the car and came to a halt against the curb. "You know, I believe it's been, let me see, five years since I've been in your home? Can you imagine that?"

"I think," Nebraska answered quietly, "it's been 'most ten years."

"Ten?"

"And my place is such a wreck now," Nebraska said, protesting. "It looks like a cyclone runned through it. Junior was here from up east and he and his wife brought their two adopted chirren and they made corned beef hash out of my livin' room."

Vivian opened her door. "Are you coming in?" she asked, laughing. "Or shall I just go in by myself?"

Abraham sat in the living room, on the couch, eating cereal and watching a football game on TV. He stood abruptly, nodded, and looked about uneasily. "Didn't expect you, ma'am."

Vivian, nodding, entered as in a trance and looked around. "It *has* been ten years, Nebraska. My, to think all that time has gone by without my seeing your place."

"Yas'm." Nebraska spoke with her back to Vivian as she went around the room rapidly, wiping mantels with her palm, straightening pictures.

Vivian looked closely at the photographs of Todd and Junior and Wenda June and Abraham and Mary. She looked at three porcelain plates hung near the photographs; one plate bore in its center a portrait of John Kennedy, another Robert Kennedy, the third Martin Luther King, Jr. Like a sleepwalker, Vivian moved to a chair in the corner of the room, a green-and-yellow wing chair, and said, "I remember this chair. I gave it to you years ago when we changed the den around. Oh, how pretty it looks here!"

"Thank you," Nebraska said softly.

"And look at this beautiful portrait of Viv taken at her Lafayette High graduation. That's the photograph Edward took, isn't it?"

"Yas'm."

"It's *so* striking."

"Thank you." Nebraska swallowed hard, but did not know exactly why.

"Care for somethin' to drink?" Abraham asked.

"Yes," said Vivian, "but let me get it. Y'all sit and relax. I'm just family." She called from the kitchen, "Any ginger ale?"

"Yas'm," Nebraska said, trudging back, watching Miss Gold, who was standing near the oven and searching for a glass. "I'll have to rinse a glass for you," she said apologetically.

"*I'll* rinse it," Vivian declared. After fishing up an unwashed glass from the sink and beginning to wash it, she paused and lifted the glass to the light. "The filling-station glasses! My word, honey, I threw these glasses out twenty-five years ago. Remember, you even once asked me where they were from and I said—"

Nebraska heard the sheepishness in her own voice. "I think that's the only one still good."

Why did she grow tense? The sight of Miss Gold standing at the Waterses' sink washing a glass did not make Nebraska feel as she had always thought it would: noble and grand, as when she fantasized of living the life of ease and having a white woman—any white woman—dust her tables and fix her meals. Watching Vivian dry the glass, Nebraska saw only herself there; and she saw herself as small and helpless, as if her life were a continuous round of fishing out a dish from a sink, washing it, drying it, using it, fishing it out, and washing it again.

After filling the glass with ginger ale, Vivian stepped back into the living room and continued to survey the apartment. "I recognize the throw rug," she said enthusiastically, "and I recognize the dress that Viv is wearing in this lovely photograph in the park. It was such a lovely, light brown dress, and Rachel was mighty pleased to know that Viv could make use of it. And I recognize . . ."

Vivian ceased to talk a moment. She paused, rapt, before the mantel filled with photographs from places around the world: Paris, Brussels, Tokyo. "This was a shot of Belgium we sent the children from overseas," she said of one. "Here's a postcard sent to us from Buenos Aires." She looked up at Nebraska, a questioning look on her face.

"I had to put them up there," Nebraska offered, feeling as if she had to make an excuse for doing something that was wrong. "I used to keep knickknacks and things like that in the drawers and photo albums, but I gots so many pitchers of Waters chirren and Gold chirren in there now that there ain't room for postcards of the world. So I put them up there." She motioned to the mantel, then turned away, suddenly embarrassed.

"Why, honey," Vivian said gently, coming around to the front of the couch and sitting and looking at Nebraska in such an amazed way that Nebraska had to look straight down at the floor. "Dear, being in your living room is like being in a room right out of my own house! Isn't that *something*?"

"Yas'm," Nebraska answered meekly, wanting, for a reason she still did not fully understand, to burst into tears. "Yas'm, I guess it is."

1975

"Miss Gold, do you remember that time Rachel threw the eggs and hit ol' Mr. Weinacker's car?"

Nebraska pushed up her new false teeth with her thumbs and said, "My, these toophes make me feel like a new woman," and went on about Rachel. "The eggs just runned on down the windshield and Mr. Weinacker came scurrying, boppity bop, after Rachel.

"Now, Mr. Weinacker hadn't been living next door too long and he didn't know Rachel good and didn't know me too good neither. So he comes round and says all high-minded, 'Are you responsible for that devil who threw eggs on my car?' And though I was plenty hot with Rachel, I got even hotter with ol' Weinacker for cursing my baby like that. So I says, 'Mr. So 'n' So,' 'cause I couldn't remember his name, 'if I had a devil who went round throwin' eggs at people's cars, she wouldn't be much devil, would she? If I had a devil, I'd make sure she took the whole chicken and whopped you side the head!' "

Vivian, counting the spoons for the Passover *Seder*, shook her head. "Do I remember! After Rachel apologized, Weinacker still wanted to sue you, me, and the whole family." She took a deep breath and burst into laughter. "Edward said we'd countersue on grounds of harassment. Have we even exchanged fifty words with them since?"

"Well," Nebraska said with a huff, "we sure ain't missin'

much." She lifted a box of *matzo* meal close to her eyes and squinted at the instructions.

Vivian glanced up at her. "You don't know how to make *matzo* balls yet? After all these years?"

"Of course I know."

"Why are you reading the box, then?"

"Is there a law against readin'?"

"Oh, Nebraska, really!"

"Just like to read up," Nebraska explained. "Nothin' more to it." She paused. "I need to refresh my memory too."

"I sure wish Rachel could have made it home for Passover," Vivian said. "Well, I guess she's busy busy, just like everybody else. I expect we'll see her first of June when she brings the kids over the bay."

"You know," Nebraska remarked, "ain't memory just like a mule? You can kick it, beat it, stomp it, but it ain't gonna do nothin' till it's good and ready."

"What?"

"Nothin'. Nothin'. Just readin' this recipe and realizing what I done forgot."

"I don't forget a thing." Vivian put down the spoons and began to count forks.

"Why are you using those ol' forks?" Nebraska asked.

Vivian glanced up again. "They're not *old*, they're *antique*."

"Look old to me."

"Just read your box, okay?"

"Already read it." Nebraska paused. "Well, I may forget a few little things, but Passover and Easter time do hope me to remember a lot o' special things. This time of year feels more like New Year's with the world startin' up and all." She broke the seal on the box and started to pour the *matzo* meal into a bowl. "You know what it always make me remember? It make me remember that sheet that flew like the wings of an angel in your bedroom. I told you about it."

"That you did." Vivian watched Nebraska's shoulders

moving slowly beneath her white uniform as she began to stir the ingredients.

Nebraska glanced back over her shoulder. "What I never told you about was the face I saw on that same sheet how many years later."

"A face? Oh, c'mon, Nebraska."

"Yas'm." She continued mixing. "I would have told you then but I didn't want to frighten you. And I wouldn't even tell you now 'cept Easter puts me in a mind to."

"I don't think I'd be frightened."

"Well," Nebraska began, "it was an afternoon when it was good and hot, so hot that even that spaniel Bop had, before it got runned over, was laying deadlike in the heat, too hot to even flick off horseflies. I had washed the clothes and sheets and hung them on the clothesline to dry. I went inside, took a nap, started some butterbean soup simmerin', and went back out for the clothes a while later. I took down the socks. I took down the underwear. I took the shirts down too. I was just balling everything into the wicker basket 'cause I was gonna iron it when I came back in. I started for one o' the sheets—and there He was."

"Was, who?"

"Was Him!"

"A strange man was standing there?"

"No'm, He wasn't no stranger. He was Jesus Christ Almighty God looking down at me from the flapping sheet."

"Nebraska, really! That's a little farfetched, don't you think?"

"You ever hear tell of Veronica's veil?" Nebraska stopped mixing the *matzo* meal and turned to Vivian. "Veronica gave Jesus this cloth to wipe His face on when He was headin' up Calvary, and when Jesus gave her back the cloth it had His face printed on it clear as a pitcher in the *Madoc Register*. Well, same with that sheet out back. Course, nobody wiped His face on it that I know of, but just the same."

"What did you do?"

"First I called the spaniel of Bop's, just in case it weren't Jesus but some kind o' hant. But when the face started smiling, I knowed it was *Him*."

"And then?"

"And then He disappeared, and this trembling came up through my body like I was being touched all over, like the way Mary felt that evening she died and Jesus picked her up right from off the bed where I was holdin' onto her. That's why I stoled the sheet!"

"Oh, dear, now I know you're putting me on."

"I stoled the sheet so you and Mr. Gold wouldn't sleep on it and maybe do somethin' to offend Him."

"We wouldn't have offended anybody, Nebraska. At least, I don't think so."

Shrugging, Nebraska sifted some flour onto her hands and rubbed them together in preparation for rolling the *matzo* balls. "Well, I don't think you'd have offended him 'tentional."

"I hope not."

"Then I grabbed the sheet off the line, bundled it up good, and took it home in my shopping bag. I bought you one identical and slipped it on the next morning. And you know what?" She was silent a moment, then shook her head. "When I got home, that sheet was gone, and I said, 'Abraham, what you done with that sheet Miss Gold gave me,' and he said, 'Why, Nebraska, shug, I took it down to the pen for my daaawgs and made them a bed from it.' His *daaawgs*! Can you imagine? So, one-two, I runned down to that pen and took back my sheet, and there was nothin' but dog hairs and ol' pieces o' bone all over it! What a fool nigger!"

"My, my, that's a shame." Vivian began to re-count the spoons. "You shouldn't call Abraham such a name, though. He didn't know any better."

Nebraska chuckled. "No'm. At the time I was full mad, but soon I realized that Jesus understood and knowed my husband didn't mean no wrong."

"*Whew*! That's some story!"

"Yas'm. I did tell Benjie. I guess he kept it a good secret."

"Well," Vivian returned, feeling somewhat miffed, "he certainly never told *me*."

"I miss that boy."

"I miss them all, Nebraska."

The room was silent a moment save for the clinking of the silverware.

The phone rang: an incessant, high-pitched ring that laced through the house. Vivian picked it up and heard the small, warm voice from two thousand miles away: "Mom, it's Sarah. Just a quick call. Some schedules have gotten changed around with the theater group. Heck, I hate to disappoint y'all, but I don't think we're going to make it down for spring break. You know how show biz is and all."

"Of course, of course," Vivian answered, striving to mask her letdown. "Nebraska and I were just saying how we didn't think we'd have enough silverware as it was for the *Seder*." She forced a laugh. "Now there'll be no problem."

"I knew you'd understand," said the small voice. "Well, look, I'll try to call late Sunday night if I get the chance. Rates'll be cheap then and we can talk good and long."

"Whenever you get the time, Sarah. We're always here, sweetheart."

Vivian hung up. She put four forks, knives, and spoons back into the case and looked out the window. Then she turned and watched Nebraska, who was rolling up the *matzo* balls and setting them out on wax paper.

"Four less chirren," Nebraska said. "Eight less *matzo* balls."

"Nebraska! What are you doing? Don't you know you're supposed to chill the batter before making *matzo* balls? Isn't that the way Rivka taught us both?"

"Yas'm, that's the way she taught us, but you only gotta chill it if it won't roll up natural. You see, the chicken fat I put in is—"

"But look how runny it is!"

Nebraska lifted up some of the batter and let it plop into the bowl. "Well, I guess you right, Miss Gold. I'm sorry. I guess I had my mind on Todd."

"Todd?"

"It's just that he said he was gonna come home for Easter, and now he can't. Junior ain't gonna make it either. This'll be a lonely Passover and Easter for us all."

"You'd think Sarah might have given us more notice," Vivian remarked, looking out the window and envisioning Sarah sitting in her own kitchen.

"Oh," Nebraska commented, "she probably gave us as best notice as she could."

"Don't defend her," Vivian snapped. "She doesn't need to be defended."

"I wasn't defending her," Nebraska said without turning around. "I was just—"

"I heard you."

Nebraska nodded and started to put the rolled-up *matzo* balls back into the batter. In another moment she spoke as though trying to sound cheery. "I can remember when both our houses were *full* come this time of year."

"Well, they're not going to be full this go-round," Vivian said, placing some spoons back in the silverware case. Like a wooden jaw the lid of the case slammed down on one of her fingers and partially ripped a nail. Grimacing, she brought the finger to her lips and sucked it. "Why don't you get me something for it!" Through the tears assembling in her eyes, she glared at Nebraska, who was hurriedly taking out ice from the refrigerator and saying, "I'll go to the bathroom and get some iodine, Miss Gold."

Nebraska's elbow caught the bowl of matzo meal and spun it about. The bowl rocked, teetered, smashed to the floor.

"Oh, hell!" Vivian bolted up, yanked off some paper towels from the dispenser with her free hand, and threw them in the direction of the *matzo* meal that oozed across the blue squiggles of the linoleum floor.

"No," Nebraska said, "let me."

"I've got it!"

"Let me!"

"I thought you were going to get me something for my finger."

Nebraska disappeared into the hallway while Vivian wiped up the meal in clumps, dropping the paper towels into the trash bag. "Oh, damn, there won't be another trash pickup until Friday."

"Friday? No'm," said Nebraska, returning with iodine and Band-Aids. "Friday's Good Friday. It won't be till Tuesday."

"Whoever heard of a garbage pickup on Tuesday, Thursday, and Friday anyway? Well, that's Madoc." Vivian stood, took a breath, tore off some more paper towels, and sent them fluttering to the floor. After putting her left foot on one of the towels she moved it in a circle.

Nebraska bent to wipe up the rest of the meal.

"Look at the grime on these towels," Vivian exclaimed. "Hasn't the floor been mopped?"

Nebraska looked up. "I mop twice a week. Have been for near thirty years. I think you tracked that in yesterday with your golf cleats. You're always trackin' in somethin' just after I mopped."

"I didn't even play golf yesterday!"

"Well, Mr. Gold must have tracked it in last night from when he was huntin' for Benjie's flounderin' lantern in the garage. Now that Benjie's not around to track up the floor no more, it looks like Mr. Gold done took over."

"I tell you," Vivian said, "we have so much trouble keeping this whole house straight, we might as well still have a bunch of kids romping around."

"But we don't, Miss Gold, we don't." With some difficulty Nebraska rose up from the floor. "I gots to sit down a minute. I just saw stars."

"Well I been seeing stars since that thing fell on my hand."

Vivian looked around. "Nebraska," she went on gently, "didn't I ask you to get me some Band-Aids?"

Nebraska's jaw dropped. "Yas'm, you did, and I done brought 'em five minutes ago."

"I didn't see them. And Nebraska, it hasn't been five minutes. That's impossible."

Nebraska, sitting now, waved in the direction of the clock. "Count fast, count slow, makes no difference to me, Miss Gold. All I know is at least my Viv's comin' home for spring break."

"Viv! Why, you didn't mention it. Will she come visit me?"

"Do you 'speck her to? She'll only be with me for a few days as it is, seein' as how she wants to spend some time in Tuscaloosa on the way back. She's so excited 'bout startin' her masters in chemistry there come June."

"No, no, I guess I didn't expect her to come visit, not if she doesn't have the time. But I did expect Benjamin. He would have to change his major twice so he can't graduate until August, and he *would* have to get a girl friend who lives in Charleston and invites him home every holiday."

"He'll be home soon enough," Nebraska assured her.

"Maybe he'll marry the girl, Nebraska. At least he wouldn't have to keep running off to visit her family. Maybe they'd move to Madoc. He grew up here. He knows where his home is. Besides, Madoc Bay's better than the Atlantic Ocean any day of the week."

"He ain't gonna marry her, Miss Gold. He's too young."

"How do you know?" Vivian, wrapping the Band-Aid around her finger, pulled off the adhesive back with her teeth.

"Sorry," Nebraska said. "Maybe I don't know."

"Well," replied Vivian, freeing the adhesive and talking with her teeth clenched on the backing, "he *is* too young. Way too young."

Vivian dropped the adhesive into the trash and walked into the hallway. She watched the walls sliding by her as they might in an aggravating dream. She went to the bathroom, ran water, and brought it up to her face, letting some of it sluice through her fingers. It ran down her arms and felt like small, pricking insects. She slapped at her elbows. "Leave the *matzo* balls," she shouted out. "We can fix some more meal later." She dried her face and hands and went back to the kitchen.

When she got there she saw Nebraska leaning against the sink, arms crossed.

"What I thought," Vivian began, "is that we should start on other things. Get the lamb ready. Make the stuffing. We can also start chopping apples for the *harosis*. And, oh, yes, the bitter herbs, the *moror*. Do we have horseradish for the *moror*? Edward would have a conniption fit if we didn't have the horse-radish! Could you look in the closet and see if we've got any, please?"

Nebraska did not move.

"Didn't you hear me?" Vivian asked, startled. "Nebraska, are you okay, dear?"

Nebraska, blinking, turned her gaze away.

Vivian waited for Nebraska to move but she stood immobile, as though pinned against the sink. Was she ill? "Nebraska! Can't you get the horseradish?"

"It's not that I can't, Miss Gold. It's just that I don't want to."

At the *Seder* there were no young adults or children present to read the Four Questions, so Edward did the honors. First he read them in Hebrew; then Edna Solomon, David Solomon, and Babs took turns reading them in English.

When Vivian heard the voice ask, "Why is this night different from all other nights?" she could think of no answer to explain why it did seem different, why the air felt closer and the crickets more strident and the streetlamp harsher through the dining room window. When it came time to open the door for Elijah, she went to the front door that was already open and, for ceremony, closed it and opened it again. She sat back down at the table and immediately heard something, heard somebody, knocking.

Was it her? Had she come back after leaving so early that day, saying no word, not even smiling, giving no hint of what exactly had been troubling her?

"I'll get it," exclaimed Vivian, and went quickly to the door.

But there was no one there, not Elijah, not Nebraska, not anyone.

❧

It was the Tuesday after Easter Sunday and Nebraska wore slacks. She had called Edward Gold's office Monday morning to say she would not be in that day because she had to see Viv off to Atlanta Technical and was "not feelin' just right, anyway," and needed a day to rest up. The slacks were deep burgundy, and though she'd bought them more than a year earlier, she had worn them only around the house, never feeling bold enough to venture past the front door onto the grounds of Golden Castles.

Today, however, she felt special, as though she were booked to go away on a holiday in some land she had always read and dreamed about, but never thought she'd really have the chance to visit. She wore a loose beige blouse over the burgundy slacks and even picked a flower near the bus stop, which she pinned on her lapel. Around her neck was a silver locket Abraham had given her; inside the locket was a picture of Wenda June.

"Why, Nebraska, you look like you's stepping out today," said one voice on the bus, and "Ooh, Miss Waters, you going to a ball or somethin'?" another voice came. When the bus dropped her off near Magnolia Court and she passed by the mailbox, walked down the incline, and moved more spryly than she had in years, one neighbor after another looked up and called, "Good mornin', Nebraska. You look fine and flashy this mornin'." And even though she heard Marsha Weinacker say to a friend, "Look at ol' Nebraska, dressed up like a teen-ager in pants," it didn't bother her in the least.

"Mornin', Marshall," she called to the yardman clipping the Bartons' shrubs. The man turned, smiled broadly, and waved his shears.

She hesitated at the garbage cans, wondering if she should roll them down the driveway into the garage as she did every trash day, getting "those unsightly things off the street after the truck has dumped them," as Vivian put it. Starting to roll them back in, she was distracted by a thought: Could Vivian Gold still be at home?

Deciding to save the cans until later, she walked down the driveway, going up the stairs lightly, peering through the kitchen window. She could see straight through the kitchen and into the living room, then the dining room, and finally the den. At the window of the den the Japanese magnolia was faintly red with the few petals that still clung to its branches.

Was it a silhouette of Miss Gold she saw against the branches of that tree? A silhouette of a woman sitting in the den near the piano and *menorah*, reading the paper, drinking coffee? Nebraska leaned her head back and scanned for the cherry-colored automobile in the garage. She did not see it.

She opened the door and called, "Yoo hoo. Yoo hoo!" Her heart fluttered. What if Miss Gold were home? Would she hand her the note? Would she, *could* she, tell her outright? Would she slip on her work shoes as though nothing had happened? "Yoo HOO! Miss Gold, you in the house?"

"IF YOU SEND JUST ONE DOLLAR TO REVEREND RICH AT THIS RADIO BOX NUMBER YOU'LL RECEIVE A THOUSAND DOLLARS IN BLESSINGS." She leaped back, bringing her hand to her chest, but just as quickly began to laugh. The clock radio, set at ten o'clock for the gospel hour, blared through the kitchen as on every morning. Had Vivian turned it loud for her?

She spotted the note:

Dear Nebraska,

I'll be back a little before 11:30. Can we start the pot roast early so Edward and I can eat in the late afternoon?

Vivian

Nebraska looked at the clock, started to pour herself a cup of coffee, stopped, and pulled the note from her own pocket. She noted a misspelling and thought to rework it. She placed the note near the sink, under a spatula, so that she would be sure to correct it. "Oh, yes," she said, fishing out a pencil from a cup of pens, pencils, and paper clips Vivian kept on top of the icebox. She bent over the draft of the note and signed, "My love always, Nebraska." She erased those words and wrote, "My love, Nebraska," then erased the words again and wrote, "Love, Nebraska."

Leaving the note there, she went to the closet and brought down her work shoes, her Bible, her copy of *Growing Up Black in Mississippi*, her measuring cup, her copies of *The Watchtower*, her shoe polish, her address book, her clippings of Vivian Gold's theater work, her knock-around handbag, and her foot pads. She reached higher and located the edge of some white cloth and pulled down half a dozen uniforms already pressed and folded. She put three of the uniforms back and stuffed three into her bag. She put the other possessions into the bag as well and started down the hallway.

Her handkerchief! The pretty, red-and-green embroidered handkerchief Rachel had sent her was in the dirty-clothes bin. She had put it there the morning she and Miss Gold had started the Passover meal, meaning to wash it on Monday. She set the bag down and reached into the bin.

As she reached and dug, pulling out socks, underwear, singlet shirts, bras, her body began to quiver. The quivering came in abrupt waves, as if she were receiving jolts from the bottom of the bin. She began to fling the clothes out, throwing them as far as the bedroom, as far as the bathroom. "Where is my handkerchief?"

Her hand latched around it. She stood slowly, the blood pounding in her head. Regaining herself, she picked up the bag and walked back down the hall and into the living room.

The living room window, the table in front of the window, the television, the lamp, the coffee table, the sofa—the objects revolved before her and pressed against her as though intent on leaving their marks. The objects dropped away and in their places came names and faces: Benjamin and Viv and Rachel and Junior and Sarah and Todd and Babs and Wenda June and Vivian and Mary and Abraham and Edward.

"Don't get all upset!" she spoke abruptly to herself, remembering she was wearing burgundy slacks and a beige blouse and a silver locket with Wenda June's picture inside, remembering this day was to be one of the happiest in her life.

"But oh, my foots do hurt!" She reached into her bag and brought out her work shoes. Her feet throbbed in the street shoes. Yes, she needed to be comfortable, to be calm, alert. For a moment she looked at the work shoes, looked at the depressed soles, the slats torn and glued together, the heels worn down on the instep. Seized by another quivering, which came more strongly and relentlessly than the one she had felt in the laundry bin, she brought back the shoe in her right hand and hurled it toward the kitchen. The shoe caught the head of the Steuben bird Sarah had sent Vivian on her last birthday. "Oh, my. Oh, my God."

Not believing what had happened, Nebraska eased toward the bird and bent above it, stroking it like a real bird whose head had been brutally severed. "Oh, Miss Gold'll be angry now. She'll be so mad . . ." She rose, hurried into the kitchen, scrabbled about in the drawer for some quick-dry cement, found it, and applied it to the head of the bird, setting it on the neck and grabbing up her bag.

The phone rang.

Nebraska stood still.

The phone rang. It stopped.

Nebraska walked out the back door and down the steps, making her way to the bus stop, her head swimming. The bus was soon before her, then the rubber runnels of the steps were beneath her feet, then she was on a seat, looking out the window, hearing some woman she did not recognize saying, "You going into town to get somethin' for Miss Gold?" and another voice saying, "Nebraska Waters, is you sick?"

She shook her head once. She shook it again. Before long she pulled the cord.

∽

"Nebraska. Nebraska?" Standing at the kitchen door with groceries in her arms, Vivian thought, Something is not right. *Something is not right.* "Nebraska," she called again, "could you please help me with these groceries?"

"Why is my heart pounding?" Vivian asked herself out loud, then set the groceries down on the floor of the foyer leading to the kitchen and started to go back to the car for another bag. She suddenly noticed an undershirt balled up against a chair leg at the end of the hallway. Mystified, she walked to the undershirt, picked it up, and saw a trail of clothes snaking down the hallway to the laundry bin.

"Is there anybody here? Nebraska, are you all right? IF THERE'S ANYBODY HERE BESIDES NEBRASKA I'M GOING TO CALL THE POLICE!"

The house answered her with a silence that crackled.

As Vivian followed the trail of clothes down the hallway, then turned into the living room and glanced out the window at the garbage cans still on the curb, images of Nebraska crowded to her: Nebraska reposing in the rocker in the den, humming a church song, the Golds' *menorah* rising behind her like a silvery vine; Nebraska sitting on the front porch, a wad of chewing gum stuck on the back of one hand while she argued with a woman who carried the Jehovah's Witnesses' *Watchtower*; Nebraska collapsed on her back in the kitchen, her legs sprawled out motionless, her marble-colored eyes staring straight up at the Holy Ghost.

"What on earth!" Vivian bent over the Steuben bird. Its neck was cracked, head contorted. She ran her finger around the neck and felt the glue still moist. "Nebraska!" she called with a flash of anger.

After pushing open the door from the dining room to the kitchen, Vivian saw her own note to Nebraska lying near a half-empty cup of coffee, then saw the other note lying beneath a spatula near the sink. She went to the note and grabbed it up, holding it close to the window above the sink to read.

Dear Miss Gold,

this is jus a note to let you know I wil not be comin in no more. Thank you for everything all these many years but I cat stay here any longer.

Love, Nebraska

Vivian read the note over again, then again, then a third time, until her eyes locked on "cat stay here any longer" and the words hobbled back and forth on their own.

She sat down heavily at the kitchen table, pouring a cup of tepid coffee, drinking a mouthful, and pouring some more. Nebraska's half-empty cup was across from her. She pushed it aside. For a moment the sight of Marshall clipping shrubs across the street distracted her. Her attention shifted to Marsha Weinacker's cane bushes, fluttering green and yellow in the April breeze.

Turning away from the window, Vivian drew the telephone from its cubbyhole and set it squarely before her. She dialed the first two digits of Nebraska's number. Her finger grew weak. She continued dialing the digits for Edward's office. Just before letting the last digit go, she slammed the receiver down and looked back out the window, taking a deep breath, letting it out slowly, and watching the cane bushes go all fuzzy as she began to cry.

❧

As Nebraska made her way from the bus to Golden Castles, she realized she had rarely been home on a Tuesday morning during the last twenty-nine years. The spryness returned to her step. How would she spend her day? Go to a movie? Go shopping? Visit a friend? She sprang up the steps of her apartment and flung open the door. Bringing her hand to her face, she found herself sweating profusely. "Abraham!" she called, but there was no answer. "I guess he's gone for the day," she murmured, pulling off her blouse, kicking off her shoes, and sitting on the sofa.

She took a magazine up from the side table and flipped through it, scanning pictures of models in bathing suits. She tossed the magazine aside. She brought out a copy of *The Watchtower* from her bag, flipped through it, tossed it to the side as well. She closed her eyes, took a deep breath, made a point to relax, then opened them. The curved glass of the television screen cast back a deep-green elongated reflection of the room. She glanced over at the clock: almost eleven thirty.

Hiking herself up with some difficulty now that she had sat, she flicked on the TV, unbuttoned her slacks, and watched a game show moderator's face come into focus.

Behind the game show moderator hundreds of people were screaming. One was dressed like a robot, another like a giant chicken, another a scarecrow. These three bounded up on the stage and began to bid make-believe money on prizes hidden behind doors. The first door opened and the robot began to scream. The contestant had won a washer-dryer. It reminded Nebraska of the washer-dryer in the Golds' house, except the model was newer and brighter. The second door opened and the giant chicken bounced up and down and yelled. The contestant had won a full set of household appliances.

Nebraska looked over at the clock: eleven thirty! She cringed, knowing the phone would soon ring, yet also knowing it would not. She turned back to the game show and thought of the Mixmaster in the Gold's kitchen. She thought of the coffeepot. Had she turned it off before leaving? And had she put a piece of bread in the toaster?

The scarecrow stood before a curtain, but suddenly the moderator announced there was no time left, that the game would be continued tomorrow. No, thought Nebraska, I want to win!

She imagined herself in the contestant's place. As she stood on stage, the anticipation overwhelmed her; the choice of curtains, of numbers and prizes, frightened her terribly.

Why didn't the phone ring? Had Vivian discovered the bird? The clothes! Nebraska recalled the clothes strewn along the hallway. Had she remembered to put "Love, Nebraska" on the note? Why had she not put "My love always"?

She chose the curtain. The announcer stepped forward. She knew by his face that what lay behind it was special, was extraordinary.

She closed her eyes and let the feeling of her own house come around her.

Discussion Questions

Nebraska Waters is black; Vivian Gold is Jewish. In an Alabama kitchen where, for nearly thirty years, they share cups of coffee, fret over their children, and watch the civil rights movement unfold on the TV screen and out their window, they are like family—almost.

As Nebraska makes her way, day in and day out, to Vivian's home where she cooks and helps tend the Gold children, the bond between the women both strengthens and frays. The "almost" threatens to widen into a great divide.

The two women's husbands affect their relationship, as do their children. This is particularly true of the youngest children, Viv Waters and Benjamin Gold who, born the same year, are coming of age in a changing South.

DISCUSSION QUESTIONS

1. What does the title *Almost Family* mean to you? Do you think that Vivian and Nebraska would answer this question differently? What about other characters in the novel?

2. Much of this story takes place in the kitchen of the Gold home, and the civil rights movement is, in terms of geography, far away. What brings the civil rights movement close to these two women? What impact do public events have on their private lives?

3. The first line of the novel is, "What you think is so different 'bout them?" How do the pressures of being "different" affect

the characters of this novel? Do they come to understand what those differences are, or do those differences act as a barrier?

4. Have you ever had an experience where, for whatever reason, you felt "different," and how have you dealt with that? Can we learn any strategies from Vivian and Nebraska?

5. How does being Jewish define Vivian? What about Edward and the rest of the family members? Does being Jewish in Alabama—a religious minority—shape their lives?

6. There are places in the novel where faith comes up for discussion, as in a scene between Nebraska and the Gold children. Does faith separate characters or bind them together? In what ways?

7. As an employee in Vivian's home, Nebraska is there because she is doing work, and she is getting paid. But what occurrences are there that also make a work relationship a personal one? Does a work relationship limit a personal relationship?

8. Nebraska's daughter, Viv, is uncomfortable with Vivian's attempt to be "almost family." Do you feel that Viv is justified in her reaction? Do you understand Vivian's feelings?

9. How do the changing generations impact each other in *Almost Family*? Do Vivian's children and Nebraska's children really get to know one another? If so, how? If not, why not?

10. What does *Almost Family* tell us about people's efforts to connect, in a deep way, with people of other backgrounds?

11. Are the lessons of *Almost Family* ones of the past, or are they relevant today? If so, in what ways?

Author photo by Nancy Mosteller Hoffman

About the Author

Roy Hoffman is the author of the novels *Come Landfall*, a Gulf Coast story of hurricanes, war, and love; *Chicken Dreaming Corn*, a Southern Jewish immigrant tale praised by Harper Lee as "a story of great appeal"; and two nonfiction books of essays and narratives, *Alabama Afternoons: Profiles and Conversations*, and *Back Home: Journeys Through Mobile*. His essays and reviews have appeared in the *New York Times*, *Washington Post*, and *Wall Street Journal*, and he was a long-time staff writer for the *Mobile Press-Register*, with a special interest in the diverse cultures of the Deep South. In addition to the Lillian Smith Award and Alabama Library Association Award in fiction for his first novel, *Almost Family*, he received the University of Alabama's Clarence Cason Award in nonfiction. A graduate of Tulane University and resident of Fairhope, Alabama, he teaches fiction and nonfiction in the low-residency MFA in Writing Program at Spalding University in Louisville, Kentucky. On the web: www.royhoffmanwriter.com.